PRAISE FOR KERRY LONSDALE

No More Words

"Lonsdale expertly maintains suspense throughout. Psychological-thriller fans will be well satisfied."

—*...Weekly*

"A perfect summer read."

—*...Crash*

"[A] mesmerizing first installment in her newest No More series . . . *No More Words* simmers with drama and secrets, sure to dazzle readers as an unmissable summer read."

—The Nerd Daily

"Lonsdale's first book in a new trilogy about love, betrayal, and the secrets families keep. Read in one sitting!"

—Frolic

"[Lonsdale] creates stories that readers will want to read again and again."

—*Write-Read-Life*

"Lonsdale is at her best with this multilayered story about three dysfunctional siblings and the secrets they keep. What a ride. I'm still a little breathless. This one was an addictive page-turner—impossible to put down. Fans of domestic suspense will EAT THIS UP."

—Sally Hepworth, bestselling author of *The Good Sister* and *The Mother-in-Law*

"Kerry Lonsdale is back and better than ever with this multilayered tale about three siblings torn apart by a series of tragic events. Nuanced and smart, filled with characters with real emotion and depth, *No More Words* is everything you've come to love from the master of domestic drama. A mesmerizing beginning to a new trilogy that will have you one-clicking the next in the series."

—Kimberly Belle, internationally bestselling author of *Stranger in the Lake*

"Full of suspense, romance, and drama, *No More Words* is a powerful story about what it means to be a family. Emotional and honest, it tells the story of three siblings, each dealing with demons from the past. I fell in love with all three Carson children and look forward to the second and third installments of this series. Kerry Lonsdale is a master storyteller of family drama, and this is Lonsdale at her best."

—Suzanne Redfearn, #1 Amazon bestselling author of *In an Instant*

"Kerry Lonsdale starts her latest trilogy off with a bang! Brimming with drama, suspense, and family secrets galore, *No More Words* will have you tearing through the pages to figure out what really happened to this broken family, and who is playing whom. With beautifully drawn, complex characters and a twisted plot that reveals itself layer by layer, *No More Words* is a stunning thriller that deserves a top spot on your 'to be read' list."

—Hannah Mary McKinnon, bestselling author of *Sister Dear* and *You Will Remember Me*

"*No More Words* burns and smolders with the tension of a lit cigarette. Kerry Lonsdale has created a page-turning story of family secrets and assumed truths that forces readers to ask what they would do if the buried past came calling at their door. Nothing and no one can stay hidden forever."

—Amber Cowie, author of *Rapid Falls*

"Every family has its secrets, and the way Kerry Lonsdale twists the truths in *No More Words*, you're guaranteed to lose sleep over this perfectly blended tale of suspense, intrigue, and emotional betrayal. Lonsdale has done it again, gripping the hearts of readers with her complex characters and layered story lines. This is a must-read thriller that will leave you stunned at the end!"

—Steena Holmes, *New York Times* and *USA Today* bestselling author of *Lies We Tell Ourselves*

NO
MORE
SECRETS

NO MORE SECRETS

A NOVEL

KERRY LONSDALE

LAKE UNION
PUBLISHING

Published by Lake Union Publishing, Seattle

www.apub.com

Amazon, the Amazon logo, and Lake Union Publishing are trademarks of Amazon.com, Inc., or its affiliates.

ISBN-13: 9781542019101 (paperback)
ISBN-13: 9781542019095 (digital)

Cover design by Rex Bonomelli
Cover image: © Poravute Siriphiroon / Shutterstock; © ArthurHidden / Getty

Printed in the United States of America

For you

1

Lucas Carson rolls onto his back and stares at the ceiling fan rotating on low, blades spinning faster than a clock's second hand melting his waste of a life. As if the Mojave Desert hasn't already done so.

He takes a mental assessment, digging up the motivation to get out of bed. His head pounds from the six-pack of empty beer bottles on the nightstand. More from the shots of tequila. The crust around his eyes that caked overnight stings. He scrapes it off. His body aches, his right calf especially. He must have tweaked it last night when they were going at it.

He drags his hands down his face, the stubble chafing, and drops an f-bomb into his cupped palms. Faye came knocking after midnight. He shouldn't have let her in.

She stirs beside him, her body going taut as she stretches her arms overhead and purrs. The sound drips with enough innuendo that Lucas can't believe it isn't intentional.

Her eyes slide open, revealing the stunning green that gets him every time she shows up at his door in a skimpy dress, mountain-high heels, and legs that go for miles. She has ten years on his thirty-three, but it doesn't show anywhere on her. She's a knockout. And he's a fool for a no-strings-attached lay.

He sits up in bed. She smiles, catlike. He swings his legs over the side. She reaches for his wrist to keep him close. He pulls his hand away and shoots up from bed, moody about when and how he's touched.

She pouts because he's slipping away. Body, mind. Interest. Until next time, at least.

"Baby." Faye's plea is breathless, heavy with the dregs of sleep.

"Got to get to work," he says gruffly, clearing his throat of morning phlegm. He grabs the orange Home Depot bucket he uses for trash and slides the empty bottles in with one swipe of his forearm. The noise shatters the morning's calm.

Faye flops onto her back with an irritated groan. "Lucas," she whines, now fully awake. She drags the pillow over her face.

He drops the bucket on the floor. The bottles clatter. "You should go. Rafe returns tonight." Her husband.

She groans into the pillow, then dramatically tosses it onto the floor and rolls to her side, propping up her head. She lets the sheet slide from her shoulders, revealing perfect breasts, thanks to some fancy surgeon in the Valley. "He doesn't leave again for weeks. Skip work. Spend the day with me." Her bottom lip pops out.

"Can't." He hobbles to the bathroom, stretching his cramped calf.

"She's lucky."

"Who?" He lifts the toilet lid and seat she'd put down. They bang against the tank.

"Izzy."

"Ivy," he corrects. His seventy-nine-year-old landlady and boss. She owns the four-apartment complex along with the market on the first floor. He works where she tells him, and he's already running late. He overslept and has the hangover to blame.

"She's all you care about."

He grunts and takes a piss without bothering to shut the door.

"'The simple act of caring is heroic,'" she recites.

Lucas rolls his eyes, no idea what she's going off about. He flushes the toilet, washes his hands, and splashes cold water onto his face. He leans on the sink and stares at his reflection, rallying the will to clean up and show up. His eyes are bloodshot, the skin around them mottled.

He hasn't cut his hair in months. It falls shapelessly around his head, the cowlick he's had since birth more pronounced from Faye messing with his hair. He swears she pulled out strands when he was pounding into her. She can't keep her hands off his head.

I need you. She palmed his face, his neck, begging for the intimacy.

He rubs a hand over his scalp. There's nothing intimate about them or what they do in the dark.

The switchblade he keeps on the toilet tank demands his attention as it does every morning since the day he arrived here feeling the lowest of lows. He scowls at it, his gaze sliding to the tub. A memory from when he was sixteen of a bathtub like this one filled to the rim with lukewarm water, him in it, fades in and out.

"Edward Albert." She's prattling on about whatever from his room. He's never heard of him.

"That actor. He was in *Falcon Crest* and a movie with Goldie Hawn. He won a Golden Globe." Her tone tells him he should know who this guy is.

Lucas shakes his head, totally uninterested. He turns away from the blade and grabs his toothbrush, smears paste across the worn bristles.

"Baby, I ache. Be a hero and come back to bed." Her voice goes all singsong on him.

He could crawl back into bed. To hell with his responsibilities.

He could also show her exactly how unheroic he is and ignore her.

He spits foamy paste into the sink. "Go home, Faye." He shuts the bathroom door.

A muffled "Lucas" penetrates the hollow barrier before he turns on the shower, and when he's finished and has wrapped a loose towel around his waist, the front door slams.

He yanks open the bathroom door and spills out with a cloud of steam. Faye isn't in his bed, and she isn't excavating his fridge for spoiled milk and month-old eggs, insisting she whip up a hearty scramble because he subsists on Coronas and Cuervo.

3

The air conditioner hums. The ceiling fans he installed yesterday in the front room and his bedroom spin.

She's gone. Thank fuck.

Hands on hips, he surrenders a relieved breath.

———

The Dusty Pantry is a convenience market located on a large parcel of barren land in California City, a town that never lived up to its founder's hype of growing bigger and more vibrant than Los Angeles. Miles of paved roads lead to nowhere, baking in the desert heat. After a postwar real estate boom, its growth tapered off until it was virtually a ghost town, which is exactly why Lucas has found himself here.

He feels like a ghost, drifting through life with no purpose. He can't figure out why he's hanging on when he doesn't have a reason to.

It's been eight months since he ditched Seaside Cove, the gated community on the Central Coast he called home, along with his older sister, Olivia; his mother, Charlotte; and the troubles that haunt him.

It's also been eight months that he's avoided the police.

There's a very real possibility he'll be sent back to prison when the authorities catch up to him. But that isn't why he ran.

When he got in his truck and drove, tossing his phone out the window somewhere along Highway 58, the market was the first place he stopped. He expected to have one last beer and drive on through. Instead he bought twelve. When the old lady behind the counter turned her back, a Reese's candy, a pack of Dentyne Ice, and a jerky stick that was probably as old as he was found their way into his pockets.

Ivy Dervish. She and her late husband, Tom, had purchased the land and built the drab multiuse structure of apartments and deli market back in the late sixties. The business has been floundering and the structure falling apart since her husband passed five years back, she told him as he paid for his beer. She'd been working overtime to keep it afloat when she should have retired years ago. He told her he was driving through, that he didn't know where he was going. He didn't see a point in hiding those facts. He wasn't planning on sticking around. But she convinced him to reconsider. There was an apartment above that needed a tenant. She'd lease it to him at half the publicized monthly rate if he helped her around the property.

He toured the sparsely furnished apartment and saw himself sitting on the worn couch powering through the twelve-pack. Then he saw himself draw a warm bath, shedding his clothes, and folding himself into the small alcove tub, and he made his decision. He accepted her offer.

This was a good place to die.

One problem, though.

He hasn't yet mustered the courage to follow through.

The Dusty Pantry lives up to its namesake. Every morning, Lucas sweeps the stockroom's floor, pushing fine, blond-toned dirt out the back door. The parking lot isn't paved, and Ivy's property in back stretches far enough that he can only see the rooftops of several single-family homes above the waist-high shrubs scattered across the landscape. The only good thing about this place is the night sky. Stars are brighter, more brilliant in the desert, where Lucas can remember he isn't anything more than a speck of nothingness in the vast universe.

He hears the familiar rumble of Sanchez's Produce. Mack drives the truck south from the Valley once a week and drops several small boxes of fresh fruit and vegetables Ivy displays in the self-serve fridge along the far wall. The parking brake drops into place, and metal doors clang open.

Lucas shuts the rear door, puts aside the broom, and pushes through the swing door that separates the stockroom from the market. He walks down an aisle of cleaning supplies, past the cash register, and unlocks the front door. He props it open with a brick.

"Hey, Mack."

"Morning, Luc." Mack drops a wood crate bursting with apples and oranges onto the sidewalk as Lucas returns to the stockroom to retrieve the empty crates from the prior week's delivery.

"Got the white peaches Ivy ordered," Mack says when Lucas hands off the crates. Lucas can smell the fruit's sweetness wafting from the truck's refrigerated box. Mack tosses the empty crates onto the truck.

"Thanks, man." Lucas mechanically bumps the fist Mack holds up before he takes the fruit inside.

"See you next week," Mack hollers after he slams the rear doors. Lucas grunts over his shoulder, dropping the fruit-laden crate by the self-serve fridge for Ivy to sort when she comes downstairs.

Mack leaves for his next delivery, and Lucas retrieves the other two crates in front. Closing the door behind him, he takes the fruit to the fridge in back. The door separating the stockroom from the market swings wide and sticks, remaining open. Lucas leaves it. His hands are full, and the market doesn't open for another twenty minutes.

He packs fruit into the fridge, tosses the crate aside, and starts on the next when a bell jingles. "We aren't open yet," he hollers. He's about finished with the second crate when he hears another noise, a can falling off a shelf. It rolls across an aisle.

Lucas sets down the crate, closes the fridge, and scopes the market from the doorway. There, along the far wall, he spots a head of dirty blonde barely visible above the aisle. He opens his mouth to tell whoever ignored him that the shop is still closed. But something stops him.

The figure appears around the endcap, Lucas going unnoticed. She's too fixated on the products displayed, Snickers bars and M&M's. Hot Tamales and Lay's chips. Dirt-smudged cheeks and greasy hair, wearing an oversize hoodie too thick for the Mojave's heat, she keeps her eyes averted as her fingers trail over the products on the shelf. They skim everything she passes. Every so often, her hand dips to her side.

Lucas's gaze narrows at her retreating back. He knows exactly what she's doing because he's done the same since he was eleven. It started with a Hot Wheels car he lifted that he regrettably let his younger sister, Lily, take the heat for. Next it was a candy bar, then a shirt he swiped from Big 5 just to see if he could do it. Until finally it ended with a six-pack of beer and a gun that didn't belong to him. His reward? Six months in juvenile detention bunking with five guys in an overcrowded cell who'd committed acts ten times worse than him.

He wasn't the guilty party, not entirely. But his friends, his football teammates since they were kids, let him take the fall.

He's still falling. Flailing.

He wouldn't wish his experience on anyone.

Face hard, he watches her disappear around the endcap. Lucas strides up the neighboring aisle to confront her. Ivy doesn't have cameras. He needs to catch this little thief in the act with the merch still on her.

She comes around the corner and gasps. Lucas snatches her wrist, startling them both, and flips her hand. Clutched in her palm is a pack of Juicy Fruit. His gaze drops to the loaded kangaroo pocket before flying up to her face. Large hazel eyes, haunted and deep, sit atop a wave of freckles bridging her nose. She can't be more than fifteen, sixteen at the most.

He lets go of her, stunned.

The girl doesn't hesitate. She sprints from the store with her loot.

2

Lucas looks up and down the road, hand raised to shield his eyes from the sun's glare. The girl is fast. She's disappeared, and that's not easy to do around here. Everything is spread apart, nothing but dirt and dust between sporadic clusters of buildings. No place to hide.

He should return inside, finish unloading the fruit, prep the deli counter. Take stock of what she took. Ivy will need the inventory numbers. But he can't unsee the girl's astonishment when he caught her, those hazel eyes that look so much like Lily's.

He recognized that haunted look. Frightened but determined. She's running from something—or someone—but driven to survive. And for a split second the past merged with the present, and he thought she was Lily, the little sister he hadn't rescued from their father. He hadn't tried to help her.

He thought that his sister was here. The one he'd let run away.

Disturbed, Lucas rounds the building and gets into his truck. He flips down the visor, and the key fob he hides there drops in his lap. He takes a right, cruising in the direction she ran. Nothing but an open field on his right, an abandoned strip mall on his left. He coasts around the building that's boarded up tight and can't find a crevice she could have slipped into.

He passes a gas station, a bar, an open lot with a faded **FOR SALE** sign that's been there since the eighties. The space is littered with abandoned cars rusting under the sun.

He wonders where she could have gone, where she sleeps at night when the temperature drops and the vagrants come out of the shadows to sift through the day's garbage with no qualms about taking advantage of an unaccompanied minor, lost, frightened, and alone.

Would anyone miss her if she disappeared?

He drives with the windows open and thinks about the terrible things that could happen to her, what probably happened to Lily. Things he could have prevented if he'd cared enough to intercede.

Eight months ago he learned Lily, who ran from home sixteen and pregnant, had survived on her own, when her thirteen-year-old son, Josh, a nephew he'd never met, showed up alone at their sister Olivia's house. He was looking for help to find his mom. Through a flood of texts from Olivia he read before he ditched his phone, he knows Josh and Lily reunited. He also knows Lily now goes by the name of Jenna Mason. Author, animator, and screenwriter.

She's a bigger success than Olivia and Lucas combined. Though Lucas's achievements, or lack thereof, don't count for much.

But that slice of unexpected news—locating Lily and knowing she didn't just survive but raised a son while launching a flourishing career—doesn't make up for what he didn't do: help her when she needed him.

Lucas keeps driving, looking out his windows, making U-turns, retracing his route, as he begins to wonder if the little thief was a mirage. She was never at the market. He was hallucinating, damn hangover. It wouldn't be the first time he thought he was seeing things. His temples throb, and his mouth is cotton dry.

Hot, brittle wind cuts through the truck's cab. Sweat drips into his eyes. He swipes his forehead. She has to be around here somewhere. He'll find her, throw some cash at her. And if she's homeless and willing, drop her off at a shelter. Things he hadn't done for Lily.

He circles the city center, crawling past storefronts and restaurants, looking in windows and back lots. When he reaches the park, the phone

Ivy insisted he carry when he's out and about buzzes in his front pocket. He didn't want the phone at first. He got rid of his for a reason. No phone, no connections back home. But this one meant he was sprouting roots here. He kept it on him for convenience, and admittedly, so Ivy could reach him. She was getting old.

He slides out the device. "Yeah?"

"Where are you? I came downstairs, and the door's wide open, there's stock on the floor, and your truck's gone. Did you leave for good?" Ivy's panic rings in his ear.

He slams the brakes in the middle of a two-lane road. The truck comes to an abrupt stop. What is he doing? A car swerves around him, horn blaring. The driver flips him off through the rear window. A second later, another car swings around the corner. Lights flashing, it heads straight at him at high speed.

His stomach caves in at the sight of the police cruiser. Sirens wail, lights blaze, and Lucas locks up, his apology to Ivy lodging in his throat. They've found him.

Instinct pushes him to split. Run! But he stops himself from gunning the engine. The cops wouldn't come at him like this, not head-on. Unless they've been tailing him, which he'd know. They don't know where he is.

Yet.

The cruiser blows past, and he exhales harshly at the near miss.

"Lucas? Lucas! Are you still there?"

He drags a hand down his face. "Yeah. I'm here."

"Are you coming back?"

Pause.

"Yeah."

"Thank goodness. You know I can't manage without you." Ivy's voice shrinks, making him feel small real quick.

But Lucas never fully committed to Ivy. He didn't sign any employment docs or a lease. They didn't even shake hands. Skin on skin makes his skin crawl unless it's on his terms. She pays him cash, which he puts right back in the register when he loads a bag of food, taking the goods and a twelve-pack of Coronas upstairs. What change is left in his pocket he deposits at the bar three ridiculously long blocks up from the Dusty.

He can't blame Ivy for how she feels. He lives like he'll pack up and take off any moment, and she worries he will. But he never anticipated remaining here for as long as he has. If he had, he wouldn't have used his given name, and he would have abandoned his truck. But when he crawled to California City like a wounded animal intent on dying far away from his sisters so he wouldn't hurt them further, Ivy visited him his first night here. He was four beers in. But she'd brought home-made lasagna, the best he'd eaten. Somehow she knew he was famished. Somehow she knew he shouldn't be left alone.

He didn't have the courage that night to follow through on his plan, or any night since. He hasn't gathered the will to leave either, even with a bleak future.

"No, I haven't left. I—" He stops. How to explain what he's doing when he doesn't understand it himself?

What if he found the girl? What did he expect to do with her if she didn't want to go to a shelter? Feed her? Ha. Let her use his shower? No way. Turn her over to the cops for stealing?

He almost barks out a laugh. Lucas has always had a precarious relationship with the police. In simple terms, he doesn't trust people in positions of authority, especially if they're after him.

"I'm headed back," he says.

"You had me worried there." A relieved laugh. "I don't think we've had any customers yet. But hurry." As in *nobody has stolen anything yet*.

Wait until he tells her about the sunshine girl, the kid with the filthy blonde hair and sticky fingers who visited that morning. He imagines that under all those layers of dirt, her tresses are golden like the sun, her smile high wattage.

He's been driving over an hour and hasn't seen a dirty speck of her. She got away. And he shouldn't give a damn that she did.

"I'll be there in a sec," he tells Ivy before tossing the phone on the seat beside him. Heading back in the direction he came, he tries not to spare Sunshine Girl another thought.

3

Fifteen-year-old Shiloh Bloom crouches inside a dumpster and watches the guy from the market drive away. She remains there, swatting flies, and waits. As soon as his truck disappears in a haze of heat, she climbs out and ducks behind the large bin, sitting cross-legged in the shadow. The metal is getting hot, the day even hotter. Sweat trickles down her back underneath the thick sweatshirt, but she doesn't take it off. She won't risk losing it if she must run, not with the stuff she swiped buried in the pocket. Food she needs to last for a few days.

She rubs her wrist where the guy had grabbed her.

That was close.

She's been lifting merchandise, picking wallets, and slipping fingers into pockets since she was ten. Her mom didn't give her a choice. What cash Harmony earned from clerking the third shift at The Fog—a vape and smoke shop around the corner—went to her fix, and Shiloh had to eat. She'd try to get her mom to do the same. On a good day she would. She'd devour the entire bowl of mac 'n' cheese Shiloh prepared and have a burst of energy. They'd take the bus to the art museum at the university. It was free and open to the public. They'd walk to the park a block up from their apartment, sit on a bench, and watch kids swing on the same set her mom used to push Shiloh on. Shiloh would share with her mom what she'd learned in her high school design class, and her mom would add to her list of unfulfilled promises. She'd buy Shiloh a laptop of her own so that she didn't have to use the school's. They'd move to Hollywood or San Francisco, where Shiloh would be closer to the very people who created the animated shows and characters she adored. A dream Shiloh knew would never come to fruition. Her mom could barely make rent on their apartment, let alone afford to live in California.

Then things changed. Her mom started a relationship with her boss, the owner of The Fog. Ellis Radford became a permanent fixture on their couch. He didn't do much other than visit his shop a few times a week and order supplies. But he watched a lot of television, and her mom liked having him around. He kept the fridge stocked with beer and paid the rent. Her mom cut back her hours and started taking more hits, injecting instead of smoking the heroin he supplied her. And when her mom would pass out, Ellis turned to Shiloh, more fascinated with what was developing under her shirt than the woman sleeping off her rush in the next room. Shiloh started avoiding going home after school. She would spend her afternoons at the library and evenings in cafés sipping black coffee that never cost her more than a buck.

Until the one evening the cafés closed early for the Easter holiday, and she had nowhere else to go but home.

Her mom was really out of it, and Ellis wasn't doing anything about it. But he came into Shiloh's room when he thought she was asleep, and after he smacked her around a bit when she gave him some lip and fought off his advances, she kneed him, grabbed her backpack, and ran.

Finn—a guy she'd been videochatting with on Interloper, an app that matched them over their common interests of animation and music—was in California. He was her ticket to Hollywood, and she was crushing hard on him.

She hitched from Rio Rancho, New Mexico, to get as far from Ellis as possible, but only made it as far as this desolate dump when Moonstar, the woman she hitchhiked with, got handsy. Moonstar felt her up when she stopped to fill the car with gas. Bracelets stacked up her forearm jangled like bells when she rubbed her palm across Shiloh's chest, cupping her breast. Her silver-adorned fingers tweaked a nipple.

Shiloh didn't have any money, and Moonstar wanted payment for the lift. Shiloh smacked her hand. Moonstar kicked her out of the car, calling her a square bush for an eighteen-year-old.

Shiloh had lied about her age, so what. She bailed, gladly, but she's been stuck here going on twelve days by her last count, too spooked to hitch again, bathing in public restrooms and stealing food when she can get away with it.

Before today, she's never been caught. She's been invisible, living under the radar, unnoticed. Frightened, starved, and alone. Vulnerable.

But so far, lucky.

She prays that luck won't run out.

She looks up the road, trying not to freak. She's anxious to return to the sandy lot of abandoned cars. It had taken her less than two days to discover where the drifters slept, and another three to find an empty car of her own. But if she runs there now, she risks getting caught. There isn't any cover. Market guy could turn around. Then he'll know where she's been living. He'll take back what she stole. He might even turn her over to the police, who'll send her home. The one place she knows she isn't safe. Her mom chose her boyfriend over her own daughter. Harmony believed him, not her. She even called Shiloh a liar when she told her mom Ellis had been touching her.

Shiloh watches movies and reads a lot of books. She knows what heartbreak is, that crushing, hollow feeling when someone you love, someone you look up to, dismisses you, rejects what you say is true. But she'd never felt it firsthand until then. Betrayal hurts. Bad.

She needs to get to Finn in California, but what she wants more than anything is for her mom to put her first for once. Not Ellis, and not her addiction.

Shiloh looks at her hands. They're grimy and reek of filth. Chipped purple paint peels off dirt-caked fingernails. She spits in her palms and rubs her hands, smearing the dirt, cleaning them the best she can, then wipes them on her jeans. She tallies her winnings: a pack of Juicy

Fruit—she was desperate; she hasn't brushed her teeth in two weeks—a jerky strip, three packs of mixed nuts, four fruit strips, and a Snickers bar. She rips the wrapper and bites off a mouthful before the chocolate melts. The other snacks will hold in the heat.

This morning wasn't the first time she's cased the Dusty Pantry. She's been able to avoid going when the guy is there. He's too observant. His watchful eye too keen. The old lady is clueless. Shiloh steals right under her nose. And she's been there enough times to know where everything is located. Before she goes in, she plans exactly what she'll steal.

But this morning she grew impatient. She hasn't eaten in two days, so she took the risk and she almost lost everything. Her loot and her dreams. Getting caught also meant no Finn. No Finn meant no place to live in California.

Ten minutes pass, then another five, and the truck hasn't returned. Shiloh tosses the candy wrapper into the dumpster, brushes dirt off her rear, and runs the mile back to her car through a dirt field speckled with tumbleweeds and spurge. She keeps away from the road but watches for market guy's truck, ready to dive flat among the brittle growth if he comes back before she makes it.

Of all places to be abandoned, this one sucks. There isn't a single tree for cover or shade. But the one thing Shiloh has in her favor is her speed. Five years of pickpocketing has taught her to haul ass when she needs to.

She's drenched in sweat when she reaches the lot, her flared jeans coated in a thick layer of dust to her knees. She runs her fingers through her hair, scooping it off her damp face, and twists the tangled mess into a topknot with the rubber band on her wrist. She whacks at her jeans until a cloud billows. Her white Chucks are up the creek. They've turned the color of the sand that wants to bury this town before the sun set on her first day here. She doesn't even try to clean them. It takes too much effort, energy she doesn't have, not after that run. She barely had enough energy for the sprint here.

Close to thirty cars in various states of disrepair and decay are scattered over several acres, each one occupied. Shiloh's is near the back, a four-door gray Ford Fiesta from the eighties she found by chance. When she first stumbled upon this lot, she followed the woman who used to occupy the vehicle, curious about her comings and goings. They don't teach Homelessness 101 in high school. But she'd seen the woman around town and trailed her back to the car, desperate to learn how she was surviving. Overnight, Shiloh learned to blend into her surroundings to avoid danger, and to sleep on top of her backpack with it still strapped to her back so it isn't stolen. She learned to avoid other homeless so they don't exploit her because she's female and young.

But most of all, cops hate the homeless, especially when they're teenage runaways. And if she isn't careful, or causes trouble, other homeless will report her.

The two most beneficial things she's learned are to use the library during the day and to walk neighborhoods the night before garbage collection. Bins are free pickings, and that night she followed the homeless woman, Shiloh found the sweatshirt she's wearing and a blanket she keeps stowed in the car. Also that same night, the woman she'd trailed had stood over a bin she'd been riffling through, made a strange gurgling sound, and keeled over. She collapsed right there on the road.

Shiloh tried not to panic as she checked for a pulse. In another life she might have tried to revive the woman. Under other circumstances she would have alerted a neighbor to call an ambulance. But Shiloh was one hair shy of losing it. And she'd already lost so much: her home, her mom, her security. She couldn't lose her head. But if someone found her with the woman, they'd find out she was a runaway; then they'd send her home.

She checked the woman's pockets, disgusted with her own actions. But she picked up a few crumpled dollar bills and a smashed trail bar before sprinting back to the lot, where she cleaned the waste and filth from the car the woman had been living in. Then she cried herself to sleep over the woman nobody would miss, for the meager food and cash that felt tainted yet she badly needed, and for the mom she lost. Not the version she left, but the one Harmony was when Shiloh was a young girl. Loving and nurturing and secure. Shiloh's world.

Catching her breath, Shiloh walks the perimeter to avoid Ricky's henchmen, as she's come to think of them. Ricky and the two men who never leave her side live in a trio of cars in the middle of the lot that circle a firepit. They keep the flame low at night, blocked from view by Ricky's Camry. The three of them sit in worn beach chairs under a lean-to of sorts made from plastic pipes and old sheets, sharing a bottle of JD. Ricky wears nothing but a red bikini smudged with dirt, her crepey skin on full display. Her face collapsing in on itself, her nose and chin protruding, she waves at Shiloh, her triceps flab swinging like a kids' jump rope in the schoolyard. Henchman Bob throws a bunch of lewd gestures her way while Barton, the one who creeps her out, stares. His eyes follow her. Fear nudges her to hurry along.

Shiloh looks away and jogs to her Fiesta.

Door wide open, her neighbor Itchy Irving sits in the torn front seat of his Chevy Caprice wearing the same saggy, dull-brown tighty-whities that have taken on the hue of the desert she met him in a couple of weeks ago. He complains anything else he puts on irritates his skin. He's always scratching.

Bent over his legs, his hair pulled back in a colonial ponytail, his gray-speckled beard reaching his navel, he preps the dirty syringe he uses daily to shoot up between his toes.

"Hey." Shiloh shouts to get his attention. She veers over to him and grabs the syringe. "You want to get high, not comatose." And she needs him somewhat coherent. His presence keeps away the creeps.

When she first met Irving, he offered her a hit off the joint Ricky passed around the camp. Shiloh gagged at the thought of sharing, shaking her head. She's indirectly been high before on several occasions when her mom smoked weed. She didn't like the feeling or what it did to her mother. Irving just laughed and invited her to sing "American Pie" with him. He got one verse in, and she broke down crying in the dirt. The song reminded her of her mom. When Shiloh was young, Harmony would play it on repeat. They'd dance, spinning as they circled the room until they fell to the floor and gazed up at the popcorn ceiling, pretending the pockmarks were stars. *Make a wish*, her mom would whisper. Shiloh had made many. Only recently did she learn she couldn't rely on her mom to help her make them come true. She was on her own.

Her tears irritated some from the encampment. Ricky wanted to turn her over to the cops, believing Shiloh had a home to return to, since she's young. But Irving didn't pester her. He just let her cry and continued to sing. He smelled. The joint stank. But his presence oddly didn't frighten her. If anything, she felt better having him near. When she calmed, he pointed at a star and told her NASA sent him there on a top-secret mission. She laughed, feeling a little less sad.

Since that first night, he insists she check in with him whenever she leaves the encampment. She reminds him of his daughter, Daisy Ray, he's told her. She married some wealthy tycoon who stole her away. They live in a compound somewhere in the Mediterranean. He also told her he's an astronaut and has flown with Richard Branson and Elon Musk to the moon, and that he's dated Halle Berry, but she dumped him for Daniel Craig. His stories are outrageous, but she enjoys them. They make her forget how scary her life has become.

Irving's head falls back. His yellow-stained smile spreads wide and slow. "Too late, Daisy Ray."

Shiloh looks at the empty vial and swears under her breath. Irving already took a hit predawn before she left. He melts back onto the seat, legs dangling over the side, hands on his chest, fingernails scratching at the wiry silver hair. Eyes closed, he hums a Radiohead song Shiloh recognizes as another one of her mom's favorites, "Fake Plastic Trees." She misses her mom, but not enough to return home, not while Ellis is still around. With Irving out of it for the day, there isn't anything she can do about it other than leave until the euphoria passes. She's on her own for now. The camp isn't safe with Bob and Barton watching her so intently, and they've always made her feel uneasy.

She returns the syringe to the tin box on the front seat floorboard. Irving smells of stale sweat and something sour she can't place that burns her nostrils. The car reeks of rotten fruit, but she leans in to get the cardboard pieces he stores in the back seat. She presses them against the windshield, holding them in place with the visors, so he doesn't burn as he sleeps off the drug, and leaves a pack of mixed nuts she stole in the cupholder. Then she turns to her car and freezes. The four side windows have been smashed in.

"No!" *No, no, no.* She runs over to her car in a panic.

The windows blocked the wind. They made her feel safe from the other vagrants. She could lock the doors and keep them out. Now anyone can get to her while she sleeps. They can steal her things. Harm her.

She grips the door where the window had been and bites into her bottom lip. Shattered glass covers the seats. Her blanket is missing. She wants to scream. Then she remembers the backpack she stowed in the trunk.

Popping it open, she cries out. The backpack's been ransacked. What clothes she has—a shirt, two panties, a pair of shorts, and a bra, each just as filthy as the articles she's wearing—her Sharpie, earbuds with the knotted cord, and a small notepad filled with her doodles are strewn about the trunk. But the money she's slowly been collecting is gone.

"Irving," she cries, terrified at how much the loss has set her back. He promised to watch her car if she got him something to eat. It took her over a week to pickpocket the thirty-two dollars she had. People don't carry cash, and she's too petrified to get caught using a stolen credit card. But worse, if whoever did this to her car did it in broad daylight, imagine what they could do to her at night.

Irving doesn't answer. He raises his arms, waving side to side as if he's at a concert, singing to himself.

She looks over her shoulder to see who might have taken her things. The lot appears desolate, with everyone hunkered in their cars to escape the direct sunlight.

Shiloh holds in her scream. She pounds the car with her fists when she'd rather beat Irving instead. Where's she supposed to sleep tonight? There isn't anywhere else to go where she won't run into someone who'll report her. People call the cops on underage kids like her. They all think teen runaways have a home to go back to, that they're spoiled brats who think they know everything.

Near tears, Shiloh repacks her bag, adding her sweatshirt and the snacks from the Dusty Pantry, and slams the trunk. After she uses a small piece of cardboard to sweep the glass from the seats, she returns to Irving and kicks his shin. "I'm leaving," she says when he grunts.

He gives her two thumbs-up before his hands flop onto his chest.

What should have been a dull day trying to escape the sun, one day closer to getting out of this hellhole, has turned into a disaster. A scream builds in her chest, and frustration burns her eyes. She's never going to get out of here. At this rate, she'll be homeless forever.

Shiloh kicks a rock.

Then she shoulders her backpack and starts walking.

4

After mounting the bracket and setting the length of the downrod, Lucas wires the ceiling fan he's installing in Ivy's living room. They closed the market after the lunch rush of three customers. But Lucas recently installed a doorbell for customers at the market's entrance that rings in Ivy's apartment, giving her the freedom to come and go as she pleases and Lucas the time to repair and improve the property.

Her odd jobs keep him busy and his anxiety-ridden mind occupied. He left his meds in Seaside Cove. Renewing his clonazepam prescription would alert authorities to his location. Yes, improving the property in exchange for a reduced rent and no signed lease is their arrangement. But he works to keep the edge off.

He attaches the blades and bulbs and steps off the ladder. He flips the circuit in the juncture box in the hallway, restoring power, and flicks on the switch. The blades slowly spin, picking up speed.

Ivy joins him from the kitchen where she's been baking cookies. She stands under the fan, face uplifted, savoring the breeze. "That's nice."

"Told you." Lucas folds the stepladder and leans it against the wall by the door to take with him. He packs up the tools that once belonged to Ivy's husband and breaks down the ceiling fan's box.

"Decision made. I want fans in the two rear apartments and my bedroom."

"On it." He'll swing by Ace where Ivy has a line of credit before he meets up with the guys tonight at the Lone Palm for a beer.

"Start with Mike's old place." Mike, a longtime friend of Ivy and Tom who'd lived in apartment three for almost twenty years, moved out a couple of months ago. He and the girlfriend he met while grocery shopping purchased a house near the ballpark. The apartment has been empty for weeks despite Ivy's ads and the sign in the market's front window.

"After that, give yourself a break."

"Beg your pardon?" Unease twists in his gut.

"You've been working nonstop since you got here. And I'm not talking about today."

So far he's installed new carpeting and linoleum, and painted all four apartments. In addition to general maintenance around the property, he's also updated Ivy's kitchen and bathroom.

"I like the work." He needs to work.

"You'll run yourself into the ground."

It's a miracle he's still aboveground.

"I don't mind."

"You remind me so much of my Tom. He never knew when to quit."

If he quits, he'll die. The only thing keeping him alive is her odd jobs, his guilt, and a deep-seated wish for his sisters' forgiveness he doesn't deserve. He failed Lily and he left Olivia without a word. He knows they're worried sick.

But also, he wouldn't want to leave the old woman high and dry. He's all she's got.

Ivy returns to the kitchen that smells of melted chocolate and butter, exactly what he once believed a home should smell like, not the toxicity he grew up with. Her entire apartment is homey, with knitted blankets draped over tweed couches and frilly pillows used as seat cushions at the dining table. Nothing like his barren apartments, the one here and his place back in Seaside Cove.

She drops a handful of cookies in a brown lunch bag, rolls the opening closed, and gives him the bag. The slight tightening of appreciation he feels in his stomach is unexpected, but he digs in, finishing a cookie in two bites.

"You need to sell these in the deli," he tells her, not for the first time.

Her gaze swerves to the doorbell's chime box. "It would make sense if I had enough customers to buy them. They'll get stale. Do you think it's broken?"

"The chime box?" He shakes his head. "It works."

Her mouth turns down. Today has been slower than most. It's why he hasn't told her about Sunshine Girl. Not because he doesn't care what happens in the market on his watch. He doesn't want to deal with the aftermath. Oh, he knows exactly what Sunshine stole, and that today's sales barely make up for the loss of those items. It'll break Ivy's heart. Hard to entice prospective buyers for the property when a business isn't profitable. But sales should pick up in a few weeks when schools let out for summer and people return to the road for vacations. Either way, she'll be upset. Maybe he can convince her to install cameras to deter further thefts.

Ivy returns to her baking as his phone buzzes with an incoming text from Faye, one of many she's sent today. First she spewed a chain of insults over how rude he was this morning when he shut the bathroom door in her face. Apparently she'd gotten out of bed to join him in the shower. He hadn't noticed and frankly didn't care. If she knew him, she wouldn't have wasted her time insulting him. He didn't care about that either.

Then a stream of apologies flew in over the next hour. She didn't mean what she'd said. Last night had been wonderful. He hadn't been rude this morning. It was a simple misunderstanding on her part. Could he forgive her?

Uh, no. Because he had been rude. And if she didn't see that? He shakes his head.

He reads Faye's latest text. Rafe's getting in late. She wants to come over. She'll make him dinner, bring a bottle of his favorite, El Tesoro Anejo, a tequila he can savor, not the cheap crap he tries to drown in.

He can picture it clearly. She'll cook taco meat in the nude, lick sour cream from his chest. They'll never get around to eating. Heat spreads from his center. He feels a curling down low.

"That your girl?" From the kitchen, Ivy gestures at his phone with a spatula.

Lucas grunts. Faye's anything but. It's just sex. She's already attached, so she can't get hooked on him. If he were wise, he'd block her number.

He slips the phone in his pocket, leaving the text unanswered like the others.

"We're a tight community, Lucas." Her back to him, Ivy transfers cookies from the baking sheet to a wire rack to cool. "Everybody knows everybody."

And they're all up in each other's business. With a population under fifteen K, how could they not be? There's not much else to do here. Aside from Mike who used to live in apartment three and a buddy of his Lucas meets at the Lone Palm over conversations of baseball, trucks, and dirt bikes, he keeps to himself. The permanent scowl on his face does wonders keeping people at a distance.

"Faye knows a lot of people. You also aren't her first . . . indiscretion, to put it delicately. Don't think her comings and goings go unnoticed." She glances at him over her shoulder, brows high on her forehead. *Just saying.*

He grunts again, latching up the old metal toolbox, the red paint scuffed from decades of projects. If people are noticing, then he has to stop seeing her.

"Her husband's a trucker and out of town a lot. Makes cheatin' easy."

"I'm not the one who's married."

"She is, and Rafe used to work at the prison."

Not one of his brightest decisions, especially for a guy hiding from the type of people her husband associates with. Call him a masochist. He's been called worse.

Lucas tucks the stepladder under his arm and picks up the toolbox. "Your point is?"

"A lot of those guards are his friends. And the Lone Palm is their favorite watering hole."

He knows. They're there every time he is, playing dice in the corner table. But Lucas can't seem to stop himself from tempting fate.

He twists the knob on the front door, itching to bail. He needs a shower. "Say what you gotta say, Ivy."

She sets down the spatula and turns around, hand on hip. "Don't be foolish. There's a good chance Rafe already knows about you."

And he's a big guy who packs a gun and probably owns a few rifles.

But Lucas is taller and wider. He's also faster, and he knows when it's time to make an exit.

He shrugs a shoulder.

"I'm just watching out for you," Ivy says.

When he was a kid, he longed for someone who would. For years he tried to get his father's attention, get him to show that he cared. Parents should love their children unconditionally, but Dwight cared only about himself. Next on the list came Olivia. Dwight loved Lucas's older sister beyond reason, and Livy basked in the glow of it.

Lucas had been envious of that attention. He excelled in sports, seeking Dwight's praise. He aced his classes, was even on track for a scholarship at USC, hoping for a hint of approval from him. When nothing worked, when he hadn't even received a pat on the back, he started picking fights. He resorted to stealing, and even held up a clerk at gunpoint at a minimart. And when those hadn't worked, Lucas gave up caring what people thought of him, how they felt about him. His dad, especially.

Then Ivy had to go on and show that she cares. And it's leaving a weird sensation in his chest cavity. He doesn't know what to do with it.

"Don't waste your worry on me." He opens the door. "I sure don't."

She levels with him with a look. "One of these days you're going to tell me why you left wherever it is you came from. You'll tell me what you're running from."

He grimaces. Doubtful.

An image of his dad's mangled car comes to mind, along with the guilt and self-loathing.

His thoughts then flash to Olivia and the last time he saw his older sister. The way she shoved at his chest, got in his face. Practically thrust her arm down his throat to drag a confession from him about their father and his involvement in his death. He'd broken down, teared up in front of her like a pansy ass. But he hadn't admitted fault. Instead, he'd gotten in his truck after spending hours staring at the bay, visualizing fragments of his life, his mistakes, his wrongdoings, willing them to float away. But they'd clung to him. Dug their claws in him. So he drove away, his demons going along for the ride.

He didn't call or text goodbye. She'll be livid if he ever sees her again.

"If not me, then tell someone else. Your troubles will eat you alive," Ivy says.

His nostrils flare with a forced exhale. They already are. And there isn't much left for them to chew on.

"Goodnight, Ivy."

He shuts the door behind him.

Back in his apartment, Lucas eyeballs the switchblade on the toilet tank while he waits for the shower to warm. Sunshine Girl comes to mind again despite his efforts to not think about her. His reaction when he grabbed her wrist unsettled him. He'd thought she was Lily.

Impossible, he knows. It's been years since she ran. She's thirty now. But the memory was instant and strong. His guilt over failing her even stronger, a baseball bat to the cheekbone. He felt like he was going to black out.

He looks at the tattooed vine riddled with thorns that twists up his forearm. His thumb traces the rigid scar hidden underneath that he's had since he was sixteen. A devil lurking in the shadows.

Disgusted with himself, Lucas steps under the scalding spray and yanks closed the moldy curtain.

5

Shiloh arrives at the library a muddled mess of anxiety and despair. Her shirt is drenched underneath a backpack empty of cash. Mortified by her appearance, she takes a left down the hall, scurrying past the circulation desk to the restroom before she's noticed. Sweaty and filthy, she hasn't cleaned up in several days.

The women's bathroom is unoccupied. She locks the door, drops her backpack on the floor, and strips off her shirt. Using paper towels and soap from the dispenser, Shiloh washes her hair, face, and torso. Her cheeks are sunburned, and the tip of her nose is peeling. She looks like a kid who spent too much time at the pool. She scrubs her hands and fingernails until her palms feel raw, then rinses her shirt. She wrings out the water, twists up the shirt, and swaps it for the less dirty one in her backpack. She'll hang it to dry at the encampment, assuming she returns. With the windows broken, the car she's been using doesn't offer the security she needs. And she has a feeling Bob and Barton are just biding their time with her. Which scares her almost as much as returning home to Ellis. She's alone, helpless, and out of her depth.

After she runs a broken hairbrush she found last week in the gutter through her hair and knots it atop her head, she wipes up the water on the floor and cleans the sink, pausing to study her reflection. She looks twelve without makeup, the squeaky-clean girl next door. She's Zooming with Finn at three. He'll guess she's been lying about her age and won't let her stay with him. She can't let him think she's younger than she's led him to believe. He's a total snack, and she really has it bad for him. She's also counting on him. But more than that, he's her only option for a place to live.

Shiloh heads to the kids' reading area where a small table sits in the corner with a basket of crayons and felt-tip pens. She picks out black and brown pens and a couple of skin-toned hues, then settles at a computer. While it boots up so she can log on to her email, she retrieves the pocket mirror from her backpack and colors her eyelids, licking her fingertip to blend the shades, fills in her brows with the brown pen and slashes the black across the base of her lashes, hoping Finn won't be able to tell the difference from her usual made-up face.

Satisfied she's added a few years to her looks, she logs into her Gmail account. Eight new messages from her mom. Her stomach compresses into a tight, queasy ball. She wants to read them, but they probably say the same as the first one she sent. Come home, baby girl. Momma misses you. Ellis swears it was a misunderstanding. He's an honest man. Just come home.

She wishes she could.

She wishes her mom would stop taking drugs and break up with Ellis.

But no. Her mom betrayed her when she didn't believe Ellis attacked her, and she rejected her when she chose him over her own daughter. Even if she could go back, Shiloh doubts she could ever forgive her.

Hurt as hot and raw as the first time she felt it surges in her chest.

She deletes each email with a hard click of the mouse. She then opens the message Finn sent late last night after his gig. Can't wait to see your beautiful face. See you at 3:00, shy girl.

A thrill of anticipation shoots through her. She smiles at the screen. Finally something good today. Her gaze slides to the time in the lower corner of the monitor. Four more hours.

Four hours to kill before she and Finn can figure how to get her from here to there.

If only he had a car.

If only she hadn't chucked her phone out the window at the New Mexico–Arizona border so Ellis couldn't track her through her mom's phone. She could call Finn anytime.

She closes her email and pops over to YouTube, elated to see another *Tabby's Squirrel* short has dropped. After plugging in her earbuds, she watches the clip, copying characters from Jenna Mason's latest animation into her notebook as her own quirky characters take shape in her mind. Shiloh has dreams, big dreams. Her head bursts with stories.

Months ago, she emailed episode ideas to Jenna for *Tabby's Squirrel*, but never heard back. That hasn't stopped her from storyboarding. Animated characters cover the pages of her notebook, from original superheroes to a mad murdering otter. Video animation is her dream. Her imaginary characters kept her company when her mom couldn't. Before she ran from home, she'd been practicing 2D renderings. Her digital design elective in high school was her favorite class. One day, her own animated feature film will debut. She just doesn't know how to start or where. She's too nervous to upload her work to social media, afraid it's not good enough.

That's why she needs to get to Hollywood by Saturday. Jenna Mason is signing her books and giving away merchandise at the Grove in Los Angeles. It's a huge publicity event ahead of the movie's premiere. Large crowds are expected. But if she can chat with Jenna for even a minute, she could get the advice and encouragement she needs to share her quirky characters with the world. Jenna's stories helped Shiloh feel less lonely. She wants her own stories and characters to be that for someone else. Someone like her.

Shiloh passes time doodling and watching videos. She peruses the bookstacks and flips through the few graphic novels available to check out. Older editions of The Umbrella Academy and Fables. She's read them before and will read them again. And when the librarian turns her back, Shiloh nibbles on a fruit strip, making it last. Hunger gnaws at her like a bear stripping meat off a bone. But it's all she'll allow herself to eat until tonight.

Three o'clock comes, and Shiloh logs on to her Zoom account, excited to see her guy. She hasn't seen Finn's face since their last Interloper chat. She'd called him right after Moonstar offered her a ride and just before she dumped her phone to tell him that she was on her way. That Ellis got too friendly.

Finn wasn't cool with her hitchhiking, but couldn't wait for her to arrive. They'd share a bed. They'd make breakfast together in the mornings and gorge on carne asada tacos from the food truck parked around the corner. He'd help her find a job and make connections. His bandmate knows a guy who knows a guy who works at Disney Animation Studios.

Shiloh starts the meeting and waits for Finn to join. She refreshes the screen, chewing the Sharpie cap, and waits some more. Ten minutes go by, and worry seeps in. Is he ghosting her? She spits out the cap. He wouldn't. He's crushing on her. But what if he is? He's the only person she knows in California. Where would she stay? She can't live on the streets there. She wouldn't have a chance.

At a quarter past the hour, she sends him an email. She sends another at half past the hour, then again at three forty-five. *Where are you?* She's online. She's waiting. They go unanswered. When it reaches four o'clock, her stomach sour from hunger and despair, she realizes he isn't joining the meeting.

Her day just went from bad to worse.

Shiloh logs out, clearing her search history. Fighting tears, she yanks off her earbuds, stuffing them in her backpack. He forgot her.

Maybe he was held up at the Vinyl Hub, the vintage record shop where he works, or rehearsal ran late. Maybe his roommate took his laptop, and Finn couldn't use it. He doesn't have his own computer or car. He can barely pay his rent, he explained when she asked him to Venmo her money for a bus ticket before she left New Mexico. He borrows everything, waiting for the day the Sunset Strips have their big break. He plays bass in the band, and when they make it big, he'll treat her to whatever she wants.

What she wants is to leave this place.

What she needs is a phone.

Shiloh slings on her backpack and approaches the circulation desk. The woman behind the desk sorts books on a cart. She smiles at Shiloh, her brown eyes big behind green-framed lenses. Her oversize teal tunic hits her knees. Underneath, she wears paisley leggings. "May I help you?" Her voice is soft, almost a whisper.

Shiloh clasps her hands on the counter. "Can I borrow your phone?"

The librarian's gaze dives to the black-office phone on the desk below the counter. "I'm sorry. This phone is for staff only. There's a pay phone at Maria's Deli."

A mile back the way she came.

Shiloh chews her bottom lip, worried. "My friend's late. He's supposed to pick me up here, so I can't leave." She taps the countertop, her eyes nervously scurrying about, and sighs heavily. She was hoping to talk with Finn about what happened today. He might have an idea on what to do.

"You don't have a cell phone?"

Shiloh shakes her head. "I dropped it. The screen shattered, and it won't power on."

The librarian's brows meet in the center. "Are you all right, dear? You've been here all day. Is there someone I can call for you?"

Her arms tingle with unease at the woman's concern. "I'm fine," she says with an uptick to sound better than she feels. If she doesn't act like her situation is worrisome, the woman won't think it is. She won't pry. "I just need . . . I need to call my friend. Can I use your cell? One call, that's it. Then I'll go."

The librarian's lips pinch. "Just this once," she decides, going to her purse. The worn brown-leather bag sits in plain sight on a chair, wide

open. "I don't usually allow customers to use it. But in this case . . .
I'm worried about you. I've seen you here before. How old did you say
you were?"

She didn't. "Eighteen," she says, itching to dip her hand into
the woman's purse. The overstuffed wallet is right there, dollar bills
poking out.

She looks at Shiloh for a beat, her eyes narrowing, and for a second
that seems like eons. Shiloh is sure she doesn't believe her. She'll call the
cops, and they'll write her up for truancy. But she holds the phone to
her face to unlock the screen, and Shiloh lets go of a breath that makes
her sound suspiciously relieved. "Here you go." She gives Shiloh the
phone, only to pull it back at the last second. "You're sure you don't
need help?"

"I'm cool, really." Just give her the darn phone.

"One call."

"One call," Shiloh repeats, taking the phone. She taps in Finn's
number. The librarian hovers close. Shiloh turns around for some privacy and waits for Finn to answer. "Pick up, pick up, pick up," she
whispers, afraid he won't because he doesn't recognize the number.

He answers after the fourth ring. "Who's this?"

"Finn, it's me."

"Shy, baby?" His voice rises with surprise. "Hey, guys, it's Shy," he
yells to the room. Shiloh hears shouts. "Did you get a new phone? This
your new number?"

"I borrowed it."

"Where're you at? You here?"

"No, I'm still stuck in Cal City." She cups her hand over the phone
so she's not overheard.

"That sucks."

"We're supposed to Zoom today. Where were you?"

He groans and slaps his forehead. She hears the smack over the line.
"That's riiiiight." He swears. "Sorry, Shy. The guys had me. Beck wrote

a new song. We had to work it out, took all afternoon. We're playing tonight at the Silverlake. This is a big deal, Shy. This could be it, our big break. You understand?"

She understands she was supposed to see this performance. But she's stuck in the desert, broke, starving, and hasn't had a shower in over a week. This is not where she expected to land when she ran.

"I thought you'd take the bus, and I'd meet you at the station. You said you had enough for a ticket."

"Someone stole my money."

"How?"

"I left my backpack in the car when I—" She glances over her shoulder at the librarian. "It's just gone."

"Shyyyy . . ."

"I know. It was stupid of me." She never should have trusted Irving to watch her stuff. "Can't you borrow a car and come get me?"

"Not today. We got the thing tonight."

"Tomorrow, then? I'll get a job in Hollywood and pay you back for gas."

"Babe, no."

"Why not? Don't you want me to move in with you? You said you loved me." She's trying hard to be brave and not sound as scared as she is, but she can't help it. She's terrified and desperate. She also can't understand why Finn isn't more alarmed. Why isn't he making an effort to get her out of here?

"I do love you. Of course I want you to move in. I dream about you, Shy. The things I want to do . . ." He groans.

"I want to do that with you, too. But Finn, *please*. You have to come get me."

"I can't."

"Yes, you can. I'm only three hours from you. You don't start playing until nine—"

"For fuck's sake, Shy. I can't drive. I don't have a license."

35

Shiloh's hope bottoms out in her stomach. "Oh." She didn't expect that. This isn't good. This isn't good at all. Why hasn't he told her before?

"You gotta come to me, babe. You can do that, right?"

How? She needs cash. But she sucks up the tears she wants to shed and murmurs, "Okay."

A shout comes through the phone.

"What was that?" she asks.

"Gotta run. Guys are loading up. Can I call you at this number tomorrow?"

"No. I . . ." She peeks over her shoulder at the librarian. She stacks books behind Shiloh, pretending she's trying not to listen. "I'll email you when I book my ticket."

"Cool. Can't wait. Wish me luck tonight."

"Good—" He hangs up. "Luck," she mutters.

Defeated, Shiloh deletes the call from the log and returns the phone, wondering where she can find cash and fast. She doesn't want to spend another day like today here.

"Everything all right?" the librarian asks, tucking her phone in the tunic's front pocket. Shiloh nods, and the librarian picks up a stack of books, hesitating before she carries them to the cart, her head shaking.

Shiloh eyes the wallet in the purse. An easy grab. She'd have the cash out and wallet dumped in a trash can before she leaves the premises, she's that quick.

Her gaze lifts to the surveillance camera aimed at the front desk, and her shoulders round. With nowhere to go, the encampment a question in the air, she returns to the stacks. She's thirsty, filthy, and broke. Back pressed to the shelves, she slides to the floor and hugs her knees. A sob bubbles up, and she covers her mouth to drown out the noise, but she can't stop the tears.

6

Lucas didn't plan to meet Mike and Oscar at the Lone Palm. He just knew they'd be there. Permanent fixtures at the bar, the Cliff and Norm of California City. Val is tending. She sends him a smile before going back to the cocktail she's mixing. Some guy nursing a beer chats her up. She's only half listening, hardly interested, and walks away to drop off a drink while he's still rambling.

The Lone Palm is a stucco box on the side of the road with a marquee-style sign above the door that features the night's cocktail special in lights. The parking lot is asphalt covered in an inch of desert dust. There used to be a lone palm in the center of the property, but the winds of '96 split the tree, leaving a fifteen-foot toothpick. The bar never changed its name or bothered planting another tree.

A couple of marked transport trucks from the prison are parked out front. Rafe's buddies. Lucas almost turns around when he sees them. He isn't in the mood for trouble. But given his luck, trouble would find him anyway. One of these nights Rafe will confront him, and Val will call the cops on the ruckus that follows. Then that'll be the end of the road for Lucas.

But fuck. He needs a drink. So here he is.

Lucas settles onto the leather stool beside Mike. Oscar's on Mike's right. Val approaches, handing off the drink she mixed to a woman in jeans and a cowboy hat. "Usual, Luc?" Blue eyes meet his. Long brown hair falls lower than the neckline of her ribbed tank. Tattoos that mean nothing to him but probably hold stories of their own run up her right arm, ending with a floral burst that coats her shoulder.

"Yeah." He pops a few pretzels from the community bowl into his mouth.

"Another round, boys?" Mike grunts with a nod, and Oscar slaps the bar in approval. "Coming right up."

"Ivy listed my old apartment yet?" Mike asks, finishing off his whiskey sour. He slides the empty glass to Val's side of the bar.

"It's listed. Still empty. Building hasn't sold either." Palms flat on the sticky wood surface, Lucas plays it like a keyboard, anxious for a drink. He wouldn't call Mike and Oscar friends. More like unintentional drinking buddies. He shows up. They're here. They drink and shoot the shit, Ivy a mutual acquaintance. In fact, Mike confessed Ivy told him to strike up conversation with Lucas when she learned he was spending his evenings at the Lone Palm. That woman's always looking out for him.

"Hard to sell without tenants."

"Yep." Hard to sell when Dusty's can't move product, or said product is swiped from under his nose.

"I thought about buying it," Mike says. Lucas quirks a brow. Mike shrugs. "It was a thought."

"You're supposed to be retiring," Oscar pipes up.

"I am retired. Sitting behind a cash register chatting with folks is retirement. Janie wants to travel."

Oscar works a toothpick in his teeth. "Don't blame her. I wouldn't want to be stuck making subs either. Though Ivy's are the best in town."

Val returns with their drinks. She sets a Corona with a lime and a side shot of Jose before Lucas. He drains the tequila before she serves Mike and Oscar their drinks.

"Want another, baby?" Val asks as Lucas pushes the lime slice through the Corona's narrow neck.

"That would be great."

The second shot arrives quick. Val touches the back of Lucas's hand. "Good to see you here tonight. You doing okay?"

His gaze drops to their hands. Silver rings adorn her fingers. A leather cuff hugs her wrist. Her finger traces his thumb before she lays her hand a mere inch from his. He forgot how soft her skin feels, how silken her hands are despite the repetitive washing as she works the bar.

He feels a buzz in his center. Instinct demands he pull away. But he pushes past the urge to retreat and luxuriates in the split second of human contact she offers him, that he allows himself to feel. He skims the back of his fingers along her forearm before reaching for his beer. When he doesn't feel repulsed by the contact or break out in a sweat, he nods. "I'm good." Tipping back the bottle, he takes a long swig.

"Let me know if you need anything." She taps the bar, her eyes meeting his again, and leaves to help another customer.

"So Janie's got a thing tomorrow night," Mike says. "A pampered something or other."

"What of it?" Oscar picks up his Ferrari, a mint-and-orange concoction Lucas has never acquired a taste for.

"I have an extra ticket to the game."

Lucas tosses back his second shot, motions for a third, and chases the Jose with his Corona. "I'll take it." California City doesn't offer much, but for three seasons it had a lower-division baseball team. Mike went to every Whiptails home game. When the team folded, he bit the bullet and bought tickets for the Bakersfield Train Robbers. Lucas wouldn't mind the hour drive. The desert is wearing on him. He's used to fog and sixty-degree highs. Bakersfield won't offer relief, but it is a change of scenery.

"What if I want the ticket?" Oscar asks.

Mike looks at him. "You want it or not?"

"Yeah, I want it."

"Darts," Lucas says.

"Darts?"

Mike pounds the table. "You heard the man. Winner gets the ticket."

Lucas stands. "Another round, Val." He circles his finger to encompass the guys.

"Sure thing, baby." Val sprays soda water over ice.

Mike snags the cup of darts from behind the bar, and Oscar moves chairs to clear the area in front of the board. Lucas hears his name. He looks over his shoulder at the group of men seated at the table in the corner playing Ship, Captain, Crew. A few of the guys Lucas recognizes as friends of Rafe watch him, but nobody acts like they'd called out to him.

The compulsion to leave not just the bar, but town, surges upward. He's lingered too long, pushing his luck. Trouble will find him. Or the law. But the town and the people have been growing on him. And Ivy would probably kill him herself if he deserted her.

When he deserts her, he amends.

He can't stay here forever. Either he sucks up the will to end it, or the cops will sniff him out. One or the other will put him out of his misery. He just doesn't know who or what will get to him first.

He turns away from them, reasoning he was hearing things. Feeling paranoid after dallying with Faye. Mike hands Oscar three darts, gives Lucas the other three. "What'll it be, weasels? Five-oh-one or Shanghai?"

"Around the Clock." A challenge that requires them both to hit every number on the board before they aim at the bull's-eye. "Highest goes first." Lucas throws a dart and lands on the eighteen.

Oscar gets a five. "Fucker."

Lucas grins. "You can give up now. I'll take the ticket."

"Not a chance." But Oscar moves to the side, giving Lucas space. Lucas throws his three darts, landing one on the one, another on the two, the third on the five, and Mike tallies the numbers.

Val comes over with their drinks during Oscar's round. She moves close enough to Lucas that her arm brushes his chest. He takes his drinks off the tray, his fingers skimming the side of her breast. His eyes dip to those breasts, linger for a sec before lifting to hers and holding. Her smile is an invitation before she turns away to deliver Mike and Oscar their drinks.

They're several turns and another round in with Lucas in the lead when the back of his neck tingles. He steps up to the line, knowing he's being watched. He aims his dart, catching his name as he cocks back his arm. Grinding his teeth, he looks behind him, and Paul, a prison guard Faye once mentioned was a good friend of Rafe's, gives him the finger.

Lucas flips him the bird before he can think better not to, Ivy's advice ringing in his ears. Yeah, time's up with Faye. Trouble is here. That's one hookup he never should have started, let alone allowed to linger.

Marshall, the bar manager, relieves Val for her midshift break. She removes her waist apron, catching Lucas's eye, and retreats down the back hallway.

"Give me a minute. Gotta piss." He hands off his darts to Mike and follows Val past the restroom and storage closet, and out the rear. The thick metal door bangs shut behind them. The back of the bar is dark, but for a single wall lamp, and thankfully void of people.

Val turns around, and Lucas's mouth lands on hers. She tastes of Jack and Coke. Her arms twine around his neck. The kiss is wet, hungry, and wordless. An unspoken agreement. A mutual consent. His hands move up her torso under her tank, scouring her sides, and squeeze her breasts. She moans into his mouth, pushing her pelvis against his hardness, and he groans. He can't get over how soft her skin is. Such a contradiction to his coarse fingers, rough from years of labor. Her palms glide down, tracing his ribs, his abs. Her fingers trail under his shirt hem, teasing, tormenting. The sensation goes straight to his groin.

Lucas breaks the kiss, catching her eye. She smiles, her chest rising and falling. Then their hands are moving. Belts come unclasped, buttons undone, and zippers pulled. Val pushes down her jeans and thong, and Lucas frees himself, spinning her around. He bends her over a stack of wood pallets, rips open a foil packet and sheathes himself, and pushes into her in a breath.

She gasps. He growls a curse. Then he's moving. Slowly at first until she accommodates him, adjusting to his size, then he's pounding into her. His hand reaches around to her front, and she cries out.

They're loud, they're rough, and at this point, they don't care who sees them.

Lucas's fingers dig into her hips, his thighs shaking as Val braces her weight against the pallets, pushing back as he tries to fuck away his guilt and shame. To take off the edge.

It's over as fast as it started.

And as always, sex just numbs the pain that never leaves.

His forehead drops onto her damp back, and for a moment they're still except for their heaving lungs as they catch their breath. For a moment Lucas gives himself over to the simple pleasure of touching someone else without shirking away. If he plans it, expects it, is mentally prepared for it, he revels in the contact. Relishes worshiping a woman's body. Softly, timidly, he kisses her back along the bumpy ridge of her spine, denying he craves the contact past experiences won't allow him to enjoy.

Val rears up. Lucas steps away, giving her space. She pulls up her pants, zips her fly. "Thanks," she says, reminding him exactly what this was. A mindless release.

Lucas's walls shore up. "No prob." He tucks himself back in, flinging the used condom into the dumpster.

She gives him a sexy grin, her tongue moistening her bottom lip, and returns to the bar.

Hands on his waist, still catching his breath, he looks at the sky. The stars are dim with the light over his shoulder. But he knows they're there, a constant. Just like the memories in his head, the screams trapped in his chest.

God, he thinks, his chin dropping. If his younger self saw him now—living off one-nighters and bedding married women, starved for affection but incapable of allowing himself anything meaningful . . .

He shakes his head.

Nothing he can do about it now. He smells of Val, but he needed that. He came out here to purge Faye, and that's what he did.

Next time he sees Rafe, he might not feel as disgusted with himself. Val's beautiful in a rough-around-the-edges way, but she's also single. No one's breathing down his neck after he screws her. No one will give him trouble.

Lucas rolls his shoulders and returns inside to win the game.

7

The library closes at six o'clock, and Shiloh is forced to leave. She wanders the streets, aimless, cautious not to linger too long in one spot before someone wonders why her clothes are filthy or why she's out alone when it's getting dark. No LOITERING signs hover overhead in almost every strip-mall parking lot. They'll realize she's homeless. Someone will call the police or CPS. And the possibility of going home to Ellis scares her more than starving to death. She doesn't want to die, but she'll choose that over Ellis invading her bedroom again while her mom sleeps off her high in the next room.

As the sun sets, she catches her reflection in a shop window. The felt pen she'd applied earlier has mixed with her sweat and bled over her cheeks, giving her a serious case of raccoon eyes. She looks clownish and sad. How many nights after working a late shift at The Fog had her mom come home with her mascara smeared? She was always tired and had a terrible habit of rubbing her eyes when she grew jittery after her fix wore off. The darkened skin around her eyes added years to her thirty-three. Shiloh hated watching her mom descend into her addiction.

Harmony used to promise life would get better. That they'd move to California after Shiloh graduated high school. There Shiloh would attend a community college or apply for scholarships at surrounding universities. Her mom would find a job, or two. Three, if need be. She'd continue to support Shiloh until she became the successful video animator they both dreamed she'd become.

But the exact opposite happened when Ellis entered their lives. He convinced Shiloh's mom to stay whenever she talked of finding an apartment to rent near the beach for her baby girl. Shiloh has dreams Harmony wants her to fulfill. But Ellis argued he was just as important, that he had dreams, too. He'd give her a gram of heroin and promise he'd buy her a house with a pool. He'd supply another gram with a promise they'd vacation in Mexico. Harmony wanted to ride horses on the beach. And when she stopped talking of California, when Shiloh's dreams were no longer part of her own, he provided her with an endless supply.

Whatever Harmony wanted, he'd get for her, so long as she stayed in Rio Rancho and he could stay with her.

Shiloh tried, but she couldn't convince her mom to leave him. "He's good for us," Harmony would murmur, sighing deeply with the initial rush of an injection. She'd been close to her mom before the drugs, before Ellis. But now she hated her because of those drugs. Because of Ellis. It's going to take more than a promise in an email for Shiloh to forgive her.

Shiloh's pace quickens just thinking about Ellis, and what he tried to do to her. She shivers as if she can still feel his fingers on her thighs. It wasn't the first time he'd touched her when she ran away. But it would be the last.

She crosses the road to the park and slips into the public restroom. She washes her face with cold water and foaming pink hand soap. The soap stings her eyes, but she scrubs until the felt pen comes off.

She dries her face with a stiff paper towel and stares at her reflection. Her face is red, especially around her eyes, and she's back to looking younger than her age. Squeaky clean. Girl-next-door fresh.

Every promise ever made to her has been broken. Finn won't borrow a car and come get her. He can't even drive. Her mom gave up on her. She can't rely on either.

She only has herself.

With a fresh wave of resolve, Shiloh pushes her arms into her hoodie and leaves the bathroom. She comes across a woman and her young son feeding ducks at the edge of the pond, her purse on the ground behind her, the mouth wide open. Shiloh stumbles, apologizing when her shoulder nudges the woman's hip, surprising her. She helps Shiloh to her feet.

"Are you all right?"

"Yes, sorry." Shiloh timidly backs away.

She turns around and keeps walking, opening the woman's wallet. She removes three ones, tucking them into her pocket, and tosses the wallet into the first trash bin she passes, before she's tempted to use the credit cards. She risks getting caught if they've been reported lost or stolen.

Across the road she enters the Dollar General, dropping her backpack off with the first cashier. She paces up an aisle, down another. A woman reads the ingredients on a box of rice. Her shopping basket rests at her feet, her purse inside. Shiloh crouches, grabs a box of rice from the bottom shelf, and keeps walking. She rounds the end cap, returns the box to another shelf, retrieves her backpack, and leaves the store. Once she reaches the sidewalk, she opens the woman's wallet, removes a single dollar, and drops the wallet in the trash.

She wants to cry over the measly pickings, but she keeps walking.

The sky darkens, the hour growing late.

Shiloh enters a restaurant, a seafood and steak eatery. Grilled meat and fried fish assail her. Her stomach cramps with hunger. She asks for a menu as she scopes the layout for dine-and-dash potential. Handbags on chairbacks she can lift. But the hostess looks down her nose. Shiloh isn't only underdressed, her clothes are filthy. Her shirt reeks of body odor.

Embarrassed by her appearance, she steps back from the hostess stand. "Where's the bathroom?" she asks.

The hostess points behind her.

Shiloh moves quickly down the hallway only to abruptly stop at a door marked EMPLOYEES ONLY. She eyes the kitchen behind her, the emergency exit at the end of the hallway. An alarm will sound, but she's alone in the hall. She peeks inside the room, finding it empty. Her stomach rolls with nerves. It's risky, but she slips inside, desperation making her bold. The door winks shut behind her.

Lockers cover one wall, and most have combo locks. Blood pulsing in her ears, she tries each accessible locker, leaving the doors open so she doesn't make too much noise, and strikes gold on the last one. A man's brown-leather billfold hides in a pile of neatly folded clothes.

The door behind her opens. Shiloh whirls, wide eyed, the billfold disappearing into the folds of her sweatshirt. The hostess stands in the doorway.

"You're not supposed to be in here." Her gaze swings to the opened lockers behind Shiloh.

"Sorry, looking for the bathroom." Shiloh pushes by and runs from the restaurant, the hostess hollering after her.

Terrified, she sprints a block, then two, unaware and uncaring of where she's running, only that she needs to put distance between her and where she's been.

Several blocks down, she veers into a parking lot and ducks behind a hedge to inspect the wallet she snagged. A five and two ones. She adds the bills to the others and throws the wallet into the bushes.

Eleven dollars over five hours.

This city sucks.

She runs again, a full sprint in the only direction she knows. The encampment.

Sweat drips into her eyes, and tears drench her cheeks as her arms pump. Her lungs strain, and her breath comes in bursts. She cries out with a sob, hating what she's done. She shouldn't have raided those lockers. The man she stole from will report her. The hostess knows her face. When the women from the park and Dollar General report their stolen wallets, the police will know there's a thief among them. They'll know it's her.

They'll be looking for her.

And she's still a few bucks shy of catching a bus to Lancaster, then another to Hollywood.

She'll have to lie low for a while unless she can convince Irving to part with a few of his greens.

He'll want more food in return. He might make her negotiate another gram from Barton.

Mentally counting the food she has on her from this morning, wondering if she can manage sharing, she cuts across the road.

A truck screeches to a halt mere inches from her. Shiloh pulls up short, a scream lodged in her throat. Someone almost hit her. Too shocked to move, she stares dumbly at the driver, watching as his own shocked expression wears off. His eyes narrow to slits. His open mouth snaps shut into a firm line. Nostrils flare. Her heart pounds in her throat.

Shit. Market guy.

The gear shifts into park, and the brake drops. He opens his door. A boot lands on the road. He's talking, asking her something, but she can't hear him over the blood rushing in her ears.

No way is she sticking around.

Shiloh bolts across the pavement and sprints into a field, disappearing into a cloak of darkness.

8

Lucas glares at the waif stone immobile in his headlights. Mouth unhinged, eyes moon-size with wisps of hair framing her face like an angel's halo, she gapes at him.

Lily.

No, not Lily. His sister's hair is brown.

Fuck, he's more buzzed than he thought.

After Val, he'd taken a pit stop, then returned to Mike and Oscar to finish their game. Several rounds of Corona and shots later, he killed Oscar in darts and left the Lone Palm hours earlier than his usual 2:00 a.m. departure with a Train Robbers ticket for tomorrow night's game in his pocket. He settled in his truck knowing he shouldn't drive. Better to sleep off the alcohol in the parking lot. But he closed the door, blinking at the dry, open space beyond the bar, a dark expanse of nothingness, belched, and started the engine.

He really shouldn't have driven. But he didn't want to sleep in the parking lot either. So he peeled onto the road, speeding toward his apartment only to slow down so he wouldn't attract attention. He rolled through a stop sign, sped up, then bam. A white blur shot in front of him.

He squints at her light-blue sweatshirt, dirty backpack straps, and dusty jeans. Her shoes are filthy. Her clothes just as dirty.

Their gazes meet and hold. He swears.

Sunshine Girl.

What the hell is she doing out here on the edge of town at this hour? Why's she in the middle of the road? He almost hit her.

Reality check. He could have killed her.

She would have been the second person he's killed.

Bile brews in his belly, lighting a fuse to his anger.

He throws open the door and steps down from the truck. "I could have killed you." Thank god he'd reacted fast enough.

At least he reacted at all, unlike the night Lily ran away, sixteen and pregnant.

That night he was home, hunkered over his desk in the apartment above his parents' garage. Windows opened, he heard Lily screaming for him.

He went to check what was going on. It wasn't unusual to hear shouting coming from inside the house. His parents argued constantly, and they often took their anger out on his baby sis. He was just rounding the back corner of the house to enter through the kitchen slider when Wes Jensen, Lily's friend from school, burst from the patio door at a full sprint.

He wasn't alone.

Lucas's dad, Dwight, tailed him, close on his heels. It was dark, the fog thick as soup, but the flash of patio lighting off the gun his father aimed at Wes as they ran was unmistakable. Lily blew past him, chasing them both, screaming for him to help. But he didn't think she saw him. Wouldn't she have stopped if she did?

He didn't move. He couldn't.

From a short distance came the sound of shoes running on the metal dock where he kept his kayaks tethered. Then he heard their voices above the gentle splash of the bay lapping the pylons. Through a sheer force of will, he moved closer so that he could hear. Silhouettes appeared in the fog. Wes was pleading for his life while Lily cried for their father to spare him. But Dwight wouldn't back down. He wanted Lily's baby-daddy's name or he'd shoot Wes.

Then they exploded into motion.

Lily lunged at Dwight. The gun fired. Wes went over the rail. There was a splash.

Then Dwight did what he had done best. Manipulate. He convinced Lily she'd killed her friend. He then told her to run. She had. She ran past Lucas without realizing he was right there.

To this day, Lucas regrets not interceding. He should have run after Lily and taken her to his apartment to keep her safe. Heck, they should have driven to San Francisco that night and moved in with Olivia.

But no, he just stood there. He did nothing.

But he can do something for Sunshine.

He reaches for his wallet at the same time wondering if anyone bothered helping Lily, then thinks better of it. What if he throws some cash at this girl and she blows it on drugs? Aren't all homeless addicts? Vagrants used to hang out behind the dumpster at his mother's real estate agency. She would make Lucas take out the trash when he came asking for money to party with his friends. Used needles littered the ground.

His eyes narrow on the girl. She could use a new sweatshirt. Pocketing his wallet, he reaches into the back seat for the USC sweatshirt he keeps in the truck. When he turns around to toss it at her, she bolts like a spooked deer.

"Hey!" he shouts after her, but the darkness swallows her whole.

He looks around to get his bearings. She's running toward the abandoned cars the homeless use for shelter. Half those guys are strung out on heroin. He'd bet the others are one crime shy of changing their address to the prison up the road.

He pictures Lily living in such a place and he wants to punch his truck.

But Sunshine Girl isn't his sister. She's like him, stealing to survive, living in the shadows. He sees himself in her and accepts that she can handle herself. She knows what she's doing. She doesn't need him. Yet the mere thought of her living in such a place makes him want to vomit. It's the last place any unaccompanied teenage girl should be sleeping.

"Fuck." This time he does smack his truck. He gets back in and takes it off road. He doesn't have a plan. No clue what he'll say to her. But he can't sit back like he did with Lily.

He drives slow. Tumbleweeds and bramble scrape the underside of his truck. Tires roll over rocks. Windows down, he breathes in dust. It coats his nostrils, stings his eyes.

When he reaches the first car, a dented Chrysler with a missing hood, he understands the lot is more of an encampment than it appears from the road. Several barrel fires burn, roasting something. His stomach turns at the thought of living off dune rabbits and ground squirrels. Flames reflect off sunken faces. Protruding eyes follow him as he coasts along the perimeter. One guy flips him off. Another yells for him to turn off his lights.

His high beams cut through the back window of a rusted-out Malibu. Two heads pop into view, eyes squinting against the glare. A flash of baby-blue sweatshirt bursts into his peripheral. There she is.

Sunshine Girl ducks behind a vehicle. When she believes he doesn't notice her, she runs, crouched low, and ducks behind another car. Lucas slows to a stop and waits, knowing she can't see him against the glare of his lights.

She crouch-runs and ducks again, then again, until she reaches a Ford Fiesta, looks around, and slips inside.

Lucas throws the truck in park, blaming the alcohol for dragging him out here. If he had his head, he would have driven straight home. He watches the car Sunshine Girl climbed into and waits for a sign that this isn't where she's been sleeping. But she doesn't come back out. The entire encampment has gone still, holding its breath as if waiting to see what he does next.

Her side windows are gone. Anyone can get to her while she sleeps. Two men standing at a nearby barrel, flames crackling between them, point at her car. They laugh. One guy nudges the other in his ribs and does an obscene hand gesture near his groin. Disgusted, Lucas tightens his grip on the steering wheel. He can't leave her here.

All those times he thought about Lily and wondered how she was faring, if she was alive, and he hadn't done jack shit. Sure, it's easier to reflect back knowing she hadn't only survived, but excelled. It still doesn't change the fact he'd sat on his ass when she needed him.

He angles his truck so the lights flood the Fiesta and gets out, pocketing his keys. He approaches her car, staring down the guys leering at him as he tries to formulate a plan to convince her to leave with him. He'll buy her a meal. He'll take her to a shelter. Resting a hand on the hood, he peers inside her car where the rear passenger window should have been. Sunshine Girl lies on her side hugging her backpack to her chest. She has the hood pulled so tight over her head that he can't see her face.

He clears his throat. "Hey," he says gently.

She doesn't move or let on that she heard him.

He raps his knuckles on the roof.

She lurches up with a squeak. The backpack falls to her lap. Through the hood's small peephole, one eye stares back at him.

He folds his arms on the window opening and leans in. "What's up?"

9

Shiloh backpedals like a cornered raccoon until her spine hits the door opposite him, her heart beating furiously in her throat. She hugs her backpack close, the entirety of her worldly possessions. How did he find her? What does he want from her? Her mind flashes back to Ellis, his hands searching and finding their marks, and she wants to scream. But that'll only alert Bob and Barton that she's here, and this terrible situation will go from worse to catastrophic with that one breath.

She didn't even want to come back here. But market guy threw her off. She thought he was pulling out his phone to call the cops, not his lame wallet. Terrified, she didn't know where to run but here. Now he and his headlights have alerted the entire encampment that she's here. Might as well put a billboard above her with a flashing arrow pointing at her car.

She unties the hood and pushes it off her head. Wisps of hair flutter around her face, waving with static electricity. She feels the charge, the tickle against her skin. "What do you want?"

His gaze roves over the car's interior, taking in the torn pleather seats, the filth on the floor. Snack wrappers and apple cores. The meager sustenance she's been living off. Fear rises like an ugly beast. She shakes with it. Will he turn her in now that he's found her?

Market guy's gaze finds hers again. His eyes reflect his shock and disgust. "You live here?"

"Go away." She throws what food she has left at him, giving back what she took so he'll leave. A nut pack hits his forehead, startling him.

He catches the Juicy Fruit gum she flings at him. Two fruit strips miss his face and fly out the window.

He drops the gum on the floor where the nut pack landed and retrieves the fruit strips. "I don't want your food."

But they're his. She stole from him. "Then what do you want?" Men always want something.

He drags a hand down his face, and Shiloh catches the stale scent of beer and something harder. Her armpits sweat. Jitters prick her neck. Ellis drank, a lot. He was drunk the night he came into her room. The sour smell of cheap whiskey is permanently stamped in the back of her nose. She swears she can smell him in her sleep.

She reaches for the door handle behind her, thinking she can make a run for it.

But where would she go? She's fast, but this guy is bigger and stronger. He also has a truck. And there's no place to hide for at least a mile. She doubts anyone in the encampment would come to her defense.

"Keep the snacks. You've got to be hungry."

She's famished, but she shakes her head only for her stomach to betray her. It growls loudly. He hears, and her face heats with embarrassment. She throws the cash she stole at him, that desperate for him to go. "Would you leave?"

"Nothing's open at this hour except McDonald's. Let me buy you a burger."

Her stomach growls again, and she glances out the back window. She really is hungry. But taking him up on his offer means getting into his truck. Once she's buckled up inside, he can do anything to her, take her anywhere. Moonstar had. Even though she'd escaped, the memories of that woman have Shiloh squirming.

She makes a face and market guy scowls. "Please don't tell me you're one of those woke Gen Zers who only eat Impossible meat. Fine, fries. I'll buy you as many as you want. Get a shake while you're at it. Just come with me. It isn't safe here." He opens the door.

Shiloh shrieks. She dives for the door handle and pulls it closed, smacks the lock. A piece of glass slices the tip of her finger, and she cries out. She sticks her finger in her mouth to soothe the ache.

"Please just go," she says, near tears, afraid he'll overpower her. He can do anything then: touch her, hurt her. Take her to the police.

He gives her a long look before backing away from the car, palms in the air to show he's not a threat. If she wasn't petrified, she'd laugh. Yeah, right. She's not that gullible.

Then he glances around, sighing with exasperation and something else. Alarm skitters down her back, sensing his unease when he turns back to her.

"You need to come with me," he orders.

She can only imagine what he has in store for her. Ellis made that picture clear. She retreats to the far corner, hugging her knees to her chest, willing to confront the dangers here rather than go with him.

He drags both hands down his face, clearly frustrated with her. "Fine. Stubborn idiot," he grumbles into his cupped palms. "Have it your way."

"You're a jerk," she says.

"I'm trying to help you. It's not safe here."

"Not your problem."

"I'm making it mine."

She frowns at that. "Why? What's it to you?"

"I don't know," he says more to himself, staring off to the side. "Look. You don't have to ride with me. Walk." He points east. "It's just a mile up the road. I'll be waiting in the parking lot. You want something to eat? Come get it, whatever you want. On me."

She could use a hot meal, con him into buying a few extra burgers. But he'll want something in exchange. They always do.

"I'll give you an hour. You decide." He backs away, holding her gaze, until he turns to leave.

He retreats, but not in the direction of his truck. Shiloh lifts to her knees and peeks out the back window. She can barely make him out, but guesses he's with Bob and Barton and getting in their faces. Their voices rise, and Ricky joins them. She moves them apart, saying some words. Market guy leaves. Bob flips off his back, but Barton isn't watching him. He's staring at her.

The hair on her forearms lifts. Her mind warns her to flee. She slides down the seat and curls on her side. What did market guy say to them? Nothing good, she suspects. He's just causing her more trouble. She collects the cash and snacks she hurled at him, pulls the hoodie over her head, and hugs the backpack to her chest.

Shivering more from fear than the cold, she listens to the night. She hears the occasional cough and Irving's snoring in the car next to hers. Heart hammering, she startles at every noise. Without windows, the night is louder, the desert more sinister. She tries to distract herself with thoughts of Finn, imagining she's safe in his arms. Her stomach cramps from hunger pangs, and she can't think of anything but market guy's offer. She could meet him at McD's, place her order, and leave. She doesn't have to get into his truck. She could walk there and back.

But since too many people she thought she could trust have taken advantage of her, it's hard to trust anyone at all.

Gravel crunches nearby. Shiloh inhales sharply, sitting upright. She looks out the windows, wondering where the noise came from. It's too dark to see anything beyond a few feet.

More crunching, then a scrape on metal. The sound reverberates through the car. She yelps, afraid of who or what is outside.

Shiloh doesn't wait to find out.

She throws open the door and flees.

10

It's after midnight, and McDonald's closed at ten. The drive-through is open until one, but good luck convincing Sunshine Girl to get in his truck when he orders food. Assuming she shows. He doesn't even want her in his truck.

Lucas almost turns around for home, wondering what he's doing. What good can he do beyond feeding her or finding her a safer place to sleep? She didn't want anything to do with him. After he left, he pictured himself in her place and saw their exchange go down from her point of view.

"What a dick," he says to the night.

The last thing she needs is some guy creeping on her, exactly what she probably thought he was doing. Hard not to notice he scared her. She probably thought he'd turn her over to the cops for stealing.

He swerves his truck into the drive-through and orders a Big Mac, Coke, and extra-large fries, something to soak up the alcohol. He didn't eat anything except the half-dozen cookies Ivy sent him home with.

He has no idea what Sunshine Girl would want, so he orders a variety of burgers, two fries, and the shake he mentioned. She seems like the strawberry type, so he gets that when the clerk asks the flavor. It was Lily's favorite. He used to take her to McDonald's after her swim practice. Their parents practically starved them. They were too busy to shop, so there was rarely food in the house. Lucas would swing by his mom's office to get cash so he could buy himself dinner. He always shared what he had with Lily.

Lucas pays for the food, parks his truck, settles on the curb with his order in the parking lot, a dried-up bush behind him, and waits. He promised an hour. That's what he'll give her.

He finishes off his burger and drains his Coke. Twenty minutes in, and Sunshine Girl is a no-show. If she ran, she'd be here by now. If she's walking—he glances at the time—it could take her another ten to fifteen minutes.

He crumples his trash and stuffs it in a bag, lets loose a long belch. Every few minutes a car pulls into the drive-through; otherwise the parking lot is deserted. He imagines what it's like during the days, crowded with cars, weary travelers passing through. Bikes leaning against the building, kids lined up inside filling up on fries after baseball practice. Everyone going about their lives while he's been contemplating whether he wants a life.

He thinks of the blade in the bathroom and why it's still there. Why hasn't he used it? It isn't like he can go home. He doesn't have a life to go back to.

He killed his father.

Olivia would never forgive him.

The police will be on him in a heartbeat if he returns. Honestly, he's shocked someone hasn't located him already.

Movement in his periphery brings his attention back to the parking lot. Sunshine Girl walks briskly toward the entrance.

Lucas blinks, even rubs his eyes, hardly believing she came.

She yanks on the entrance door, finding it locked, and he hears her cuss up a storm. She cups her hands around her face and peers inside. Then she looks at the door and reads the operation hours.

"Shit," she cusses again. Back slumped, face drawn, she turns around. Her gaze finds him, and even from his distance, he can't miss her relief.

"Got you a shake, Sunshine Girl." He lifts the cup to show her. "It's melted but drinkable."

She hesitates, her gaze slinging all over the place before she decides to approach him. She reminds him of a stray pup eager for scraps, yet skittish of humans.

"It's strawberry, my sister's favorite." He scowls, wondering why he told her that.

She snatches the cup from his hand, backing out of reach, and doesn't bother with the straw. Removing the lid, she gulps down the shake. Faint-pink foam coats her upper lip when she's done. She wipes it off with her sleeve.

"I like chocolate. This was okay, I guess."

He huffs. He'll take that as a thanks.

She stuffs the lid and straw into the empty cup and drops it on the ground.

He holds up a bag. "Got you burgers and fries, too."

She snatches the bag and again moves away. She looks inside at the hamburger, cheeseburger, quarter pounder, and Big Mac. Two extra-large fries on top.

"I didn't know what you liked, so I got one of each."

Her tongue peeks out, her hunger making her eyes extra bright.

"Thanks," she mutters. She closes the bag and turns to leave.

"Where do you think you're going?"

"What's it to you?" She got her food, and she has no intention of sticking around, that much is obvious to him. Itching to go, she can't stand still. Her feet shuffle as if the encampment has a line hooked into her. She starts walking away.

"You're being rude."

She turns around. "And you're drunk."

True, but he's sobering real fast.

"Your burger and fries will be soggy by the time you get there if they aren't already. Eat here." He doesn't like the idea of her going back to the encampment. Maybe he can talk her into camping out elsewhere. He takes out the order of large fries he saved if she came.

She glances over her shoulder, then eyes the curb beside him.

"Sit over there if you want." He gestures at the curb across from them. "Just sit. I know you're starving, you've got to be exhausted. You'll be dead if you run another mile without eating."

Shame flames her face. She dips her head and sits down, surprisingly only a few feet from him. Close enough for them to have a conversation. Far enough for her to bolt if he tries anything, which he won't. He's not one of those guys, never has been.

But he knows the type firsthand. The memories pollute his mind.

She starts with the cheeseburger. Lily would have, too. And the nostalgia of it collides into him. He looks at the ground by his feet and waits until she's finished and starts unwrapping the hamburger before he asks through a constricted throat, "What's your name?"

"Why'd you call me Sunshine Girl?" she says around a mouth full of food.

He frowns. He had?

"When I first got here. That's what you called me."

He shrugs. The hell if he knows. "Cause you looked sad when I first saw you?"

"That's weird."

"You're filthy."

"Piss off, Millennial."

He lowers his head, runs his hand up his nape and into his hair. "How old are you?"

"Eighteen."

"Bullshit."

Her face scrunches up. "Whatever." She bites into the burger.

"What's your name? Your *real* name."

"Hannah."

His eyes narrow. Liar. Doesn't know how he knows. Just that he does. He lets it pass.

"I'm Lucas. Call me Luc if you want." His sisters do.

"Like Skywalker?"

"What? No. Luc with a *C. L-U-C*, that's it. Where you from, *Hannah*?" he asks sarcastically because he knows the name she gave him is a load of crap. "How old *are* you?"

"How old are you?"

"Thirty-three."

"My mom's thirty-three. Or, she was."

He looks her over, feeling an ache over her loss. "When did she die?"

She ducks her head, bites into the burger.

"What about your dad?"

"Never met him. Died before I was born."

Poor kid. She's on her own.

She finishes off the burger and starts on the Big Mac. Her face screws up. She presses a hand to her stomach and releases a large belch.

"Nice." Lucas holds up a fist for a bump. She gives him a death glare and goes back to the burger.

His hand drops. "I know you're hungry, but you might want to slow down."

Staring at him, daring him to say something, she jams the rest of the Big Mac into her mouth.

"Jesus," he mutters, then slurps the dregs of his soda. He waits until she finishes chewing before he says, "So, you're an orphan."

"Something like that."

"Any aunts or uncles?" She shakes her head. "Boyfriend?"

"Finn. He's in a band."

"Where's he?"

"Hollywood. He's coming to get me."

"When?"

"When he can get here."

"Does he know you're living in a car?"

She ignores him and starts on her fries.

"Where'd you meet him?" He's curious about this guy and wonders if he really exists. Why hasn't he helped her?

"Interloper."

"What is that?"

"An app." She stares at him like he's an idiot.

With a mix of concern and curiosity, he looks up the app on his phone. Posted across the top of his screen in weighted bold lettering is a single title: Talk to Strangers. The page goes on to detail how the app randomly pairs users with another person based on common interests to talk one-on-one. Perfect for people looking to make a friend.

That's how she met this guy? Oh, hell no. He couldn't imagine Lily letting Josh on this app. But Sunshine Girl is an orphan. She doesn't have anyone to warn her that guys prey on girls like her through these kinds of apps.

"Have you met Finn in person?"

She shakes her head. "Not yet. But he's cool. I know everything about him."

There isn't anything cool about this. "How old is he?" He's willing to bet Finn lied about everything, including his age.

"Nineteen." She flings the empty Big Mac box off her lap. It flops onto the ground and bounces to Lucas's boot.

Nineteen, his ass. "And you believe him?"

"Why wouldn't I?" But her gaze shifts away. She has doubts. Either that or she's been lying to this guy, too.

Damn, this girl is naive. And she's living on her own? He's shocked she's survived as long as she has.

He glances at the time. It's almost 2:00 a.m. "Grab your stuff. You're coming with me." He stalks to his truck.

"What?" Her face pales. She doesn't move.

Lucas rolls his head, loosening his shoulders. "You can't sleep out there. I'm taking you to a shelter." There has to be one around here somewhere.

Her face screws up. "I'm not getting in that truck with you."

He doesn't want her there either, but he's not leaving her here.

A police cruiser turns into the parking lot, catching him unawares. Panic explodes in his chest. Every time he sees the police, he's instantly thrown back to the night he was arrested for holding up a minimart. The red-and-blue lights, the cops in his face, the cold metal of the handcuffs. The fear consuming him. And now that he killed his father, he's terrified that he's fated to repeat the experience. He'd been so focused on Sunshine Girl that he hadn't taken care to watch his surroundings.

The cruiser stops in front of them, blocking Lucas's truck. A window drops down, revealing the stern cop inside. His gaze sizes up Lucas, then Sunshine Girl. Lucas watches his mouth move when he speaks, but he can't make out what he's saying over the roar in his head. Why hadn't he been paying attention?

Sunshine's immobile, but she recovers first. "Nothing much, Officer," she says evenly. "Just having a late dinner with my dad."

"That right?" The officer's eyes narrow on him. Lucas coaxes his hands to relax so he doesn't appear threatening.

"Yes, sir." His voice is a forced calm, belying the terror brewing inside him. He sends up a prayer of gratitude for the dark or the cop would see how filthy Sunshine is. He'd know right away something wasn't right between them.

Lucas holds his gaze, silently willing him to move along. But the cop unlatches his seat belt. "I'm going to need to see some ID."

His stomach crashes into his feet like a dropped bag of rocks. Bile churns, and he has to physically force himself to keep the sickness down. In his mind, he's already back in his cell, reliving the horror his bunkmate Morris put him through.

Sunshine's feet shuffle. She meets his eyes, and Lucas slowly shakes his head. If she runs, they're screwed.

He probably already is. The cop will run his ID and find the warrant for his father's murder. He'll be cuffed and behind bars within the hour.

Thoughts bounce around chaotically in his mind. His gaze wildly searches for an exit.

He steps back, primed to run.

The cop opens the door, and a dispatcher's voice crackles over the speaker about a domestic dispute less than a mile from them. The cop doesn't even glance at them. He shuts the door and guns the cruiser toward the scene.

Air whooshes from Lucas's lungs. He clasps his hands behind his head and swears under his breath. That was too close for comfort. He turns to Sunshine to tell her to get into his truck so they can get out of here, but she's gone.

11

Arms folded, Lucas stares out the Dusty Pantry's front window at the empty parking lot, fighting off a yawn. After last night's close call with the authorities, he slept fitfully, tossing until his alarm went off. He woke with a throbbing headache, fire behind his eyes, and a gut full of worry. That cop almost ID'd him. He might not be so lucky next time.

If he had any sense, he'd leave town, ditch his truck, and change his name. But that's more work than his life is worth. And last he checked, he wasn't interested in living. But he's tired of hurting, exhausted from a past that torments him and he can't change. Factor in what he did to his father, and he can't see what he has left to give.

So why can't he stop thinking about Sunshine Girl?

He worried all night she didn't find a place to sleep. Still worries. So much concern for a girl he doesn't know when he couldn't spare an ounce for his own sister.

No thanks to him, though, Lily survived. Aside from a speech impediment, his nephew, Josh, seemed to get on well. A wise and talented kid. His sister raised him well. She's done well for herself. *Is* doing well. Somewhere along the way, someone must have helped her, given her a chance to survive and thrive. Opened her world to opportunities she didn't hesitate to take. She overcame odds he's never hurdled.

There are days he wishes he knew what happened to her. Other days he regrets tossing his phone. Yes, he could reach out to his sister Olivia to get Lily's number. But he doesn't want any connection to the past, including his family. As dysfunctional as they are, he'll only hold his sisters back. If they know where he is and don't turn him in, they could be charged with aiding and abetting a criminal.

So yeah, maybe he does care about something: his sisters.

His thoughts circle back to Sunshine Girl.

What should he do with her?

Ignore her. She's not your problem.

He drags his thumb and forefinger across his eyelids and sighs wearily. Why does he even care? He didn't the night Lily ran. He didn't the night he killed his father.

Lucas looks at his hands. They shake as another memory surfaces and he no longer sees his hands as they are now. They're bloody with shredded knuckles. Fists that pulverized his dad's face. Then Olivia is in front of him getting into his face. She's asking what happened to their father. She wants to know what Lucas did.

I don't know. I don't know, he shouts, vaguely recalling the night he found his father at a wine symposium in Carlsbad and followed him up to his hotel room. How his father knocked him over the head with the hotel room's metal trash can when Lucas physically accosted him because he was fed up with how Dwight treated Lucas's mom. He despised him for how he'd abused Lily and hated him for all the years Lucas couldn't live up to his expectations. He delivered a punch to his father's jaw, his cheekbone, and his right eye socket. One for each of them. But when Dwight fought back and pushed him off, his father grabbed his keys and ran from the room. Missing the elevator Dwight took, Lucas raced after him down ten flights of stairs, bursting into the parking lot as Dwight's Mercedes squealed around a corner. Then there's a large gap in his memory, because next he was sitting in his truck parked on the side of the road, staring at his bloody hands, his father's car crumpled in a ravine below him. Lucas doesn't remember how they got where they were, or how the accident happened. Though he feels the truth to his core: Lucas hated his father for what he did to Lily. He despised how Dwight belittled and abused her and how Lucas could never live up to his expectations. He loathed Dwight's affection for Olivia, the prince-*sis* who could do no wrong. When his mother insinuated that Dwight emotionally abused her, and that she wanted him taken care of and wouldn't blame Lucas if something befell Dwight on his business trip, Lucas realized how much he wanted to hurt his father. How badly he desired his father to die. So, he murdered him. And now there's a warrant for his arrest. Traffic cams somewhere must have recorded what went down.

No, he can't go home.

He won't go back to prison either.

So he's biding his time. For what, though?

He doesn't know anymore.

"A watched pot never boils," Ivy says from behind him where she's arranging and rearranging merchandise on the shelves to keep busy. Not much else to do around here when customers are scarce.

Lucas glances over his shoulder at her, confused.

She gestures outside. "Staring at the parking lot won't make the customers come."

He'd wrapped eight sub sandwiches and rung up thirteen customers since he opened the market at six thirty this morning, thirty minutes early in case Sunshine Girl returned. He'd consider this a profitable day compared to others, except his thief hasn't shown her face.

He turns away from the window, feeling uneasy and hating that he's worrying. He strides over to the deli counter. He splits three Dutch crunch rolls and smears on mustard and mayo. "Ready for me to start on the kitchen in Mike's apartment?" He needs a new project.

Ivy shakes her head. "Not enough money yet. I owe Keith from the work you did on my place." She ran up a tab at Ace. He didn't realize she was still paying it off. "I need to find a tenant first."

"I'll cover it." He brought cash with him. He keeps it in a boot in his closet. Not like he has plans to spend it.

"Thank you, Lucas, but I can't accept. I won't be able to pay you back."

"Consider it my treat. You've done plenty for me." He meets her eyes to say what he can't out loud. He's grateful for the home-cooked meals she prepares him at least once a week. He'd be dead if she hadn't sat with him that first night, and he wouldn't be here to keep her company. He tells himself she needs him and that it's not the other way around.

He slaps on roast beef, salami, and ham. Adds pickles, jalapeños, and shredded lettuce. A splash of oil and vinegar. Ivy collapses an empty cardboard box and turns to him.

"You've worked nonstop since the day we met."

"I like the work." He wraps the sandwiches. He puts two in one bag with chips and extra pickles, the third in another.

Ivy plants a hand on her hip. She's a petite thing with protruding veins on the back of her hand. Her lips purse.

The corner of his mouth pulls into his cheek. "Spit it out."

"You keep up with these projects, you'll only convince me you want to buy this place."

He takes in his surroundings, the scuffed concrete floor and sputtering air conditioner. The antique cash register. Once upon a lifetime ago, he would have leapt at the opportunity to remodel such a place. That past version of him, young and naive with stars in his eyes, aspired to study architecture at USC. He dreamed of designing cities and building skyscrapers, but only got so far as starting his own paint contracting business. Admittedly, installing Ivy's kitchen cabinets and tiling her bathroom reignited that spark. But not enough to tie him down to this place.

"I'm the last person you'd want to sell to."

Her shoulders round, and he looks away, her disappointment affecting him more each time she brings up the subject. She's been asking him to take over for months.

He packs up the deli counter, putting away containers in the under-counter fridge. When he's done and looks up, Ivy is sweeping an aisle she'd swept earlier in the afternoon. An unfamiliar emptiness pulls at his chest over her slow, methodical movements, when it strikes him. They're both trapped by their circumstances.

He could change their fates in a heartbeat. All he has to do is say yes. His work on the property hasn't been anything more than chores, maintenance, and upkeep. But they've spoken to a part of him gullible enough to believe he can still dream.

But he isn't being fair to Ivy. He's hiding his past, and she'd never offer him the place if she knew his secrets.

"Mind if I cut out early? I'm picking up Mike for the game."

Ivy waves him off without looking up from the floor. He finds himself waiting for her to say something, but when she doesn't, he grunts and picks up a Sharpie. Uncapping the lid with his teeth, he writes *Sunshine Girl* on the bag with the single sandwich. He says goodbye to Ivy and drops the bag just outside the front entrance when he leaves for his truck.

He feels guilty not checking on Sunshine after she took off last night, which pisses him off. You only feel guilty when you care.

12

Standing outside Maria's Deli in a strip mall near the city center, Shiloh stares at the only pay phone she's seen in town, wondering how to make one of those collect calls her mom once talked about. Long before Shiloh had a cell phone and Harmony had a steady job, her mom hadn't paid the phone bill. The landline was dead, and her mom needed to make a call to schedule a job interview, but she couldn't find a pay phone. There weren't any around anymore. She ended up borrowing the neighbor's phone, a gruff guy named Graham who had more hair on his back than his head and face and collect called into her interview. She didn't get the job.

Last night freaked Shiloh out. She's desperate to get to Hollywood and needs to convince Finn to come get her now. She can't spend another night here. Finn would have made money from last night's gig. Maybe he'll spare her enough to convince his bandmate to drive him and pay for the gas.

She picks up the receiver and wipes both ends on her sweatshirt before pressing the phone to her ear. The steady hum of the dial tone tickles the tiny hairs inside her ear. If there were ever instructions on the phone on how to make a collect call, they've long since faded. Taking a chance, she presses the zero. That number always gave her a live person when she'd call her school.

An automated attendant answers and lists her options. Shiloh selects *Make a Collect Call* and dictates Finn's number. She prays he wakes up and answers. It's not even eight in the morning.

A shrill tone rings in her ear, and an automated voice informs her collect calls cannot be made to cell-phone numbers.

Shiloh slams down the phone, flustered and embittered. Now what?

The library opens in another hour, and she debates sending Finn an email to set up a Zoom call for later. But she can't go back today after spending all day there yesterday. The librarian will grow suspicious. She already is.

A guy around her age unlocks the deli's entrance and pushes the door open. Curly auburn hair covers a thick neck under his ball cap. He's round in the middle, and his gray khaki pants sag in the rear. His Nike sneakers are brand-spanking-new white. He props open the door with a door stopper and drops a case of Pepsi beside the entrance. He brings out several more, stacking them beside the door. The outline of a phone bulges in his front pocket.

She gives him a slight wave.

"Hi." His smile comes slowly, as if he's surprised she noticed him. He is plain looking with drab attire. "We're open now if you want to come in," he offers.

"I was hoping I could borrow your phone."

His smile shrinks as he takes in the sight of her, the greasy hair, dusty clothes. Each day it becomes more obvious she's living on the streets, which only adds to her shame and bitterness. His gaze shifts around as if he's assessing where she'd take off to if he lent her the phone. How fast could she run? Would he catch her?

Shiloh doubts it. She'd be across the parking lot and around the block before he could blink. But that's beside the point. She isn't interested in stealing anything that could track her.

"I'm not going to steal it. Here, hold this." She slides off her backpack and offers it as collateral.

"You can't use that?" He gestures at the pay phone behind her.

"You can't collect call a cell phone."

"Oh." He slips out his phone. "How many minutes?"

"Five?"

"I guess that's okay. My mom monitors my usage." His face pinkens. He takes her pack and gives her his phone.

"Thanks."

She hastily moves a few steps away and calls Finn. He answers after the fourth ring.

"The eff. It's early, man."

His sleepy voice is a gush of relief. "Don't hang up. It's me."

"Shy Girl. You're my sexy mystery woman. Whose number you calling from now?"

"Don't know. Some guy's."

"What guy?" He's suddenly alert.

"I don't know. Some guy I just met."

"He good looking? He better not make a move on my gal. I'll fuck him up."

"Finn, stop. I'm just using his phone." She doesn't want him to get fired up. He'll go on a rant, acting all protective, until he has to end the call because something else more important than her is pulling him off the phone. She hates that he gets jealous so quickly, yet at the same time makes her feel wanted.

"How was last night?" she presses, feeling around for how much money he made.

"Epic. You should have been there," he says drowsily.

She would have been if Moonstar didn't freak her out or if Finn would get his ass here and pick her up. "I wish I could have seen you play."

"You will, babe. Hey, I'm tired. Can we talk later?"

"Um . . . okay," she says, disappointed he's hustling her off the phone again and liking herself a little less that she puts up with it. But she can't help it. She loves him, and up to this point he has been good to her. He kept her company many nights during their video chats listening to her as she vented about her mom and Ellis. "Wait . . . before you go." She pulls the hoodie string. "Did you make any money last night? Think you can spare some and ask Beck to drive you here? I'll pay you back when I find a job. I want to get out of here. I miss you."

"Mmm, miss you, too."

"Then come get me. Please, Finn," she begs, desperate and on the verge of tears.

"Shit, Shiloh. Have you seen the price of gas? It's over six fucking bucks a gallon. I owe people money, people who'll make my life hell if I don't pay up. You understand that, don't you?"

She's starting to understand that Finn might not be as into her as he led her to believe. If he loved her, he'd go out of his way to come get her, wouldn't he? She doesn't have much experience with guys when it comes to love. Only what she's read about in books and seen in movies.

"This place is creeping me out," she gives in, confessing her fear. "I'm sleeping in a car."

"You're lucky you've got one."

His retort is a backward shove into a cement wall. "It doesn't work. God, Finn!" She wants to stick a fork in his face. Doesn't he realize how dire her situation is? But he's all she's got, the only option she has if she wants a place to live in California. She forces down her tears. Teeth gritted, afraid of the truth, but needing to ask anyway, she says, "Do you want me there or not?" If he doesn't, she needs to stop wasting time and find another option.

"You know it. I've made space in my closet, cleared out some drawers. It's all yours, baby." He pauses. "Listen, I'm sorry I snapped. I'm tired and grouchy. It's not your fault you're stuck there. I just wish I could be of more help." He pauses again. "I'll ask around for a ride, see what I can do, but . . . Can't you ask someone for money?"

She glances over her shoulder at the boy behind her. She doesn't know what it says about her, but she's always found it easier to steal than ask, even with the guilt. Asking draws attention.

But if Finn asks around for a ride like he says he will, she should pull her weight on this end.

"I'll try," she concedes.

"Excellent. Call me tonight and let me know how it goes," he says on a yawn. "Gotta go. I'm beat." He hangs up.

"Done?" the guy asks as soon as Finn ends the call.

She nods. "Thanks for the phone." She exchanges it for her backpack.

"I'm Theo."

"Shiloh," she mutters.

He tilts his head to the side and squints at her. "You okay?"

She shrugs, too ashamed to come up with an answer.

"Want something to eat?"

She struggles to meet his eyes. "Do you, uh . . . Do you have any cash?"

"For what?" His expression turns wary.

"Bus ticket to LA."

"How much?"

"Twenty." An easy amount to steal, but Shiloh hasn't been so fortunate since what she had was stolen.

Theo checks his pockets. He pulls out a crumpled one. "Will this help?"

Anything will. She takes the dollar while looking at the ground, reluctant to let him see she's disappointed that's all he has. "Thanks," she mumbles, disgusted she's begging for cash like the homeless she's seen holding cardboard signs. Maybe that's another reason she's been reluctant to ask. Subconsciously she doesn't want to put herself in the same category as them. She technically has a home. Just not one she wants to live in.

Theo holds up a finger. "Wait here a sec." Then he goes inside and returns with a bag of Fritos and two Lärabars. "Take these."

Shame tangles with gratitude. Her stomach knots with hunger. But she's near the end of her rope. She takes the handout. "Won't you get in trouble?"

He shakes his head. "My mom owns the store. She's always giving freebies to her friends."

She opens a bar, resisting the urge to devour it like an animal in front of him. "Thanks."

"I have to get back to work. See you around?" His expression is hopeful.

"Yeah, see ya," she says, turning away, knowing they won't. She can't risk him knowing more about her. He's kind, but if word gets around she's been stealing, and he connects it to her, he'll call the police.

She crosses the parking lot in a rush, finishing the first bar and opening the Fritos. She tips back the bag, greedily eating a mouthful as she admits to the cold, hard fact that she's the one stalling. Has been for days. Moonstar's advances had been unexpected and unsettling. But if she really wanted to move in with Finn, she would have used the cash she'd accumulated before it was stolen to buy a bus ticket to Lancaster. She would have reached Hollywood last week. She'd have a bed to sleep in, a roof over her head. A place to shower and wash her clothes. She would have seen Finn play last night. When it comes down to it, she's been stuck here through no fault but her own. She's scared. What would stop Finn from wanting the same thing from her that Ellis did? She dreams of kissing Finn, of making love with him. But is she ready?

No, she isn't.

Not only that, but their phone call has also made her realize she's been thinking of him as her white knight. Her only solution. Everything about her situation would go away when she moved in with him. But he's had every excuse not to come charging to her rescue on his gallant steed. He doesn't even own a steed or know how to ride it. And things will only get worse once she gets there if she's looking to him for all the answers. Unless she can live fully independent of him, he'll want something in return like Ellis wants with her mom, or what he wanted from her.

Shiloh needs to live with Finn until she can afford her own place. But until then, she needs some financial independence so that she isn't freeloading off him. Before she makes it to Hollywood, she needs more money. A lot more than a few measly bucks for a bus ride. She estimates she'll need at least several hundred, enough for gas and groceries and some clothes.

She counts the bills in her pocket and cries with frustration. Twelve lousy dollars. She has a long way to go and a long day ahead.

Sticking to the shadows, she keeps her head down and cases the city. She picks a wallet at the grocery store and a billfold in a gym bag at the park. Her hands dip into the tip jar at Starbucks. For a town with a prison on the outskirts, people sure are trusting of their personal belongings while out in public. Lucky for her.

When the day draws to a close, the sun setting on the dry landscape where the air tastes like chalk, Shiloh is exhausted. She hasn't been sleeping well in general. But last night when the cop showed up at McDonald's, she couldn't get away fast enough. She ran in the opposite direction of the encampment, so Lucas wouldn't find her again, and ended up at the park. She slept on the grass behind some trees, only to be startled awake at five in the morning when the sprinklers went off. She made a dash for it before she got drenched.

But what about tonight? She could return to the park where she's exposed and vulnerable and risks getting caught when the police patrol the area. Signs specifically state no overnight camping.

Or she could sneak back to the encampment after dark and slip into her car unnoticed. She'll leave before sunup, and Ricky, Bob, and Barton would never know she was ever there. Plans made and time to kill, she starts walking, kicking pebbles and chasing lizards out of pure boredom. When she's several hundred yards up the road from the Dusty

Pantry, she notices Lucas's truck is gone. The old lady will be working, and she's betting Lucas didn't tell her about the theft.

Thinking of the **FEED THE HOMELESS** jar loaded with change and the candy bars she could lift for dinner, Shiloh makes her way there only to find the market closed.

"Damn." She shoves the bolted door then smacks the glass. Why'd they close early? She walked all this way.

A cruiser speeds past, and Shiloh slams her back to the glass on a terrified gasp, afraid it's the same cop from last night. When the car is long gone, she slides to the ground. Knees up, she drops her head in her arms, exhausted and hungry. Her hands flop to her side, her left hand landing on a paper bag. She looks down and sees that dumb nickname Lucas gave her. *Sunshine Girl.*

Glancing around, double-checking his truck hasn't returned or he isn't watching her from who knows where, she looks inside the bag and finds a six-inch wrapped sub. Shock and wonder widen her eyes. Her stomach lets off an angry growl. The sandwich is unwrapped and in her mouth before she's on her feet.

Shiloh crosses the parking lot, biting into the sandwich, feeling only a little weirded out that Lucas guessed she'd be back.

13

"One beer, on me." Mike exits the truck, shutting the door.

The Lone Palm is not where Lucas wants to end the night, but Mike wanted a beer to celebrate the Train Robbers' win over the Tucson Saguaros. And Lucas could use a drink.

He gets out of the truck as a car he swore was behind him when he pulled into the parking lot drives past the other way. His eyes narrow on the nondescript Honda, and he fists his keys, the metal teeth digging into his skin. Had that car been tailing him on the highway? How far back? Bakersfield?

"Everything cool?" Mike rounds the truck bed.

"Yeah." Lucas pockets his keys, rubbing his palm. Whoever it was could have been at the game, made a wrong turn, and is circling back another way. But he can't shake off the feeling he's mistaken and that he'd been followed. He debates leaving, but Mike tugs him into the bar, Lucas's thirst for alcohol overriding his impulse to flee.

It's packed. Music thumps with Kacey Musgraves's twang from speakers tucked behind photos of military planes and paraphernalia commemorating the base nearby where the sound barrier was broken. Shouldering through bodies, he tucks himself up at the bar. They sit on the same two stools at the end they did the other night.

Mike nudges him with an elbow. "I'm buying since you did the drivin'. What do you want?"

"Usual's fine."

Two guys man the bar, and Lucas scans the place for Val, surprised she has the night off given how busy it is. When his gaze lands on the table in the corner, he accepts how much he wished she'd be here when he sees the one person he hoped wouldn't be. Faye.

The table is full of the usual suspects. Rafe and his squad. Faye sits perched on her husband's lap. The lone trucker among a table of men who spend their days herding convicts from cells to the mess hall and the yard outside. Lucas doesn't know the guards, but he doesn't respect them. Guards hadn't protected him; then they buried the incident in the system.

Faye's eyes fix on Lucas, and a sanguine smile pulls at her plum-tinted lips. She slides off Rafe's thighs and onto strappy heels so high they could be used as a weapon. She saunters toward him.

Lucas groans and turns back to the bar. He doesn't want to deal with her right now.

"What?" Mike asks.

"Nothing," Lucas says with a head shake. Faye had better not cause trouble.

Mike flags down the bartender working their end. Stu, a scrawny guy in his early twenties with a buzzed head and tats circling his neck.

"Corona with a lime and a Miller."

"Anything else?" Stu asks, popping tops and sliding over the bottles.

Mike flashes his fingers. "Cuervo. Two shots."

"Coming right up."

Faye arrives as Stu's pouring. She leans between Lucas and Mike, her breasts brushing Lucas's arm, her hand warm on his shoulder as she plucks a cocktail napkin from the stack. Her palm sears through the thin material of his shirt. His skin ripples with unease, and he instinctually leans away.

"Evening, boys."

"Faye," Mike says, tipping back his beer.

Lucas shoves the lime slice into his bottle and wills himself to remain seated. He can't risk making a scene and for the cops to come. Mike also needs him for a ride home.

Faye eats up the space he put between them and leans in close. "Miss you, darling." Her breath tickles his ear.

Anger sears his throat. She's deliberately provoking her husband. Payback for ignoring her texts, he figures.

He tips back his beer, taking a deep swallow. His body vibrates with restraint when her hand glides up his spine before she saunters back to her husband. Lucas glances over his shoulder, watching her go. His gaze lifts, meeting Rafe's. He glares at Lucas with hard eyes, a hand fisted on his thigh.

"Uh-oh." Mike sees the whole exchange. "Warned you Faye was trouble," he says, turning back to the bar.

"That you did." Lucas clenches his jaw. Trouble always finds him, even when he doesn't consciously go looking for it. He'd seen Faye when he frequented the Lone Palm in the first months he rolled into town. Mike or Oscar might have told him her name and who she was at some point or another, but he didn't remember when he had been trashed one night several months ago and brought her back to his place. They've been hot and heavy since whenever Rafe leaves town.

He's also known since day one who Rafe associates with. He'd never vocalize it out loud, but there've been times he's wondered if he hooked up with Faye exactly for that reason. He wants to bring attention to himself. He wants the authorities to find him and force his hand.

The scar underneath his shirtsleeve pulses. He rubs his forearm.

"It's over," he says.

"Faye know that?"

Lucas shakes his head. It's over for him, and that's what matters.

He lifts his shot glass. "To the game. Thanks for the ticket."

"You bet." They toss back their shots, and Lucas wipes the moisture from his mouth with the back of his hand.

Mike claps Lucas on the shoulder. "Gotta piss. Back in a sec."

Lucas finishes off his beer. Another arrives, and Lucas asks the guy in the ball cap and boots beside him to watch their seats. He gets up to go relieve himself. He just reaches the men's room down the low-lit back hall when he's pushed hard from behind and manhandled out the rear entrance. Two large hands shove him away. Lucas stumbles a few steps before regaining his balance. No sooner does he turn around to say he doesn't want any trouble when Rafe throws a punch at him. His fist connects with Lucas's jaw, throwing his head to the side. Sharp pain bursts through his skull. Rafe punches him again in the temple, knocking Lucas to a knee.

Damn, he hadn't expected that one.

He blinks away the stars.

Rafe is big. But Lucas has several inches on him. He's almost twice as wide. But he takes the punches, absorbs the punishment. Relishes the pain that reverberates through bones and muscle upon contact, the sting that sends shock waves through his system. He deserves it. Then he tells himself this is what he's wanted since the day he first laid eyes on Faye.

Rafe bounces in front of him, fists raised. "Fight me back, asshole."

Lucas stands, shaking his head. If it were anyone else besides Faye's husband, the guy wouldn't have gotten in a second punch, let alone the first. He would have leveled the guy for breathing on him. And if Rafe had brought out his friends to hold him down, anyone other than Jim, who guarded the door, Lucas would have gone berserk. Restraining him during a fight triggered too much bad shit.

Rafe punches him in the gut, doubling him over. Lucas gasps, hands planted on his knees.

"Touch my wife again and you die." Rafe growls the threat, and a sick part of Lucas wishes he would finish him off. Rafe spits on the ground and turns to leave.

"How'd you find out?" Lucas gasps, curiosity getting the better of him. He lifts his head from where he's bent over. Peeks at Rafe through the hair that's fallen into his face. Faye wouldn't have given him up. Until her stunt tonight, he was her dirty little secret.

Jim's chest puffs up. "Saw her leaving your place the other morn wearing the same getup she had on at the bar the night before."

Lucas nods. He figured as much would happen. His apartment faces the road. Anyone driving past sees who's coming and going.

"Next time I bring my gun."

Please do.

He'd take the decision out of Lucas's hands.

Rafe throws open the thick metal door, and Jim follows him inside. The door bangs shut behind them.

Lucas straightens with a groan and rubs his stomach. He'll be sore tomorrow.

The rear door flies open. "I leave for two minutes to take a piss, and you get hammered." Mike stomps over, grabs Lucas's chin, checks his face.

Lucas thumbs his swollen bottom lip and winces when he sees the pool of blood collecting on the tip of his finger. "How do I look?"

Mike's expression is wry. "Better than McGregor but messed up nonetheless. Told you to keep your dick in your pants."

Lucas swats away Mike's hand. "Back off."

Mike arches a brow. "Something eating at you, son?"

Always. Every second of the day. Every secret he's kept. What he did to his father, what was done to him in juvie, it all wants out. And he's not sure how much longer he can keep the pain contained.

"You're lucky Rafe didn't call the cops on you."

He wouldn't call them, not at first. He'd just let loose his prison-guard buddies on him like a pack of dogs. Then he'd bring in the police only after they left him bruised and broken.

He takes out his keys, gives them a shake. "Let's close out. I'll take you home."

14

It's late when Shiloh makes her way to the encampment. She moves stealthily around the perimeter toward her car. Heart thumping in her head, she tries not to make noise. Barrel fires have burned to a smolder, and most of the inhabitants have fallen asleep or passed out, depending on their poison. When her car comes into view, her pace quickens. She rounds Irving's Chevy Caprice and trips over a lump on the ground.

She swears out loud before she can stop herself. Wide eyed, she claps a hand over her mouth and waits. An owl hoots, and a mouse scurries past underfoot. She dares a look down. Passed out by her feet, Irving lies facedown in the dirt. He's naked except for the dingy tighty-whities. Frail with loose hanging skin, he doesn't move.

She toes his elbow, afraid he's dead. "Irving?"

He moans.

A pained noise rumbles in her throat. This isn't the first time Irving's passed out on the ground. But why tonight of all nights? She just wanted to get into her car and hide. But she can't leave him like this. He could die out here, and she'd never forgive herself, even after he allowed what happened to her car the other day.

Dropping to her knees, she gives his shoulder a shake. His skin is too cold. "Irving," she whispers harshly.

He groans, shifting his legs. His knee connects with the metal tin he uses for his drugs and syringes. It clatters across the dirt.

Shit, shit, shit.

Shiloh grabs the tin and feels around for the lid. Her palm lands on a used syringe, and she jerks back before cautiously picking it up. As quietly as she can, she puts the tin in the car and tries to flip Irving over.

He groans louder, pushing up on his arms until he flops onto his back.

"Shhhh." Shiloh waves her hands to get him to quiet down.

His eyelids lift to half-mast. "Daisy Ray?" He shouts his daughter's name.

"Quiet." She looks around, terrified that Bob and Barton will hear them. She tries to haul him up, breathing in his stink and hating that she's getting the smell of him on her. "Get up. You'll freeze to death out here."

"But I like the stars."

"I know." She grunts, getting him to his feet.

Irving tumbles into the back seat. Shiloh finds his blanket on the ground. She shakes it out and drops it over him.

He grasps her hand before she moves away. Her heart rate jack-knifes. But he smiles dreamily. "You've always been good to me, Daisy."

Irving's delusional. If his daughter was good to him, if she cared for him, he wouldn't be homeless.

If her mom cared about her, she would have kicked Ellis out months ago. She would have believed her when Shiloh told her Ellis was touching her, which hurts more than the emotional trauma Ellis put her through. She feels unseen and unwanted. Worthless to her own mother.

"Good night, sweetheart."

She pulls her hand free of his dry and brittle palm. "Night, Irving."

Glancing around, she holds her breath. Someone snores. Someone else coughs. But all seems undisturbed.

She tiptoes to her car and as quietly as possible opens the rear passenger door. It creaks once before she dives inside and comes face-to-face with Ricky's gummy grin.

A startled scream expands her throat.

"Wonderin' if you'd be returning, sweets. This is my car now."

"But . . . no." Her breath gushes with fear. "No, it's not." Where the hell else can she go?

"It's mine." Ricky lunges across the seat and smacks Shiloh's cheek. The contact is sharp, stunning Shiloh speechless.

"Mine, mine, mine," Ricky yells.

Shiloh covers her cheek, shocked the woman hit her. "It was you. You broke my windows." Not Bob and Barton, the two scumbags always leering at her.

Ricky sneers. "You don't belong here."

If Shiloh were smart, she'd make a run for it. But she's fed up with people taking advantage of her, and she snaps. "You bitch. Get out of my car." She grabs Ricky's ankles and drags the woman across the seat.

Ricky kicks madly, knocking Shiloh's chin. Her head snaps back. She sees stars.

"Thief! Thief!" Ricky shrieks. Her screams pierce the quiet night.

Hands snake around Shiloh's chest and pull her from the car. Barton's face appears in front of her. "Hey, there, sugar. We were hoping you'd come back."

She blinks up at him, her vision blurring.

He starts dragging her away.

White-hot terror slices into her. "Let me go!" She squirms in his arms but can't get her footing.

"Not so fast, girl. You're ours tonight. Bob, grab her feet."

Her screams cut through the night. If Bob and Barton drag her off, she'll never see her mom again. She'll never get to Finn. This can't be happening. She screams again, kicking at Bob where it counts. But they're big guys. He blocks her foot and picks her up with ease. Again she screams, and again, struggling in their grip as they effortlessly carry her like a pig on a spit into the dark, dark desert.

Nobody is coming for her. No one cares what they'll do to her.

She's going to die out here.

Shiloh sobs, wishing for the first time she'd taken Lucas up on his offer to take her to a shelter. Being sent home to Ellis couldn't be nearly as horrific as what these guys have planned for her.

15

"Get some ice on that eye," Mike says when Lucas drops him off at his house.

Lucas grunts and lifts his chin to say goodbye before driving off. He cruises back through town, past the Lone Palm, past the homeless encampment, and straight to his apartment, where he sees that same car from earlier is parked across the street. His pulse rate rockets.

Someone's found him. He needs to leave town.

Survival mode kicking in, he starts to turn around but notices the sandwich he left for Sunshine Girl is gone.

She did come back.

He looks around, momentarily forgetting about the car across the road, his concern for a homeless girl, a stranger, outweighing his fear of getting caught. Where is she now?

A mixed bag of relief and anxiety has him rubbing the back of his neck. He's been worried about her since she took off last night.

Looking off in the direction of the homeless encampment, he prays she didn't return there. But it's the best place to start. He doesn't know what he'll do when he finds her, but he admittedly feels like he wronged her. It was his fault she ran off last night, just as it was his fault Lily ran away. He needs to check on her. Then he needs to get out of town.

With one last glance over his shoulder toward the Honda with the darkened interior, he leaves his truck behind, reasoning he can get there and back quicker without it, and jogs the mile across the open field, moonlight guiding his way.

It's late, and the encampment is still. Barrel fires have burned down to a flicker, but the full moon casts a mystical glow, and the dirt under his boots appears to shimmer as if alive.

Sweat dripping down his spine and coating his hairline, he canvasses the outer rim until he reaches Sunshine Girl's Ford. At the same time he hopes she's there and that she's not. If she is, he won't have to spend the rest of the night looking for her. If she isn't, she's probably in a safer spot than this haphazard parking lot. Still won't stop him from searching for her.

He knocks gently on the roof, so he doesn't startle her like he did last time. The lot is so damn quiet, she's got to be asleep. When he doesn't get so much as a grumble from her, he knocks a little louder. This time he gets an annoyed groan.

His shoulders tense. That doesn't sound like her.

He sniffs the air. The smell is off.

Frowning, he leans into the window, flashing his phone light. A woman with missing teeth and thinning hair shrieks. Her clothes are filthy, and she smells worse. She holds her hands up against the light.

"Turn it off! Turn it off!"

Her yelling stirs others nearby. Someone has a coughing fit. Someone else shouts for them to shut up.

"Where's the girl?" Lucas demands, swallowing his panic as he tries not to think what it means that someone has commandeered Sunshine's car. Did she give it up willingly? Or is this what happens when someone leaves the encampment for the day?

Or didn't return the previous night.

His hands clench, and he fights the urge to punch the door.

His fault she lost her car. He convinced her to meet him at McDonald's last night.

"Where is she?" he repeats when the woman covers her face with her hands and shakes her head, refusing to answer. "Tell me." He roars, smacking the hood, his anger startling even him. He doesn't understand the urgency overtaking him, only that he needs to find her. She shrieks louder.

Heads peek out windows. Same guy as before swears at him to shut up. He's trying to sleep.

As if Lucas cares.

"The little bitch is getting what she deserves. Wouldn't stop taunting my boys."

His stomach drops with dread.

The guys standing around a barrel fire he'd seen leering at Sunshine last night? This *is* his fault. He warned them to leave her alone. Instead he'd worked them up.

There isn't a fire tonight, just an orange glow at the barrel's mouth from whatever is smoldering inside. As he'd done with Lily, he screwed up. Now another young girl would be traumatized because of him.

"Go away." The old hag spits at Lucas, her body twitching. He rears back so she misses. Damn, she's higher than a kite.

A scream cuts through the night, followed by a guttural bellow. Then a shriek that raises the hairs on Lucas's arms. The sounds come from beyond the perimeter, out in the darkness. They sound just like Lily had all those years ago.

The woman cackles, and Lucas takes off at a full sprint, driven by rage and fear. He failed Lily once. He won't fail again. When he comes upon them, Sunshine Girl and the two men that made him uneasy, he finds the guys on their knees and Sunshine pulling down her sweatshirt.

Pulsing hot rage rips into him at the thought of them touching her, and memories from his time in juvenile detention crash to the forefront, mixing with the present. Hands touching him. Sweaty bodies pressing in on him. The foul breath of the one on him.

Sunshine grabs her backpack, swings it at one guy's head. He's hunched over, cupping his groin and whining like a toddler. Upon impact, he lurches to the side, but catches himself before he face-plants in the dirt. She then takes off running.

The bigger guy drops forward, supporting his weight on an arm. Blood oozes from his mouth in thick strings. There's enough to make Lucas wonder if he bit through his tongue. He's grumbling up a storm at Sunshine Girl.

Hearing Lucas's fast approach, he looks up, and his eyes bulge. He starts to stand, but Lucas, channeling years of anger and shame, punches him in the cheekbone, splitting the man's face. He still manages to stagger to his feet and raise a fist at Lucas. Lucas doesn't give the guy a chance to take a swing at him. He delivers a roundhouse kick to the head. His boot connects with the man's skull, knocking him out cold. The guy drops like a stone.

"Who the fuck are you?" The shorter guy sneers at him, still cupping his balls. Obviously, he's already forgotten Lucas got into their faces last night. He's also in a lot of pain. Sunshine Girl kneed him in the balls. Good for her. His clothes hang on his unwashed body. Lucas can smell his stench from several feet away. Liquor and something foul that burns his nostrils. Familiar, distasteful odors that imprinted on his brain when his bunkmate and others overpowered him. His stomach turns.

The guy goes to stand.

"Down. Stay," Lucas yells ferociously, treating him like the dog he is.

The guy lifts his hands and drops back to his knees. He's half Lucas's size. Lucas can dust him with an uppercut, but he takes off after Sunshine before he loses her. She's heading toward town, and she's fast.

But Lucas is faster. He spent his childhood as a tight end chasing wide receivers. He kept up his workout routine long after he was forced to drop from football. Running and lifting helped in two ways: sweat out the alcohol and take off the edge when he couldn't deal with life.

She hears him behind her and glances over her shoulder. She shrieks, her eyes widening, and she cuts across the field, zigzagging toward the road.

"Stop," he hollers, giving chase.

To his amazement, she picks up the pace.

She's scared, he gets that. She probably doesn't realize it's him. But she's running out of steam. He can hear her breath coming in harsh bursts as he closes the distance between them. If they don't stop this madness, one of them is going to catch their shoe on a rock or shrub and go flying. Break a wrist or ankle. It's too damn dark to be running at this speed.

"Sunshine, wait!"

Her step falters, and he snags her arm, using her momentum to swing her around to face him. Her fist comes with it, connecting with his jaw. His head snaps back, but he doesn't lose his grip. He easily grabs her other wrist. Shit, she's strong.

She screams, struggling to get away. Her shoe catches his shin.

"That hurt," he growls. His grip tightens. "Calm down, Sunshine."

"Stop calling me that." She throws her head forward. Lucas leans away before she connects with his chin, giving him a good impression of what she'd done back there to escape.

"Then tell me your name."

"I already did."

"Your real name. Tell me your name, and I'll let you go."

She twists her wrists, trying to loosen his grip. She whimpers in pain, and it kills him she's willing to hurt herself to get free of him. But for the life of him, he's not letting her sleep on the streets one more night.

"Stop it. You're only going to hurt yourself."

"Go to hell." She spits.

"Already there." He wipes his cheek on his shoulder and swings her around as if they're dancing. Then he holds her back tight against his chest, the stuff in her backpack digging into his ribs, before she can cause further damage to either one of them.

She grunts and kicks, breathing heavily.

"Would you just chill? I'm trying to help. I'm not going to hurt you," he says with forced calm, letting her work through the shock. Giving her mind time to catch up with everything that happened. To realize she's safe. Or, at least, safer with him than she ever was with them. He knows. He's been there. And eventually, slowly, she surprisingly does calm down.

She takes a deep defeated breath. Then she whispers, "Shiloh."

"Shiloh," he repeats. He likes her name. It suits her.

He releases her wrists and cautiously takes two steps back.

Shiloh remains still, shoulders hunched, chin dropped, before she turns around to face him, her shoes scraping in the dirt. She sniffles, her hazel eyes lifting to his face. She digs the base of her palms into her eyes as if trying to plug the waterworks, then lets her arms drop to her sides. The tears keep coming.

"What are you going to do with me?" she asks, wary.

His face contorts with disgust. What kind of man does she think he is?

"Nothing. I . . . I don't want—I'm not like them." He tilts his head in the direction they'd run from. "I only want to help."

Her mouth screws up. "Nobody *just* wants to help. They always want something."

"You aren't trusting, are you?"

She shakes her head.

"Good. You shouldn't be." His hands drop. She also needs a cold, hard reality check. He points back toward the encampment. "Those guys would have torn you apart inside out and left you there to die."

Her face pales.

"No one over there would have cared. No one would have lifted a finger to help, no matter how loud you screamed. And nobody would have done anything to get those assholes arrested. They would have gotten away with what they wanted to do with you. Then they'd do it again, and again, and again. To you, if you didn't die during the first round. Then to someone else."

She looks physically ill. A tear tracks down her cheek, followed by another.

"Would you have wanted that?"

She shakes her head.

Good. She's scared. He wants her scared. Then maybe he can talk some sense into her.

"Did they hurt you? Did they—" He swallows roughly, and his voice comes out thin. "Violate you?"

"No," she says, meekly, vulnerable.

He loosens a relieved sigh. *Thank fuck.* This could have been much worse.

She pulls her gaze from the encampment and stares at the ground. She looks so young.

"How old are you really?" he asks.

Her teeth rattle, and he realizes she's shaking uncontrollably. She's probably going into shock. In another few minutes, her skin will be ice cold. She needs food and a hot shower.

"Fi-fi-fifteen," she whispers.

Hell.

What's she doing out here by herself?

"There's got to be a women's shelter around here. You need to go there."

"No!" Panic sharpens her eyes. But there's something else there, too. There's more to her story, and he suspects what she told him about her parents is a lie.

"Your home life crap?"

She nods. "My mom's boyfriend. He . . . He tried to . . ."

"Don't say it." He doesn't need to hear more.

She looks away, ashamed.

"Your mom still alive?"

She nods.

He swears. He can't take her to the shelter. They'll contact CPS, who'll notify her mom. She could land right back where that bastard will have access to her. He only sees one option for her, at least for the night.

"Come home with me. I have a spare room. You can stay there."

Her face pales.

"There's a lock on the door. Barricade it with the dresser, I don't give a rat's ass. But come back with me. I won't be able to sleep tonight if you're out here."

"Sounds like a personal problem."

"Yeah, smart-ass, it is. A big one. So are you gonna return to your car and risk Tweedledee and Tweedledum getting their hands on you again, or are you going to stay at my place?"

"Bob and Barton."

He tilts his head. "What?"

"Bob and Barton, those guys. That's their names."

He grinds his teeth. The fact she knows their names tells him she's spent more nights alone in that car than he cares to think about.

"And the woman I found in your car?"

"Ricky. I think she's their mom. She acts like it. She's a bitch."

"Yeah, she is."

Her mouth twitches, which makes him smile. Just a brief, strained one. God, what if he'd arrived a minute later? That thought alone will give him nightmares for the week.

He tucks his hands in his pockets and nods toward his place. "Let's go before Bob and Barton regain their wits."

"What did you do to them?"

"Finished what you started."

Her chin lifts with pride.

"Come on. It's late and I'm exhausted." He starts walking.

When he hears her shoes kicking up dust behind him, he releases a pent-up breath. He wasn't sure she'd follow.

16

Shiloh hugs her ribs and steps into Lucas's bland apartment. She warily looks around. The walls are stark white, the furniture is spartan, and an old coffee table stands on three legs. Above her a ceiling fan whirls. Frightened, stressed, and unusually exhausted, she realizes that she's alone with a stranger and worries she made the wrong decision coming here with him.

She turns back to Lucas before she registers that she's changed her mind. She doesn't know where she'll go or what she'll do, but she wants to leave. Lucas, though, is staring intently out the door. Across the street, a car is parked alongside the road. "What is it?" she asks, the fierce expression on his face making her more uneasy than she already is. She splits her gaze between him and the car.

"Nothing." Lucas shuts and bolts the door, and she feels the blood rush from her head. His response doesn't reassure her one bit. Something about that car bothers him. Not only that, now she's trapped. He holds up his hands. "It's okay."

"That car . . . Who—?"

"Not sure, but right now I'm worried about you."

"I'm f-fine."

He cocks his head. "No, you're not."

"B-B-Bob . . . ?" Her teeth chatter. She can't talk she's shaking so badly.

"They didn't follow us here. I checked. They won't hurt you anymore." He starts to close the blinds, and she whimpers.

He abruptly lets go of the curtain. "Everything's cool. I can keep them open if you want." She gives him a blank stare, unsure now what she wants. The curtains will keep her hidden from Bob and Barton in case they did follow them, but she'd be hidden from anyone who could help if Lucas tries anything. She doesn't know him. He could be lying to her like every other man she's met.

"Ivy lives next door," he says, cautiously, slowly, and on some level she understands he's doing it for her benefit. He doesn't want to scare her. "She owns the building. If you're more comfortable with a woman, I can ask if you can stay with her."

She shakes her head. The more people who know she's homeless, the more likely she'll be reported to the police.

Her teeth chatter uncontrollably. He can close the blinds. Do whatever he wants. She can't decide. But she does need to get a grip. She's about to have a breakdown. She hasn't stopped shaking since Lucas found her.

Violent tremors rack her body. She can still feel their hands on her, smell their rank breath. Fortunate for her, they were wasted, and she could move twice as fast. She had the element of surprise on her side. Bob could barely keep a grasp on her ankles. She wriggled one free and nailed him in the balls, making him howl. He dropped her other leg, throwing Barton off balance with her weight. Shiloh got her footing and shot to her feet, slamming her head into Barton's jaw. He bit into his tongue. His shout was guttural, deadly. And she feared what he'd do in retaliation.

He tried to grab her when she wrenched free but pulled off her backpack instead. Without thinking, she punched him in the mouth. He squealed in pain, eyes rolling back in his head, and dropped her backpack. She grabbed it, swung at Bob, knocking him over, then took off like the hounds of hell were on her heels. She's never run so fast in her life.

"Can I ask you a question?"

Her head whips in his direction. "What?"

"I'm not a fan of the police, but why run away and not tell them about your mom's boyfriend?"

"He threatened to hurt my mom if I did." Ellis was livid when Shiloh told Harmony about him. He smacked her mom around until he convinced her that Shiloh had been lying about him. She wanted her mom to go to the police, but she refused. She insisted they wouldn't be of help, and that Shiloh should be ashamed of herself for lying. Ellis is the most reliable man she's met. She loves him. How dare Shiloh try to destroy what they have.

Shiloh wants to believe it was the drugs talking. Her mom was high at the time. But her words didn't hurt any less. They only made her feel rejected and betrayed. Alone.

"Men like him don't deserve to breathe the same air we do," he says with deadly calm.

Shiloh rubs her arms. She can't get warm. Her skin feels like ice.

"I'm going to repeat what I said out there." Lucas speaks slowly, cautiously. "I won't hurt you. I want to help. It's not safe on the streets, but you can leave anytime. It's entirely up to you. I'm not forcing you to stay."

She stares at him, and he starts to walk away. "Why?"

He turns back. "Why what?"

"Why are you helping me?"

He looks at the keys in his hands. "You remind me of someone." Tossing the keys and his wallet on the counter, he goes to the freezer and grabs a pack of peas and a bag of corn. He gives her the peas and slaps the corn against his temple.

She stares at the frozen bag of vegetables in her hand. "What's this for?"

"We have matching shiners."

"Oh." She gingerly touches her eye, becoming aware of how tender it is. Barton had cuffed her good when she wouldn't shut up.

Lucas settles on the tweed couch, knees spread. He plants an elbow on his thigh, holding the bag against his face, and watches her, following her gaze as she scopes out his apartment. The old flatscreen. The mess in the kitchen. The stained carpeting. His laptop on the coffee table.

She inhales a sharp breath. Holds it.

She could Zoom with Finn. She could email him without going all the way to the library and let him know where she is. Would he finally come get her if she told him what happened tonight? That her life was literally in jeopardy?

No, she needs more cash before she sees him. She won't be a free-loader like her mom is with Ellis. He'll have too much control over her. Maybe Lucas has money. She could sell the laptop.

Lucas's eyes narrow. "There's no money here, and that's off-limits." He points at the laptop.

Her head snaps to him. "I wasn't—"

His eyes narrow farther.

"Whatever." She hugs herself tighter and turns away. Another tremble rolls through her.

"You're pale and shivering, and you're freaked out. That's normal."

She walks farther into the apartment. "I don't need a shrink. Just a bed."

"Down the hall, room on the right. Bathroom's right next to it."

"Whatever, Dr. Luc."

He snorts, keeping the corn against his face.

As if to prove that she isn't as rattled or nauseous with residual fear as he thinks she is, she tosses the pea bag on the coffee table and stomps down the hallway, stopping outside the bathroom door. She does have to pee, and she could use a shower. Rather, she's dying to take one. She can still feel their hands on her body. Her gaze dips to the doorknob. There's a lock. Does she dare undress in a strange man's apartment? She stares into the narrow room with the plastic shower stall and tub combo, toilet and square sink stuck in the corner. The shower curtain is white with mold spotting the bottom hem. A single navy-blue towel is draped over the shower curtain rod. The floor . . .

Her top lip curls.

The floor . . . is . . .

"Ew, when was the last time you cleaned?"

She hears him drop the corn on the table. He strides down the hallway, stopping beside her.

"What?" he asks, confusion riddling his face.

"Look." She gestures at the bathroom. "It's disgusting."

Urine stains the linoleum around the base of the toilet. There's a ring around the tub and scum in the sink. She doesn't even want to look inside the toilet. Does he flush when he's done?

"It's grosser here than the one at the park." Which was nasty. People vomited there and did who knows what else.

Red tinges his cheeks. His face twitches with embarrassment before he glares at her stonily. "Then go use that one. No one's stopping you." He steps aside so she can leave.

She takes a deep breath and slowly shakes her head, as afraid to leave as she is to stay.

"Deal with it. I don't have a maid, so clean up after yourself."

"Not if you don't."

He grunts and grabs a clean towel from under the sink. He pushes it into her arms. "I'll clean tomorrow. Shower and get some sleep."

Shiloh doesn't move. What is she supposed to wear after she showers? The clothes she has are filthy, especially the ones she's wearing. Bob's and Barton's hands were all over her sweatshirt, trying to yank it off her. If it weren't the only one she has, she'd burn it.

"What's wrong?" Lucas asks in a tone that suggests his patience is thinning. He might be regretting his decision to let her crash here. Then where would she go?

Her cheeks heat, thawing her chilled face. "I don't have clean clothes."

Lucas sighs. He does that a lot, as if she annoys him. Shiloh clutches the towel to her chest. She hasn't had a shower in almost two weeks.

She'd sleep on the bathroom floor tonight if it meant she could finally get clean and no longer smell like Irving's car.

Lucas leaves her side and goes into one of the bedrooms. She hears a drawer open and close. A white shirt with something printed on the back and a pair of basketball shorts drop in her arms. He opens a louvered door in the hallway to a small closet. Stacked inside is a washer and dryer.

"Leave your clothes. I'll wash them later so you have them in the morning," he says.

She hesitates, debating what to do. He could destroy her clothes and keep her captive. But he's already told her she can leave at any time. Should she test him? Walk out the door right now? And go where? Sleeping outside tonight is the last thing she wants to do. She also wants to get out of the clothes Bob and Barton touched.

"All right," she tells him.

She shuts and locks the door, turns on the vent and water, and when it's scalding hot, she steps underneath the spray and sobs with relief. She's alive. She'll be clean. She's going to sleep in a bed.

And right now, she doesn't want anything more than that.

In the privacy of the bathroom, Shiloh lets herself go, where the water washes away her tears before they fall. Where the vent drowns out her sobs. She cries out her fear, frustration, and trauma, bawling over her mother, what happened with Ellis, and again tonight with Bob and Barton.

And for the first time in a while, she stops acting stronger than she feels. She lets herself be the fifteen-year-old girl she is.

Homeless. A runaway.

A sexual-assault victim.

A dreamer and a believer.

The whole mixed bag.

Shiloh sinks to the base of the tub and pulls her knees to her chin. She hugs her shins and lowers her forehead to her knees.

And she weeps.

17

Lucas stares blankly at the wall across from him. The shower runs down the hall. A car drives past the building, the noise crescendoing before it fades, and he has the sudden urge to look out the window to see if the car he swears followed him home from the game is still across the road. He should be halfway to anywhere but here by now, but he can't leave Shiloh alone, not after that attack. Everything that could have happened to her . . .

Condensation drips on his knee. Plop. Plop. Plop.

They would have killed her if he hadn't intervened.

The reality of what he did tonight sinks in. He put someone else before him. He's more worried about her than that damn car out front. Someone could be following him. He could land in jail tomorrow.

He swears, tossing the corn that's rapidly defrosting onto the table, wipes the moisture off his face with his shirt, and sighs heavily. He's taking a risk harboring an unaccompanied minor. Him, a guy with a record and a warrant.

Now what's he supposed to do with her?

He doesn't know the first thing about handling kids, let alone a girl. He balked when Olivia tried to off-load Josh on him, and he's his nephew. Lucas is the worst sort of role model in a family of crappy examples. Shiloh shouldn't stay with him, and not because of the law. Granted, harboring an underage runaway in California isn't illegal unless her parents are actively looking for her. But he can barely keep his own shit together.

Yet he can't in good conscience talk her into returning home. She might have lied the other night about being an orphan. But she told the truth about her mother's boyfriend. Tonight wasn't the first time she's been assaulted. He recognized her shame and disgust. He sees it on his own face whenever he spares his reflection a glance.

He also won't notify the police or call CPS. He didn't rescue her from one lion's den only for her to land in another. From where he stands, it comes down to this: What does Shiloh want?

When he arrived home after juvenile probation, his parents never asked what he wanted. Neither did the authorities, his attorney, or the doctors. He was treated like a nonperson. Worthless and incapable of making decisions or thinking on his own. Sixteen, immature, and already a lost cause. *He screwed up his life. There's no hope for him now.* His father's words replayed so many times in his head that Lucas believed him—still believes him—so he let his parents manipulate him into every direction he didn't want to take his life.

Looking back, he was too ashamed to speak up for himself. Too damaged to care. His gut tells him Shiloh is dealing with a similar sort of shame. The last thing he wants is to take away her voice. What happens next will be up to her.

He sighs wearily, dragging his hands down his face, wincing when he irritates the contusion on his cheekbone. They'll talk in the morning. She's traumatized, and he's too tired and sore to string two words together.

The shower turns off. Pushing off the couch, he returns the peas and corn to the freezer. When he turns around, Shiloh appears in the kitchen. She looks like a drenched kitten, swimming in the shirt and gym shorts he gave her to wear. Her hair is combed back from her face and hangs long and damp down her back. Without the dirt, she looks younger than fifteen. Her eyes are huge, almost oversize for her petite face. Christ, she's a baby.

"May I use the washer?" She shows him the pile of dirty clothes in her arms, and his switchblade drops. The metal thuds loudly on the linoleum floor.

They both look at the blade, then at each other. Her face drains of color. The room holds its breath. He doesn't move. He doesn't dare twitch.

She visibly swallows. "I thought—"

"Keep it," he interrupts. "Not keep it, keep it." That blade holds too much meaning for him. "But keep it on you. If it makes you feel safer."

Eyes locked on him, she slowly crouches and picks up the blade.

"Just don't off yourself."

"I'm not suicidal," she scoffs at the same time her gaze zeroes in on his tattoo, the raised flesh underneath. Her cheeks darken. "Sorry," she mumbles.

An awkward silence hangs between them. She's the first who's remarked on his scar, however indirectly, in years.

He clears his throat, uncomfortable with his own failings. Not from the time he attempted to take his life when he was sixteen. But because he hasn't had the courage to follow through on it again, which was the whole reason he landed here in his own private purgatory. A way station between living and dying.

"I'll wash them," he offers, because he needs something to do.

"'Kay." She drops the pile onto the counter, more interested in the blade. She flings it open and closed with the flick of her wrist.

"Where'd you learn to handle a knife?" Unsettled, he takes her laundry to the washer in the hallway closet. He starts a load.

"A friend. Same one who taught me to kick a guy in the balls," she answers.

He likes that friend.

He returns to the kitchen, and she's flipping through one of his sister's *Tabby's Squirrel* books he's left on the counter but has never read. Too afraid of his own reaction, he hasn't even cracked them open.

"You have Jenna's books."

He goes utterly still. "You know her?"

She shakes her head. "Love her stuff. I want to meet her. Kind of weird you have kid books. You got a kid somewhere?"

"Nope."

"Niece or nephew?"

He doesn't answer. She takes that as a negative and makes a face. "See? Weird."

"I didn't ask for your opinion." He also doesn't like her flipping through Lily's book. She closes the cover, and he moves that book and the other aside, stacking them on his laptop.

Her gaze follows him, her fingernail picking at a piece of peeling laminate on the counter. "You know that friend who taught me about knives? His name's Jace. He was my neighbor, and his mom was a mean old bitch. She knocked him around a lot. She told him he was dumb, but he's the smartest guy I know. Anyway, when you hear enough times that you have shit for brains and won't amount to anything, you start to believe it."

A tingling swoops up the back of his neck. He knows that all too well.

"Jace and I meet at the park before school and walk together. This one time, though, a couple of years back, he didn't show, and I got this weird feeling that something was wrong, so I went to his apartment. When he didn't answer, I used the key his mom keeps in the crack in the doorframe. I found him in the . . . he was . . ." She fixates her gaze on the chipped counter. "He was in the bath."

A chill spears his spine, dry-ice cold. He knows where this story is going. He was Jace once, alone in a warm bath with a blade.

"The water was overflowing, and he had a knife. He looked at me and said, 'I can't do it.' He gave it to me. I don't know if he wanted me to cut him, but no way, man. I couldn't. I flung it out the door." Tears well in her eyes, and it takes everything in Lucas not to pull this stranger of a girl into his arms and comfort her. The urge to do so a stranger itself.

"He dried off and cleaned up, and I told him I was keeping the knife at my place. He could have it back after he taught me how to use it. I told Jace I wanted to learn how to protect myself in case, you know, Ellis tried anything. I told him he wasn't allowed to die. He couldn't leave me unprotected."

"You gave him a purpose." Lucas's throat is tight.

She nods.

"How old were you?"

"Thirteen."

So damn young. "Why didn't you go to his place when you ran away?"

"His mom would have called my mom. I didn't want Ellis to find me."

Lucas pushes out a breath. He wants to bash the guy's face in.

"What's your last name?"

He blinks, startled at the sudden subject change. "Carson. Why?"

She shrugs. "No reason."

He figures it makes him less of a stranger. "What's yours?"

"You going to call my mom?"

"We'll talk about it in the morning."

Her lips purse, her expression circumspect. She gently, cautiously rests the blade on the counter. "Bloom."

He frowns. "Your last name?"

She nods, and an odd, unwelcome ripple of unease coils in his chest, as if he's been fated to end up here just so his life intersected with hers. Two wayward, broken souls.

Bloom, like a flower. Like Lily.

"Thanks for saving me tonight," she says, her voice barely above a whisper. "Good night, Lucas."

"Good night, Shiloh." She retreats to the spare bedroom, leaving him to wonder the exact opposite. She just might have saved him.

Too bad he isn't worth saving.

18

Morning comes with the arrival of a blaring alarm. Lucas smacks his clock and realizes he has two things to be grateful for before he rolls out of bed. The other side of the bed is empty, and he isn't hungover. Then he remembers the Honda Accord.

He swiftly gets up, heart racing, and parts the curtains. The car is still there, a dull gray covered in dust. It hasn't moved, and it's hard to tell if there's someone inside. The sun is reflecting off the windows.

Backing away from the window, he tells himself he's being paranoid. That run-in with the cop the other night has him thinking everyone is following him. Surely the cops would have made an appearance by now if that was the case.

Shaking off his anxiety, he goes to the bathroom, does his routine, showers, glances at the toilet tank while he brushes his teeth and does a double take, startled the switchblade isn't there. Then he remembers why—Shiloh.

He almost forgot about the kid in his apartment. He scratches his neck. They should talk about what happens next with her, but it'll have to be later. He glances at the clock. She's probably still asleep, and he's going to be late.

He pulls on jeans and a shirt, ties up his boots, and heads to the kitchen for coffee.

"Oh, my god, you're Lucas Carson!" Shiloh shouts from where she's sitting on the couch when she sees him.

Lucas's heart explodes from his chest. "Jesus Christ." He thought she was still in bed.

"You're Jenna's brother." She clutches Lily's books to her chest.

"Give me those." He takes them from her, tosses them onto the kitchen counter, feeling ridiculous that he has them. He never should have purchased them in the first place. Anytime he sees them he gets a pang in his chest.

"What are you doing up?" he asks. It isn't even six in the morning. Normally he wouldn't be up either unless he went for a row on the bay at sunrise. But that was when he was living in Seaside Cove, and the Dusty Pantry opens at seven. He has to set up the deli counter and open the market.

"I couldn't sleep." She gets up from the couch and joins him in the kitchen, sliding onto a stool from the previous tenant. He left behind all the furniture, beds included. Up and died on her, Ivy told him when she'd shown him the apartment that first day. Everything was Lucas's if he wanted it. George didn't have family, and she didn't have the money to hire someone to haul his belongings to the dump, which is where she thought everything should go.

What George left was exactly what Lucas needed. He told Ivy to leave it.

Back home, he kept his apartment neat. His belongings were sparse, but what he did own—bikes, canoes, electronics, a couple of antique trucks—were top of the line and kept in fine working condition. He treated his things well.

Here, he just doesn't care. Hence the dirty bathroom.

He saw the room in a new light when he used it this morning.

"Is it true Jenna's your sister?" Shiloh asks, bringing his attention back to the nuclear bomb she set off. "Because if she is, that's wicked cool. Can you introduce me?"

"Who says I know her?" He drags the coffeepot off the hot pad and pours out yesterday's brew.

"I figured it out last night. TMZ did this piece on her months ago about how she ran away as a kid because she thought she'd murdered her best friend, but what really happened is she killed him in self-defense. He came at her, choking her and all that, but she thinks he did it because he thought she was her dad, who'd tried to shoot them both with his gun. Jenna said Wes, that was his name, hit his head and was out of it. He never would have hurt her otherwise. But what's crazy is that her dad died last September. Car accident or something, so they can't ask him what happened. I'm sure he would have been arrested and spent the rest of his life in prison. But—" She pauses dramatically, inhales deeply, and Lucas is immobile, a prisoner to her story. "Jenna Mason isn't her real name, not the one she was born with. It's Lily Carson. And this guy Ryder, Wes's older brother, stalked her for years thinking she murdered Wes. Isn't that wild? Anyway, I'm a huge fan, as if you can't tell. I want to be an animator just like her. I have all sorts of ideas, that's why I'm moving to Hollywood. She's super successful and has been uploading videos to YouTube forever. I've read everything I can on her. That's how I know she has a brother named Lucas Carson. Hey, don't you think that's enough water?"

Lucas looks at the coffeepot clutched under the running faucet. Water spills over the rim. His back to Shiloh, he couldn't move once she started talking about Lily. He should be asking how she's coping after last night, but what she told him about Lily left him speechless. Since Lily's return and Olivia's text about their sister's name change, he's intentionally avoided searching for news on Jenna Mason, afraid what he'd read would be too upsetting. That the life she'd led had been racked with hardships and threats. A life he could have prevented.

He smacks off the water and angles his head toward Shiloh without meeting her eyes. "What happened to Ryder?"

"Who?" she asks.

"Ryder, the guy stalking her." He remembers Ryder Jensen. He was the same year as him in high school. They had a few classes together.

Ryder used to mow the Carsons' lawn when he was a kid. He was also an annoying shit, that kid who drew dicks with Sharpies on girls' lockers. He served a four-year prison term after beating up his girlfriend to within an inch of her life.

Worry clouds his vision. Is Lily still at risk? What about Josh, her son. *His* nephew?

"He was arrested when he attacked Jenna. He tried to kill her."

"The fuck?" Lucas almost drops the pot in the sink. He slams it into the coffeemaker.

Shiloh looks surprised. "Where've you been? Don't you know any of this? You're her brother."

"I'm not—" He stops. Arguing with her is pointless. Telling her there's more than one Lucas Carson is useless, especially given his reaction. "When did this happen?"

"With Ryder? Seven or eight months ago."

Around the time he ditched the Cove. For a brief second, he regrets leaving Olivia behind. She and Lily might have needed him. He should have been there for them. He needs to read those articles. Now that he knows about Lily, he must know more.

He dumps grounds in the filter and turns to Shiloh. "Go get ready. You're coming with me." He wants to get through the day so he can look all this up.

She blinks, startled at the change of subject. Or maybe his order. "Wh-where?"

"Downstairs. Store opens in an hour."

"Can't I stay here?" Face on him, her eyes swing to the window and back.

"They don't know you're here." He understands her fear.

"What am I supposed to do all day?"

She has a point. She can't stare at the walls.

"I have a question for you." He folds his arms. "What are your plans? You mentioned a boyfriend."

"Finn. He's a musician in a band. I was on my way to his place when my ride didn't work out." She tugs at her shirt hem, and he suspects there's a story in there somewhere.

"Where does he live?"

"Hollywood."

She lived in a homeless encampment with her boyfriend only three hours away? He's more of a douche than Lucas thought. "Why hasn't he come to get you?"

"He doesn't have a car, and I need money."

"For a bus ticket? Done." He reaches for his wallet.

She stretches the hem farther. "I need more than a bus ticket. Finn is broke. He can't support me, and I don't want him to. I need a job."

"Fine. I'll give you one." Work is good. It'll keep her mind off her assault.

Her mouth falls open.

"I can't in good conscience tell you to go home." Or give her a lift to Hollywood. Finn is bad news. If one of his sisters wanted to live with a guy she chatted with online but hadn't met in real life, he'd never take them. In fact, he'd try to talk them out of that nonsense. In time, Shiloh might realize she can do better than that guy. Does he know where she's been living? "You can work in the market for as long as you want. But people I know will be curious about you. We need to make up a story."

"Like what, I'm your daughter or something?"

"Or something." A daughter is too close. Ivy will ask if he has a wife. "We'll tell them you're my niece." He notices the dark blemish spreading across her cheekbone. Her shiner is a few shades on the side of nasty this morning, as is his. He saw himself in the mirror.

He points at her black eye. "We also need a story for that." He pours her coffee and slides over the mug. "I've got mine. We don't want them thinking I knocked you around."

"What happened to you? Did Barton hit you?" She looks ill when she says his name, and Lucas realizes she's acting tougher than she's feeling. Poor kid. He understands more than she'll ever realize.

He shakes his head. "Fight at the bar."

"Over what?"

"None of your business." That's a story he won't be sharing with her. She doesn't need to know about Faye, or that he was banging a married woman.

She taps her lip. "Hmm. How about I'm your niece, and I got into a fight at school? My mom, your sister"—she winks—"is making me stay with you while I'm on suspension."

He stands in the middle of the kitchen and sips his coffee, considering. "That should work." Ivy doesn't know he has siblings. They can easily embellish a story, and he can fabricate a reason Shiloh should move in with Ivy. As to what, he'll have to figure that out later. But he can't have her living with him.

She rubs her hands together. "So, when do I start?"

19

Shiloh stands behind the deli counter with Lucas as he unpacks the fridge and spouts off sandwich-making instructions. Condiments first, cold cuts next, followed by the dressings—shredded lettuce, tomatoes, jalapeños, whatever the customer wants. Top it off with Ivy's secret sauce. And never, ever reveal what's in that sauce. Lucas doesn't know, so don't ask. Ivy mixes a batch each week. Smells like nothing special to Shiloh. Just seasoned vinegar and oil.

She stares in disbelief at the food. The irony. For two weeks she lied, stole, and scrounged for anything she could stomach. They never had much food at home, but she's never appreciated more what they did have than these past weeks. Now she can eat as much as she wants.

He slides tubs of sliced meats to her across the stainless-steel prep surface and tells her twice which slots to drop them into for the refrigerated display. She's having trouble keeping her eyes open. She hadn't slept last night because she wouldn't take her eye off the door. What if Bob and Barton followed her back to Lucas's apartment? The lock was flimsy and the door thin. They could easily force their way in while Lucas slept. So could Lucas. What if he lied to her to get her into his apartment?

At some point during the night, she snuck into the kitchen for the switchblade she'd found in the bathroom. She needed protection. But the blade was gone. She stole a steak knife instead and kept it under her pillow, but sleep still eluded her, and her thoughts wandered every which way. Does her mom miss her? Has Ellis hurt her? Do they know where she is? Will he come for her? How long will Finn let her stay with him when she finally gets there? Will anyone hire her? Should she finish high school first? Is there a real chance to meet Jenna Mason?

Her thoughts then drifted to the books in Lucas's kitchen. He's never read them, or he hasn't read them often. She could tell when she cracked one open. The spine was stiff. She wondered again why he had them if he didn't read them when it clicked. His name.

She's read many articles about Jenna, and in one she mentioned an older brother she hasn't seen since she ran away. Could Lucas be him? What are the odds? There must be hundreds of guys with that name. But the possibility excited her so much so that she blurted it the second she saw him. He was shocked. She'd caught him off guard. And if his expression told her anything . . . he *is* him.

Fingers snap in her face.

"Wake up, Sunshine. Pay attention."

She jerks her head back. "Don't call me that."

"Shiloh." He pushes tubs of prepped food into her arms. "Set these up."

She looks at the deli counter. "Where do you want them?"

"Just told you." He gestures at the slots.

"What order?" she asks, knowing he likely told her that, too, and she hadn't been paying attention.

"Tell me right now if you need to be micromanaged, and we can drop this gig."

"Nah, I got it." She needs the cash. Shiloh lines up the tubs alongside the cold cuts in no particular order.

Lucas sighs, but he doesn't correct her. "That'll do. Just don't come cryin' to me when Ivy complains. She's overly set in her ways." He looks at the shelf behind them stocked with supplies. "We need fresh bread. Wait here." He goes into the back.

Shiloh's gaze trails over the food she and Lucas put out, and her stomach growls. She hears Lucas rustling around in the back, and she wonders if now is a good time to make herself a sandwich when the front door opens. In walks Ivy, the old woman who owns this place, and her eyes widen when she spots Shiloh standing behind the counter.

"Who are you?" she asks, coming closer.

Shiloh fidgets, afraid Ivy might recognize her and their sham is up before it gets started. She'd been in a few times before Lucas caught her and stole merch right under this woman's nose. She probably should have told him that when he offered the job. Guilt sinks in her stomach. If she wasn't so desperate she'd tell Lucas to not pay her until she earned out what she stole. She looks at her feet then the back door, wondering if working here is a bad idea and whether she should leave before Ivy calls the cops.

Ivy comes over to Shiloh, nothing between them but the deli counter that reaches both their chins. They're about the same height.

"Have we met before?" Shiloh shakes her head, and Ivy tips hers, peering closer. She points to her cheekbone and asks, "What happened to your eye?"

Shiloh fumbles for words. The story she and Lucas concocted dissipates faster than a puff of smoke from Ellis's cigar.

"Morning, Ivy," Lucas says, returning to the front, carrying an armful of bread-roll bags, and Shiloh lets go of her breath, relieved he returned. "I see you've met my niece." He says it with ease.

"Your niece?" Ivy exclaims. She takes another look at Shiloh, her eyes alight with interest. Shiloh forces a smile and gives her a small wave before hiding her hands in the deep pockets of the apron Lucas made her put on. "I didn't know you had a niece. I didn't even know you had a brother."

"Sister. Two of them," he shares, slipping behind the counter with Shiloh. He warns her with a look to not mention Jenna and stacks the clear plastic bags of sourdough and Dutch crunch rolls on the shelf above the back counter. "And you didn't ask."

"I'm sure I have. Shame on you for not letting me know. I would have told you to invite them over." She smiles at Shiloh. "Welcome to the Dusty Pantry, dear. Are you sure we haven't met? You look familiar."

"No, I . . ." Shiloh shuffles away from the counter.

"She got in last night and will be staying for a few . . . for a while. All right if I put her to work? She has the tendency to get into trouble when she doesn't have anything to do."

"I do not," Shiloh scoffs.

Lucas grunts.

Ivy clutches the thin gold chain with the cross pendant on her neck. "Lucas, you know I can't afford another employee."

"Give her a cut of mine," he says, rounding the counter.

"I barely pay you enough as it is."

"I'll make do." Lucas shrugs, and Shiloh waves both hands.

"I won't take your money."

Well, she would if he leaves out his wallet. She'd be too tempted not to. But she won't freeload like her mom, taking handouts for nothing in return.

Sensing her dismay, he says to her in a voice only she can hear, "You're not taking. You're earning." He turns to Ivy. "Can I get a moment with you?"

"We should talk about this money business. Your idea is silly." Ivy retreats to the supply room, and after Lucas glances out the front window, his eyes narrowing, he follows her back where Shiloh knows he'll tell Ivy the story they fabricated this morning.

Shiloh looks out the front windows, wondering what snagged Lucas's attention. All she notices is his truck parked in front and that same gray car across the street alongside the road she saw last night. Dust covers the side panels, and the sun reflects off the windows, stinging her eyes. She can't see who's inside, if anyone.

Turning away, her gaze falls on the phone on the counter by the register. She almost whoops out loud. She could call Finn anytime she wants. She could swipe the cash in the register and leave now. Surely there's enough money inside to get her by for several weeks if she plans it right. She wouldn't have to waste time here.

"Shiloh."

Her head snaps to the back room. Lucas stands in the doorway. Her face heats as if he knows exactly what she's been thinking, what she's planning.

"Make yourself a sandwich. There's a table and chairs out back. You can eat there."

"Everything okay?" Her gaze flicks behind him, worried Ivy's figured who she is.

"All good." He leaves the door open so he can see her but turns to Ivy. They talk in hushed voices. Shiloh knows it's about her. He told her he'd tell Ivy the story they made up.

Her stomach growls.

Ravenous, Shiloh takes Lucas up on his offer and slices open a sourdough roll. She starts piling on an assortment of meats and cheeses. If anything, she'll eat better today than she has in weeks, and for that she's grateful.

After she devours the largest sandwich she's ever made, and after she's swept the aisles and straightened inventory on the shelves, Shiloh receives her first sandwich order. A woman walks in, stopping just inside the glass door. She looks around the minimart until her gaze falls on Shiloh, who's standing behind the deli counter, wiping down the stainless-steel surface for the third time in an hour because she's run out of things to do.

The woman approaches the counter, smiles at Shiloh, then lifts her face to read the list of sandwich selections posted on the wall above Shiloh's head. She's tall and skinny, with narrow hips and a flat chest. And here Shiloh thought her own boobs were small. Large reddish-brown freckles dot the woman's nose and cheekbones, which make her more intriguing than attractive, if freckles are your thing. A gray beanie caps her head, and her hair is an auburn-tinted cloud hugging her neck. Both ears are pierced, and Shiloh notices studs run up each lobe before they disappear into her hair under the cap, making her way cooler than anyone Shiloh's run into so far in this lame town.

She leans forward, catching a peek at the woman's Dr. Martens. She's always wanted a pair.

When she lifts her face, the woman is watching her, more than mildly curious. Her smile spreads wide. "Hi."

Shiloh tucks her hair behind her ear, forgetting she was using it to shield her black eye and the other scratches on her cheek, and clears her throat. "What can I get you?"

The woman's smile fades. She touches her own face where Shiloh's shiner is the darkest on hers. "What happened?"

Lucas chooses that moment to pop his head in from where he's been working in the back, sorting stock. "All good?" His eyes dart from Shiloh to the woman before falling back on Shiloh.

"Yep," she answers. She knows their story. She won't screw it up. As for the sandwich, how difficult can one be to make?

Lucas hesitates, his eyes meeting the woman's before landing back on Shiloh.

"I got this," she says.

He grunts and returns to the back.

The woman watches the door for eons before swinging back to Shiloh. "Who was that?"

"My uncle. I'm staying with him for a bit." She slaps on a smile. "What sandwich do you want?" she asks so she doesn't overshare, something she has the tendency to do when she's nervous, and it gets her into trouble. But she might have already said too much—done too much. Damn. Why is she always touching her face? She shouldn't have moved her hair. Because now the woman's looking at her like one of those abused dogs in a Dodo video. She also keeps glancing at the door where Lucas went.

The woman tucks her fingertips into her front pockets. "Turkey and cheddar on sourdough." Then she drops her voice to a whisper. "Did he do that to you?"

Shiloh stills as she's reaching for the bread. "Lucas?" She shakes her head, unable to help looking at the door to the storeroom. She pulls down a bread bag and removes a roll, slices it open. "Girl fight at school. Totally lame, but Mom's making me stay with him. Mustard, mayo?"

"Both." The woman leans on the display counter. She studies Shiloh as if she can see right through the lie.

Nerves skitter down her arms. She dips her head, and her gaze burns holes into the bread. She smears on the mustard, feeling every move of hers watched. Every twitch in her demeanor analyzed. This woman isn't someone who'd turn the other way if she saw a young Shiloh tending to her mom, high on fentanyl, doing what she can to keep her mom from overdosing. No, this woman is observant. She gets involved. She'd confront her mom. Then she'd call the cops and child protective services. The cops would arrest her mom for possession and child endangerment, and CPS would put her in foster care.

Part of her wishes the cops would arrest Harmony. Payback for bringing Ellis into their lives. For putting his needs over her own daughter's. For believing him over her when she told her mom he'd assaulted her in the kitchen while she was making mac 'n' cheese. He put his hand up Shiloh's shirt. A bold and senseless risk, the prick.

The only thing that stopped Ellis from going further that night was the steak knife she grabbed from the drawer. He laughed at her threat to slice and dice him, but he valued his looks and backed off.

"Lettuce and tomato?"

The woman's gaze darts across Shiloh's face. "Sure."

"Onions and pickles?"

"Yes. Wait." She lifts a hand.

The storeroom door swings open, and in walks Lucas with a box full of cleaning supplies. He looks at them both before he moves down an aisle. The woman watches him as Shiloh watches her, breath held. She waits for her to say something to Lucas. Maybe she won't bother and will call the police instead. Ruin everything.

"Onions and pickles?" Shiloh repeats.

The woman turns back. She smiles, and Shiloh can tell it's forced for her benefit. "Put pickles on the sandwich, and I'll know to get help," she whispers, then louder, "Hold the onions."

Shiloh's eyes widen. She can't fault the woman for assuming Lucas is to blame, and she can't help feeling an affinity toward her. They don't trust men. Under different circumstances, she might admire her. Would have been nice having a woman like her around, unafraid of helping, someone Shiloh could have run to when Ellis got handsy.

But this woman's too quick to judge. She doesn't know Shiloh or her story. And you know what they say when you assume.

Shiloh adds Ivy's secret sauce and wraps the sandwich, then slides it across the counter. "No pickles, just like you asked."

The woman holds Shiloh's gaze for two heartbeats before flashing a broad smile. "Thanks, hon. I'll take these, too." She shows Shiloh a bag of Fritos.

Shiloh nods over the woman's shoulder. "Fountain's over there if you want a soda. He'll ring you up in the front," she says of Lucas, and turns around to wash her hands, hoping the woman leaves and that she's the last one to ask Shiloh about her face. She wishes she had foundation to cover the bruises. She recalls seeing some when she straightened the inventory. Maybe Lucas will give her a discount. It would be in both of their interests that she do something to hide it. Until her eye heals, people will keep asking, and Shiloh fears she'll slip up.

The woman skips the drinks, and Lucas rings her order. She stares at the mottled skin around Lucas's left eye and smirks. She probably thinks Shiloh slugged him in retaliation for her shiner.

Lucas notices her staring at him and counters with a lifted brow as he counts out her change.

"Thanks," she says, pocketing her money.

He shuts the cash register. "Come again soon." Shiloh watches their eyes meet, and the woman looks as if she's about to say something. Shiloh holds her breath. The woman draws her gaze down his front, and Lucas just waits, eyeing her the same.

Gross. They're checking each other out.

"Great band," the woman says of the faded Jimmy Eat World shirt he's wearing.

He grunts and she flashes a smile. His gaze follows her out the door.

They both watch her leave. Lucas's expression doesn't hide his interest. He can't take his eyes from her. The woman calls someone on her phone, looking across the parking lot. Then she turns around and snaps a photo of the ad for the vacant apartment in Dusty Pantry's window. Sliding the phone into her rear pocket, she walks across the road to the dirty Honda.

Lucas scowls.

"What?" Shiloh asks. That car bothered him last night. Does he know the woman?

"You did good. Fewer words the better." He continues to watch the woman. She gets in her car, rolls down the window, and unwraps the sandwich.

"You can't stop looking at her. You were watching us from the back, weren't you?" There's a small window in the door.

His scowl deepens. Maybe he's crushing on her.

"You want to tap her ass."

Lucas turns around, appalled. "You have the worst mouth."

Shiloh presses her lips until her mouth is a thin line. It wasn't a nice thing to say. She can't explain why she did. It's something Ellis would have said, and it just came out. Disgusted, she glances away and asks, "Who was she?"

"Don't know," Lucas says, returning to the aisle to finish restocking the cleaning supplies.

Shiloh shifts her attention back out the window. The car is gone.

20

Lucas follows Shiloh into his apartment. "You did good today." He tosses his keys and wallet on the counter, then thinks better of it when Shiloh's gaze follows the cash poking from the billfold. He picks it back up.

She flops on the barstool across from him. "I'm not going to steal from you."

He counts out some cash, slides the money across the counter to her. Her eyes widen. "That's for today. More tomorrow if you want to stay." He returns the wallet to his pocket.

She swipes up the money. "I'm staying."

Relieved to hear she won't rush to her online boyfriend, he empties the contents of the plastic grocery bag he'd packed downstairs. Hot dogs, rolls, an onion, and a can of chili. Their dinner. The onion drops onto the floor he mopped during their lunch hour.

"What are your plans for school? Are you going to finish?" She'll have a hard time finding the type of work she wants if she doesn't. He picks up the onion.

She scoffs. "I've been suspended, remember?"

He glowers because he's genuinely curious about her plans. He spent half his senior year in juvie studying precalc and American lit alongside criminals hardened before they were out of diapers. It was no picnic. By the time he got out, he was messed up. Not even close to being in his right mind to finish school on campus surrounded by his peers. Just the thought of walking through crowded hallways sickened him. His dreams of a USC football scholarship and majoring in architecture scrubbed, he studied for his GED online. Does she intend to do the same?

Did Lily finish school?

The thought gives him pause.

What did she do after she ran?

The impulse to reach out to her almost forces his hand to the phone. Every day it gets harder to resist the urge to call Olivia to apologize for running off and ask for Lily's number, especially now, after what Shiloh told him this morning. But resist he does. She'd never accept his apology and doing so won't change what happened.

Shiloh spreads her hands across the counter. "So, what now?"

He drops a pan on the stove. "Now we eat."

She scopes out the food. "No salad?"

Lucas pulls a face. "This isn't a five-star restaurant." And he isn't serving a balanced meal. Should he? He looks at the food on the counter, second-guessing what he selected.

"Fine with me. I can't stand the stuff." He grunts, and Shiloh lifts a fist. "Bump for no greens."

Something about her posture, the angle of her face, reminds him of Lily pulling faces over salad. They were at the Whitmans' cabin at the time, and she didn't want to eat it.

He stares at Shiloh, astonished by how much she keeps reminding him of his sister. His gaze loses focus, and the past becomes the present. He starts to feel light, untethered, and he stumbles, catching himself against the counter.

"Whoa. You don't look so good."

Afraid he's about to black out, he abruptly leaves the kitchen. Brisk strides take him to his room. He slams the door and sits on the edge of the bed, dragging in long pulls of air. One breath. Two. One more. His racing heart eases. Perspiration on his forehead, nape, and in his pits cools his skin.

When he feels in control again, he lifts his head. The switchblade on the nightstand winks at him. He snatches the blade, flips it over in his palms. Flicks it open, closed, open again. Traces the tip down his scar, the cool metal a bolt of electricity up his ulnar artery to his auxiliary, through his subclavian and straight to his heart. A warning.

He flicks it closed and fists the blade. Plants an elbow on his thigh and rests his forehead against the blade in his palm. It's been years since he thought of their summers with the Whitmans, friends of their parents who took him and his sisters in while his father campaigned for Congress and his mother worked long hours.

But that memory Shiloh's expression triggered . . . He saw flashes of Lily in her. The smirk, that teasing glint in her eyes.

It was summer, one of the many spent at the Whitmans' cabin. They sat at the table for dinner, all of them. Blaze, Olivia, him, Tyler, and Lily. Mr. Whitman at one end, Mrs. Whitman at the other. She'd set a bowl of salad in the middle of the table. Lily didn't like salads, or anything leafy and green. She made a face. Her lips pulling in opposite directions, her tongue sticking out. It was such a visceral reaction that Lucas barked a laugh. Lily's cheeks pinkened. Embarrassed, afraid she'd get in trouble, she ducked her head. She never would have made such a face at home in front of their parents.

"What's so funny?" Mr. Whitman stabbed a fork into his meatloaf.

"Nothing." Lucas unfolded his napkin and laid it over his thighs. He wouldn't look Mr. Whitman in the eye, and it was probably one of the last times Lucas had come to Lily's defense, covered her actions. But when Olivia served herself salad, Lucas made a face back. Lily snorted and made another face. And soon everyone at the table was making faces and doubled over with laughter.

But the next day. The next day . . .

Lucas blinks away the burn in his eye as one memory tumbles into another.

The next morning Lily found him by the lake. He'd brought his breakfast outside, a paper plate of scrambled eggs and buttered toast, and left it on the ground. Distracted by a school of minnows, their air bubbles looking like raindrops on the lake's surface, he'd scooped up a handful of pebbles and started chucking them into the water, aiming for the fish. He hit a few, knocked them right in their heads and laughed.

Bored with that, he'd chucked the remaining pebbles into the water and returned to his food. Ants swarmed his plate. Livid, he yelled and started stomping the trail, killing as many as he could.

Lily came outside and ran over to him, asking why he was upset. When she saw what he was doing, she pleaded for him to stop, tried pushing him away from the ants.

He picked up his plate, and one by one, flicked the ants into the lake.

"Stop, Luc." Her eyes shimmered and he rolled his.

"They're stupid ants."

"They're living, breathing things."

"They're annoying, tiny insects who've ruined my food." Flick, flick, flick.

"Now you're just being mean." She ran to a bush and returned with a leaf. She held it steady on the edge of his plate.

"What are you doing, weirdo?"

She coaxed an ant onto the leaf. "If I can save one life, it matters."

Cradling the leaf with the ant in her palm, she walked to the bushes and set the leaf on the ground.

"You're a jerk, Lucas," she shouted, and ran inside.

Guilt had curdled his stomach. He looked at the plate. A frenzy of ants raced around his food as if they'd struck gold. He had no intention of eating it, so he hadn't wanted the ants to eat it either. He'd tried killing as many as he could, taking out the anger over his mistake on them. He let the rage inside consume him.

He'd behaved exactly like his father.

And it had never scared him more.

Disgusted, Lucas dumped his food in the bushes near where Lily had let the ant free. Fine, those stupid ants could eat it all. He stomped back into the cabin for more eggs.

Lucas jerks open the nightstand drawer, drops the blade inside, and slams it shut. He couldn't have been older than eleven in that memory. Lily would have been eight. And she was already wiser than him. Kinder and more forgiving, because she'd told him exactly that when he fixed himself another helping of eggs. "I forgive you, Lucas." Then she'd asked him to take her swimming.

Would she be as forgiving if he confessed his secrets now? Doubtful. She isn't that naive child who once looked up to her big brother.

Through the wall, Lucas hears the doorbell ring followed by muffled voices. His first thought is Ivy. It sounds like her. She'd told him this morning she'd allow Shiloh to work if he took her offer of buying her out more seriously. They could work out an arrangement if he didn't have the cash to invest or couldn't get a loan. He put her off. She's probably here to press for an answer he doesn't have.

Then again, the person at the door could be that woman from the market this morning, the one who drove away in the Honda he'd seen parked out front last night.

The same one that sent a jolt of arousal through him just from throwing him a look.

The same one his gut tells him wasn't here just for a sandwich. She came looking for him.

21

He rushes for the bedroom door and yanks it open.

Shiloh's on the other side, fist raised to knock. "Dude. You scared me."

He leaves the room and walks into the living area, making her follow. "Who was at the door?"

"That old woman from the store. She invited us for dinner. Homemade lasagna."

Lucas shoves back his hair. For a second there, he thought it was over for him. He should have left earlier today, but he couldn't make himself abandon Ivy or Shiloh. He keeps telling himself the cops would have already been here if he needed to worry.

"What's your prob?" Shiloh asks, noticing how agitated he is. He's wound so tight.

"Nothing." He's wrong about that woman. She isn't here for him. She's gone. He needs to chill and stop assuming everyone is out to get him.

Good luck with that.

Shaking his head, he goes into the kitchen and puts away the food.

"I've never had homemade lasagna. Beggars can't be choosers, but it sounds a heck of a lot better than chili from a can."

His sentiments exactly. She's scrawny from living off whatever she could lift these past weeks. But he avoids eating at Ivy's. Other than the time she stayed with him when he first arrived, he's never eaten with her. She brings him meals, at least one every week, and they always come with an invitation to join her. He declines, fearful he'll let slip what he's done, even more afraid he'll grow attached.

But she'll give him an earful if he refuses tonight and doesn't give her the opportunity to get to know his *niece*. He doesn't see a way out of this, not without Shiloh's help. Besides, the kid probably hasn't had a decent meal in weeks. They'll just have to be extra careful about sticking to their story.

He tosses the bag of rolls on top of the fridge and turns to Shiloh. "You've never had homemade lasagna?"

She shakes her head, and he wonders what her life was like before she landed herself in a homeless encampment. He suspects she was the parent in the family and cooked for her mom.

Shiloh slides onto the counter stool again and picks at the chip in the Formica. "My mom doesn't cook. I mean, she did when I was little, but never from scratch. Then she was too high to bother, and after Ellis moved in . . ." She shrugs, confirming his suspicions.

Lucas moves to the counter. If Ellis shows his face around here, Lucas will exchange more than words with him. "My mom worked too many hours to be bothered to shop. My dad just didn't care. He wasn't home much either."

"How'd you eat, then?" she asks.

"I'd buy me and my little sis McDonald's with my allowance. Sometimes I'd bike to my mom's office and ask her for money."

Shiloh looks down at her hands. "Sounds lonely."

"It was." He inhales deeply. He's never shared that with anyone. But he wanted her to understand that he gets her. "Wash up."

She snorts. "What am I, five?"

"No, but you still have grime under your nails. I can't believe I let you work behind the deli counter."

"I wore those plastic glove thingies." She curls her fingers and studies her nails. Her lip pulls up. "Be right back." She darts to the bathroom and stops up short. "Whoa, it's clean. Thanks."

Warmth spreads from his chest into his limbs. "No prob." His voice is rich with emotion. He clears his throat, unused to the feeling. Rarely does someone thank him.

He returns the pan to the cabinet, pretending what he's feeling isn't a big deal for him.

Ivy is pleased when they arrive, and again Lucas feels a tingling warmth and admits he likes the feeling, even welcomes it. The table is already set for three when Ivy invites them in, and the lasagna is cooling on the stove top. The entire apartment smells like meat sauce and basil. His mouth quirks when Shiloh's stomach rumbles loud enough for them to hear. She blushes and hugs her midriff, almost caving in on herself.

"My word, Lucas, don't you feed this girl?"

"I was just about to," he says in his defense. But she's right. Shiloh is skin and bones under the bulky sweatshirt she always wears, her arms and legs sticks poking out of his shirt she slept in last night.

Ivy draws an arm over Shiloh's shoulders and leads her to the table, where a large wooden bowl of tossed green salad is already set. Shiloh makes a face, her gaze lifting to Lucas's. He hides a smile and is on his way to retrieve the lasagna when Ivy asks him to get it.

The casserole dish is large enough to feed a team. Ivy will be forcing lasagna on them for days. Not that he's complaining. He'll eat her food over the fast food he buys any day. He sets the dish on the hot pads Ivy put on the round table and settles in a chair beside Shiloh.

Ivy retrieves a basket of garlic bread and sits down. She smiles at them. "It's so nice to have company. And you, Lucas. Finally joining me." Her eyes shimmer with gratitude, forcing him to look at his plate. The guilt's too much. She's lonely, and he's declined her invitations more times than he can count. But he just couldn't risk discovery. He also couldn't bear to disappoint her further, which will happen if she ever learns the truth of him.

Shiloh kicks his shin. His head snaps up and he glares at her. She holds out a hand for him. Her other hand clasps Ivy's across the table. Shiloh rolls her eyes from him to Ivy.

He swings a look at Ivy. She's smiling at him, brows lifted. "Will you say grace, Lucas?" Her hand reaches for his.

Lucas wants to throw up. The thought of holding both their hands, skin to skin. He inhales deeply through his nose. *Get a grip, man.* His stomach churns. He preps his mind to expect the touch. He grasps their hands and mutters, "God is great, God is good. Thank you for our food. Amen." He ignores Ivy's surprised look over his brevity and releases their hands. He wipes clammy palms on his thighs. Damn, he could use a beer. He grabs his water glass and chugs.

Shiloh digs into the lasagna, serving herself a hefty slice and humming her pleasure with the first mouthful. "This is amazing," she says before swallowing.

"Shiloh, tell me about yourself. Lucas never told me he has sisters or that he has a niece." Her accusatory gaze slides to Lucas, and he grunts, serving lasagna to Ivy, then himself. "You must tell me everything, I insist. How did you end up here?"

Shiloh's gaze meets his before she launches into a story about how her mom raised her since birth. Money has always been tight. She works nights, so Shiloh was on her own fixing meals, getting herself to school. But then her mom got into drugs, and their roles reversed. Shiloh started taking care of her. Her mom also liked men, often brought them home. But Ellis stayed, and Ellis's eyes strayed.

Lucas grinds his teeth and sends her a warning glare. She's revealing too much. But he's also mortified everything she's telling them is the truth. His heart aches for what she's had to put up with.

"Goodness." Ivy's face is pale. "Lucas, I'm so glad she came to stay with you. You should have taken her in sooner."

His nostrils flare.

Shiloh won't meet his gaze. She clears her throat and changes the subject to a girl at school who teased her about her junkie mom. They got into a fight, Shiloh explains, further embellishing her story, and Shiloh was suspended. Her mom sent her to stay with Uncle Lucas during her time off from school.

"You told me some of this earlier, Lucas, but it sounds worse than I imagined coming from Shiloh." Ivy is appalled. "You must do something about your sister."

"I've tried," he lies to his plate.

Shiloh looks at him through narrowed eyes. He shrugs, confused. What else is he supposed to say without compromising them?

Shiloh turns back to Ivy. "He is."

Both of them look at Shiloh. "Is what?" Ivy asks.

"Doing something," she clarifies, her fork nudging a chunk of ground meat across her plate. "He's letting me live here. I'm better off with him than my mom." She crams lasagna into her mouth.

For pete's sake. Why does his throat feel tight? What's with the warmth expanding in his chest? That's the third time today.

"I'm glad to hear it," Ivy announces. "I hope your uncle lets you stay as long as you need." She looks pointedly at Lucas.

"I already told her she can."

Ivy nods, satisfied for the moment.

Shiloh drags a fork tine through sauce. He begs under his breath that she doesn't start going off about Finn and her plans to move to Hollywood to live with him. The way Lucas sees it, if the guy is worth anywhere close to the sauce on her plate, he would have shown his face by now to collect her. Doesn't he give a lick about her safety?

Ivy changes the subject. "I've rented out Mike's old apartment."

That gets Lucas's attention. "You have?" The apartment has been listed for some time.

"A nice young woman passing through town who needs a place to stay for a week."

"A week? It's an apartment, not a hotel."

"I need the money. She'll be paying by the day. We agreed over the phone."

"You didn't meet her?"

Ivy's mouth pinches. She sips her water, dodging Lucas's pointed gaze.

He shouldn't care who Ivy rents to or for how long. But he's finding it hard to not care after everything Ivy's done for him. Plus he's got Shiloh. He has to think of her safety. He doesn't want some random loitering around the property.

"How much is she paying you?"

"None of your business."

"How do you know she isn't taking advantage of you?" She could be a con artist, and this is only the beginning of her scheme. She'll squat and never leave. In fact, it's unsettling Ivy doesn't know anything about this woman.

"Did she sign a lease?"

Ivy sets down her glass with a firm clunk. "You didn't sign anything."

Pot, meet kettle.

He scowls at his plate.

Ivy's hands lower to her lap. "I'll make sure she signs one tomorrow," she acquiesces, making him feel better. "But I need the rent money, however little it is. The building has been on and off the market for three years, and there've been no takers. No one in town wants to get stuck with it. You won't buy me out. I'm done, Lucas. I'm too old for this. I want to retire. Travel." She looses a heavy sigh. "Sorry. I didn't want to bring this up during dinner. I know you're tired of hearing about it."

He's starting to feel guilty for declining, and that bothers him as much as if not more than the way he's starting to realize he cares for her.

Done with her lasagna, Shiloh puts down her fork. "You want Lucas to buy this building and run the store?"

"Yes. I think he'll be very good at it. He'll turn this place around."

He'd redesign the building's facade and market's layout, bring in seasonal products that specifically targeted the needs of the locals, drew in tourists. He'd upgrade each apartment, new fixtures, flooring, and appliances. If he wasn't worried about his future, or lack of one, he'd jump at the opportunity.

"Why don't you?" Shiloh asks.

"He doesn't want anything tying him down, especially this place," Ivy answers for him.

"I thought you liked it here," Shiloh says.

His brows pull together. "When did I ever say that?"

"You didn't. Just a feeling."

Lucas grunts, unable to pinpoint exactly what he's done or said to give her that impression.

"Well, it's a done deal," Ivy says with finality. "You'll meet her tomorrow when you install the ceiling fans in her apartment."

He would have done the installation today if he hadn't spent his lunch cleaning his toilet.

Ivy reaches for the bowl in the center of the table. "Salad, anyone?"

Lucas and Shiloh both make faces.

22

After dinner, Lucas and Shiloh help Ivy clean up. When Shiloh excuses herself to use the bathroom, Ivy pulls Lucas aside.

"Shiloh is a wonderful girl. After what she told me about her mother . . ." Ivy shakes her head. "I can't imagine what she's been through."

He grunts, drying a pot Ivy just washed.

"Was your sister always like that, into drugs and men?"

"Not always." His gaze slings to the side, guilt tightening his chest. Lying to Ivy has never been easy. He wants to tell her about Olivia. She's gorgeous and kind, but a hard-ass. He wishes he could tell her something about Lily, wishes he actually knew his sister and hadn't let her run away. But doing so would expose his history, and his shame about his past is as great as his fear of being arrested again, which would surely happen if Ivy knew the truth about him.

"Well, for what it's worth"—Ivy soaks a casserole dish in water—"Shiloh is lucky to have you."

"About that," Lucas starts, clearing his throat. He sets the damp towel on the counter, his misgivings about Shiloh living in his apartment returning. "Would it be possible if she stayed with you?"

"Whatever for?" Ivy looks at him, clearly surprised by his request.

"You've seen my place. It's a bachelor's pad." Worse. "It's no place for teenage girl. I can't cook." And he drinks far too much. Besides, the time will come when he runs, and when it does, he can leave Shiloh behind with an inkling of hope she'll be looked after.

Ivy dries her hands and turns to him. "I know what you're doing, Lucas."

He shifts with unease. "What's that?"

"You're doubting yourself again."

He frowns, forgetting how easily Ivy can read him. She did it the night he arrived. She didn't ask questions and she didn't pry. But she did sit with him, sharing stories about her life with Tom through a better part of the night. He knows she stayed with him because she sensed he shouldn't be left alone.

She presses her palms to his cheeks. It takes everything in him not to jerk his head and slam into the fridge behind him. He focuses on her smile. Kind and warm and trusting, making him hate himself more because he isn't being honest.

"That girl needs you, Lucas. She needs a male role model in her life. Someone guiding her to make the right decisions. You might not think it, but you're a good man."

He shakes his head. "No, I'm not. You don't know me. You don't know what I've done." He gives in to some of the pressure that's building inside him, feeling like he owes her that much.

"Why do you believe you're so terrible?"

His jaw tics.

"Lucas," she pushes.

And she'll keep pushing if he doesn't elaborate. Which he should. She needs to understand why it's wrong for Shiloh to stay with him.

He forces out a breath. "I spent six months in juvenile detention for holding up a minimarket clerk at gunpoint. How's that for a role model?"

Her hands slide from his face, her eyes clouding with unease. Exactly how he expected she'd react. His actions even disgust him. He'd been so damn irresponsible.

After he was sentenced and served his time, he swore to his parents he'd never speak of the incident again. But he's thought about it almost every day of his life since, about how different he'd be today if he hadn't followed Tanner and Reg into the minimarket for a six-pack of beer. There had been only one security camera in the market, which was trained on the cash register.

It caught everything.

Tanner unveiling the gun he'd hidden in his letterman jacket.

Lucas yanking the gun from Tanner.

The gun firing.

The gun. The gun. The gun.

The window blew out behind the clerk's head, shattering Reg's windshield. Tanner and Reg bolted from the store. But Lucas couldn't make himself move. When he'd reached for Tanner's gun, it was as if he was watching someone else do it. He didn't understand why he'd taken it. The only explanation he's come up with is that he had been afraid Tanner would fire it. The safety had been off.

The clerk was new, but he was a big guy. He dove over the counter and tackled Lucas. The police arrived and arrested Lucas. Tanner and Reg shared an attorney, who set Lucas up to take the fall for all three of them.

Lucas's face heats with shame. He can't look at Ivy. Clearing his throat, he crosses his arms. "So, yeah. Better for Shiloh to stick with you."

"How old were you?"

He frowns. "Sixteen, why?"

Ivy's smile is melancholy. "Lucas, if we were all judged by our actions at sixteen, most of which I can guarantee were blatantly rash, our society would be in worse shape than it already is. I'll say this again because you need to hear it: You are a good man. You are good for that girl." She pokes his chest. "Better yet, you've experienced the worst that can happen. You know best how to steer your niece clear of that so she doesn't end up like your sister."

Lucas dips his chin, looking at the spot where she poked him. He experienced something far worse than getting arrested for firing a loaded weapon. But Ivy has planted a seed of hope in him he doesn't know how to fertilize. He'd give up his freedom if it meant he was as worthy as she believes him to be.

Shiloh returns, putting an end to the conversation. He's feeling weirded out he shared so much with Ivy, and he's itching to put some space between him and the conversation. He swipes up his keys. "I'll be back. Don't wait up for me."

He leaves the apartment before she can ask where he's going.

Downstairs, Lucas takes a Cuervo off the shelf only to put the bottle back and grab a beer from the fridge. He wants a drink, not to get wasted. He takes the beer out back and drinks under a partial moon that drenches the wasteland around the property in a silvery light.

He came often to the desert in his twenties, raced at the motocross track on the outskirts of town. Probably why he'd driven in this direction. He hadn't planned it, just drove on autopilot. Though he never intended to stay. He didn't plan to live this long either, and he wouldn't have if Ivy hadn't intervened that first night. If she hadn't stayed with him, talked on and on about her life with Tom, he would have drawn the bath, settled into the tepid water, and dragged the blade up his forearm, right over the scar he'd left from his first attempt at sixteen.

But he also shouldn't have stayed this long and worries he can't linger long enough for Shiloh to earn the money she needs, not if someone's onto him.

He tips back the bottle, and the moon mocks him. Ivy believes he's a good man. But she doesn't know the real him, or that he lives in fear of being discovered every day. She doesn't know what he's capable of.

Memories of his father's last night flicker to life. They haunt him, becoming clearer each passing month as his mind fills in the blanks. That was him chasing Dwight across town until his Mercedes blew off the road and flipped end over end down the ravine. That was him climbing down the slope to reach his father's car. Those were his hands wrapping the seat belt around his old man's neck.

Lucas always knew he was as monstrous as Dwight. That night proved it.

The urge to run again nips his ass.

His truck is out front, the keys in his pocket. He could leave right now.

But where would he go, and what would happen to Shiloh?

She isn't my problem.

But you made her yours, Olivia would tell him, reminding him to see the responsibilities he took on through to completion.

Admittedly, he wants to help Shiloh, even at the risk of getting himself caught, which is out of character for him. But he's been to hell and back and wouldn't wish that on anyone. He understands what she's going through. His parents hadn't helped him through his trauma, and from what he knows, Shiloh's mom didn't help her. But maybe he can.

"Fuck." He's going to get himself in trouble.

He finishes off his beer and returns to his apartment. Shiloh's door is closed, a sliver of light visible underneath. He takes a shower, towels off. He pulls on loose shorts and a shirt and only then notices the laptop he'd stashed in his dresser isn't there.

Why that little . . .

He stomps to her room and bangs on the door. "Open up, Sunshine."

"That's not my fucking name."

"Language."

"Like you're one to talk."

"Get off my laptop."

He hears her slam it closed before she throws open the door.

"I didn't say you could use it." He snags the laptop from her.

"I wasn't going to steal it."

"And you're not using it to chat with fish brains."

Her nose crinkles with ire. "His name's Finn."

He grunts and opens the laptop, expecting to find a chat window in his browser history, but paused on the screen is a cartoon squirrel midleap. His heart seizes.

"A new *Tabby's Squirrel* dropped. You know, the cartoon from those books you've got?"

He knows.

His heart pounds as he watches his finger direct the cursor to play the video, as if he can't stop himself. The squirrel shrieks, landing in a sprawl. Acorns spill from a hole in a tree, landing on the squirrel's head. A scruffy dog paws the nuts into a bucket and takes off with it across the yard.

Unaware of what he's doing, Lucas wanders into Shiloh's room and slowly sits on the edge of the bed. He can't stop watching. Lily made this. It's funny. How could she find humor in anything after what she's been through?

"Here, start at the beginning." Shiloh leans over him, and he stops short of flinching away at her nearness. "What?" she asks.

"Don't like people touching me."

He grimaces. That's two confessions in one night.

He waits for her to make some silly comment about him, but she only shrugs and says, "I don't like it either." Then she replays the video. They watch together. He even laughs at the appropriate moments. When it finishes, he feels a tightness to the point of pain in his chest. His baby sister made this.

And it's physically hurting him to stay away from her.

"Your sister has a book signing in LA this weekend."

His first thought: he wants to go.

"She's not my sister." And she won't want to see him. He closes the laptop.

"Liar."

"There are a thousand other Lucas Carsons."

139

"But if she was your sister, would you introduce me?"

"Haven't seen her in years," he mutters under his breath, standing up.

"What?"

"No, I wouldn't."

"I heard you. You said—"

"Nothing." He strides to the door, laptop in hand.

"But—"

"Go to sleep."

She stares hard at him. "You're a jerk." She gets up and goes to the bathroom. A minute later the shower runs.

Lucas drags a hand over his head. He needs to watch himself around her, or she'll be dragging him to LA before he can tie his shoe.

Back in his room, door shut and locked, he settles on his bed, his back against the wall, and does what he's put off for eight months. He looks up Lily. Rather, he runs a search for Jenna Mason, and is floored over the number of hits. Page after page of links display. Her website is at the top. He skips that and goes straight for the story that would elaborate on what Shiloh told him this morning, an article in *Luxe Avenue* written by Ella Skye. And there before him, filling his screen, is grown-up Lily in full color. She's smiling, seated at a table on an outdoor patio. A glass of water within reach, the ocean a backdrop. She looks entirely different from when he last saw her and the same. A vise grips his lungs.

When he met her son, Josh, Lucas wasn't just worried about Lily and how she and her son had been separated. He was scared for her. He blamed himself for what happened. Lily never would have been separated from Josh if he had stopped her from running away in the first place.

He scrolls down the page. More photos of Lily cover the screen. One was taken in a professional studio. She's perched on a stool and dressed entirely in black. Pants, blouse, and heels, her fingertips dipping into a side pocket. Brownish-auburn hair swept off her face, her hazel eyes gleam. The slight curvature of her mouth mocks him, as if she's flipping him off. *I survived, Lucas. No thanks to you.*

More photos show her at her desk, another seated on a couch, her arm around Josh, his face averted so only his profile is visible. It's a studio shot, from the emerald couch to the gray backdrop, but the sight of Josh is a blade across his chest. Emotion wells in his throat. He swallows it down before it escapes. But . . . *Josh.*

He made it home.

Lucas scrolls back to the top and skims the article, which is a deep dive into Lily's life. He learns the first photo was taken at Thalassa, a restaurant in Oceanside owned by her fiancé, Kavan. They're getting married this summer. Lily's movie releases in June, and she's contracted to cowrite the screenplay for a follow-up film. This is on top of book releases, merchandise, and tours. He can see why Shiloh idolizes her. Lily's accomplishments are impressive.

Then he reads what he witnessed firsthand the night Lily ran away. That she'd left. But then she'd come back. He didn't know that. She found her friend Wes, whom she'd thought she shot before he fell into the bay, only to end up accidentally killing him in self-defense. That she'd not only run away but kept on running. Ryder Jensen, Wes's older brother, stalked her for sixteen years.

Lily mentions there were people along the way who helped her. They took her and Josh in. But despite Ella Skye's attempt to extract more details about what Lily's life was like those years, Lily's responses are vague. In fact, most of the article is Lily answering Ella's questions with nonanswers and steering the conversation back to her career.

His father is briefly mentioned in that he passed before the writing of the article, killed in a single-vehicle accident, and that Lily has yet to see her brother, Lucas. It pains him to read about it. Aside from a couple of paragraphs about their lives in Seaside Cove, it's the only time his name is mentioned. No connection between him and Dwight's death is cited. He doesn't know if he's relieved or alarmed.

Though there is mention of his mother. She's a person of interest in Wes Jensen's death, which doesn't surprise him. She was inside the house when his father went after Wes. Lily believes she left the country, which is news to Lucas. That does surprise him. The last time he saw their mother, Olivia was taking Charlotte to spend the night at her house. She was distraught from learning of her husband's death, and Olivia didn't want to leave her alone. He helped put their mother in Olivia's car.

Shiloh knocks, and he nearly jumps off the bed.

"Lucas?" she asks from the other side of his door.

"Yeah?" He slowly closes the laptop, catching his breath, embarrassed he was *caught* stalking his sister.

"Good night."

"Night," he says, listening for her to leave.

A few seconds go by.

"You still there?" Lucas asks.

Another beat.

"I'm sorry."

He frowns at the door. "For what?"

"For what I said. You're not a jerk. And . . ." She stops.

He stares at the door. "Shiloh?"

A pause.

"Ivy's right."

"About what?"

"You're a good guy."

He starts shaking his head. "I'm not—"

Her door shuts, and the lock clicks into place.

A good guy.

23

Their day starts early, and Lucas is cranky, so she leaves him alone even though she knows . . . just knows he's Jenna Mason's brother. She's read every article and watched every interview she could find on her favorite animator, which isn't many. Jenna only recently revealed who she is. She hid behind caricatures up until eight months ago. But she and Lucas have the same-shaped mouth and the same color eyes. He even moves like her.

Shiloh watched him during dinner, and she overheard him and Ivy talking when they thought she was still in the bathroom. Shiloh should be afraid of Lucas, given her experience with men. But Ivy's faith in him has only reassured her that Lucas's behavior toward her is sincere. He means what he said. He wants to help her. He isn't going to send her home or report her to the cops. So she's going to stay until she can save enough money to support herself when she moves in with Finn.

She follows Lucas into the market. He turns on the lights and points to the back corner.

"We've got breakfast burritos in the freezer. Grab one if you're hungry. You can use the microwave in back."

She's starving, and after what she's experienced during the last couple of weeks, she isn't going to look a gift horse in the mouth. Feeling extra hungry, she takes two egg-and-bacons, eating both in the back lot while Lucas does whatever he does to prep the market to open by seven.

Wiping her hands along the sides of her sweatshirt, she returns to the stockroom. Lucas hands her a clipboard with a pen and an empty box.

"What's this?" She looks at the empty spreadsheet.

"Inventory. Start at the far aisle. Dump anything that's expired in the box and track what's left. Ivy wants the item name, brand, PLU code, and quantity for reorders."

It sounds like the most mundane, tedious task, and she wonders if Lucas is intentionally torturing her. "I thought you wanted me to make sandwiches." She enjoyed talking to the customers yesterday, as few of them as there were. She embellished her and Lucas's story, even came up with a few new ones, like how she spent a few weeks every summer camping with her "uncle." They've been to Yosemite and Yellowstone. This summer they plan to visit Zion. She has a hammock and wants to sleep under the stars.

As she spoke, she found herself wishing he was her uncle, or that she had one. Her mom is her only living relative as far as she knows. She's never met her dad's side of the family and doubts they know she exists. Harmony doesn't have family, or so she claims.

"I'll cover the deli today."

"You just don't want to do inventory," she gripes.

He smirks. "You got that right." He pushes through the swinging door and tosses over his shoulder, "Hurry up. Ivy needs numbers by closing, and that'll take you most of the day."

Shiloh groans and picks up the box. By ten when she takes a break, she's going stir crazy. By noon when Ivy calls down for Lucas to come meet the new tenant and install ceiling fans, she's so bored she has to remind herself why she's here and not halfway to Hollywood. She needs the money.

"Ivy needs my help. She'll be down in a minute to ring up any customers while I'm gone." He locks the cash register and pockets the key.

"Don't trust me?"

A thick brow lifts. "Would you trust you?"

Her mouth flattens.

"Work on the inventory. You'll be fine," Lucas says. "Ivy will be down in a few."

He leaves and Shiloh doesn't waste time. She drops the clipboard into the box and grabs the cordless phone on the counter, bouncing on her toes as she dials Finn. She'd taken a risk last night borrowing Lucas's laptop but was able to shoot off an email to Finn. In it, she told him she's staying in California City a little longer. She's calling because she wants to know if he's read it, and if he's cool with it.

Finn answers after the third ring. "Shy Girl."

His voice washes over her like crystal-clear spring water. "How'd you know it's me?"

"Caller ID, baby. You said you're staying with some guy above the Dusty Pantry."

"You got my email." Her gaze darts to the window, on the lookout for Ivy, worried she'll overhear.

"I don't know, Shy. I'm not sure I like you sleeping with this guy."

"I'm not sleeping *with* him. I'm using his spare bedroom. He's an old man."

"How old?"

"I don't know. Like his thirties or something. He could be my father."

"But he's not. You don't know this guy. What if he tries something like that freak show your mom's slumming with?"

"He won't."

"You don't know that. I can't believe you'd risk staying with a strange guy after what happened with that deadbeat your mom kept around. I swear, Shy, I was about ready to beat the crap out of him for what he tried to do to you. Good thing you left when you did. Can you honestly tell me this guy is any better?"

"His place is better than sleeping in a beat-up car. I was—" She stops abruptly, her confidence waning. Anything she says could spur his frustration and impatience with her. Would he accuse her of guilting him into coming if she told him she was attacked? She doesn't want to upset him. He might change his mind about letting her stay with him.

"Look, I'm sorry. I didn't mean to yell," she says when his end of the line goes quiet. "I was scared, and Lucas has given me a place to stay and a job. I can leave anytime, and I promise I will if he tries anything."

Finn huffs. "Fine. Whatever."

"I just wanted you to know why I'm hanging out here a little longer. I'm saving up money so I can help pay for rent and food, but it's still cool to stay with you when I get there, right?" She tugs the hoodie string, nerves making her speak fast.

A long pause.

"Finn?" She hears a noise at the rear entrance and shoots the door a worried glance. "Is it still cool?"

"How long do you think you'll be?"

"A couple weeks. A month at the most." She should save enough by then.

"That long?"

"I need enough for rent," she argues.

Another pause. Then a bothersome groan as if she's inconveniencing him. "Yes, it's still cool."

The back door opens.

Shiloh's heart jumps. "Gotta go." She drops the receiver into the cradle and grabs the clipboard.

Ivy approaches her from the stockroom. "How's inventory?"

She pastes on a smile so Ivy doesn't suspect she's out of sorts. "All good."

24

The door to Mike's old apartment is already open. Lucas raps a knuckle on the jamb, crossing the threshold, and he nearly trips over his shock. They're in the kitchen, Ivy and the new tenant, the woman he rang up a sandwich for yesterday, the same one who slept overnight in the Honda. He'd been wary of her before, but now he's almost positive she's here for him. She could be an undercover cop.

His heart lurches, and not in a good way. This is it. She knows what he did. But even as he thinks it, he knows it's illogical. She would have reported his location this afternoon or arrested him herself. Wouldn't she have?

The woman turns toward him and catches his surprise with an insignificant lift of her brow. Way too chill to be staking him out.

No, she's not a cop. But she is something.

Ever watchful, ever on alert, he tells himself to play it cool even as he breaks out in a sweat. He shifts his weight and looks her over, the same way she's assessing him, as he tries to figure out who and what she is. Something about her turns him on. She's tall and flat chested with narrow hips. Not really his jam. She isn't pretty, just different. There's a story to her, and he gets the impression it's as messy as his. Maybe that's why he's drawn to her. He's always been attracted to danger.

"Lucas, finally. Just the person I want to see." Ivy draws the woman forward. "I was telling Zea all about you. Zea, this is Lucas. He's . . . well, he's the one I'm trying to convince to buy my building."

Zea greets him with a smile that comes across as phony, and his nape crackles with the unease he's feeling. "Nice to meet you," she greets, wearing the same skin-hugging jeans and boots she had on yesterday. Different shirt. This one's short sleeved, and the tattoo on her forearm he hadn't noticed yesterday, same place as his tattoo, is clearly visible. The urge to move closer and read the script keeps him rooted to his spot, as do his suspicions. He tells himself he doesn't care what poetic passage has meaning to her. She isn't hanging around for long, not with a by-the-day rent. That in and of itself is sending him into a quiet panic, until he recalls that he, too, hadn't intended to remain here this long. But her skin. It glows underneath the dewdrops of reddish-brown freckles spilling across her nose. His fingertips tingle with his desire to touch that skin.

Whoa. Where is this coming from.

He grunts a welcome, unnerved by the push-pull urge he feels around her. It's confusing. He wants to fervidly plan what he should do—stay or go?—while at the same time he wants to know more about her. Conflicted, he decides to do neither and looks at Ivy. "Start in the bedroom?"

"Do you want fans in this room and yours?" Ivy checks with Zea.

"That would be great." Zea smiles, her gaze never leaving his. He wonders what she wants from him. Anything? Could he be reading too much into this?

Lucas breaks eye contact first and retreats to the bedroom with his toolbox and ladder. He sets them down and returns downstairs to retrieve the boxed ceiling fans he'd picked up the other day. As he works, he hears Ivy and Zea conversing in the front room until Ivy leaves for the market. He's just removed the ceiling-light fixture when he senses Zea in the doorway. He feels her watching him, which sends his nerves firing off again, and peeks at her from under his arm as he unscrews the light-fixture plate. She's leaning against the doorframe, an arm loosely casual along her side. He tells himself he can do casual, too. "Can I help you?" His tone is even. His heart is banging in his ear like a repeatedly slamming door.

She smiles, and this one appears genuine. "Ivy tells me you're the guy to call if I need anything repaired."

"Yep." He removes the plate, exposing the electrical wires, and steps down from the ladder. Squatting, he slices through the packing tape with a box cutter and starts removing ceiling-fan parts.

"She thinks very highly of you."

"She thinks highly of everyone." He climbs back up the ladder.

She chews her thumbnail and inspects the cuticle. "Who's the girl I saw you with yesterday? Is she your daughter?"

His nape tingles again, but he keeps his tone level. "Niece."

"She staying with you?"

"Yep." He hooks the fan up to the electrical.

"For how long?"

He glances at her. "You ask a lot of questions." Ones he doesn't care to answer. Her presence makes him nervous, but her interest in Shiloh isn't sitting right with him. That sets him on edge.

"Sorry. Just trying to be neighborly. I'm new around here." She looks at him expectantly as if she wants him to ask where she's from or tell her about him. Even though he wants to know more about her, he doesn't bite. With a grunt, he returns his focus to work.

"She makes a good sandwich," Zea says after a moment. "She's what, fourteen?"

"Fifteen." He folds the ladder when he finishes and packs up the toolbox, dumps the old light fixture in the empty cardboard box, then moves on to the next room.

Zea follows. "Does she go to school here?"

"She's taking a break." He unpacks the next ceiling fan.

"Is that a thing now?"

"She's on suspension," he says flatly, staying consistent with the story they told Ivy last night.

"Ah," Zea says after a brief pause when she realizes he isn't going to elaborate. "Well, I'll leave you be." She retreats into the kitchen, where she scrolls through her phone.

Lucas pushes out a long breath. He can be chill. Just act normally. He keeps telling himself if she was here for him, she would have acted on it by now. He's just on high alert and excessively suspicious because he's always looking over his shoulder. He reasons Zea's just an ordinary woman looking to make conversation, and returns his focus on the install. Every now and then, he feels her eyes on him, and does his best to ignore her. When he finishes, he packs up his tools and wipes the sweat off his neck with a stained rag.

"All done?" Zea asks, joining him in the front room.

"Yep." He retreats when she moves into his space. They're almost eye to eye, and she studies him curiously.

"You don't talk much."

"Nope." He folds the ladder and looks around. "You don't have any furniture."

"Is that a problem?"

It is. All of it: the lack of furniture, the length of her stay, her questions. He really isn't sure what to make of her.

She shrugs. "I'm just here for the week. As for my things . . ." She glances around the room. "I travel light."

"Huh." He did, too, when he found himself here, which makes him wonder if she's running, too. From who and what?

He picks up the toolbox and tucks the stepladder under his arm. "Unless there's anything else you need, I'll see you around."

She shakes her head, but he only makes it to her door. "Will I see you at Ivy's tonight?"

"She making dinner?"

Zea nods, walking to the door. "Everyone's invited, I'm told."

He grunts, his standard nonanswer, and leaves her apartment. He filled his dinner-party quota for the year last night. He makes it halfway down the stairs when she calls out, "Bring your niece."

He looks back over his shoulder, catching her watching him. She quickly puts on a smile and waves.

25

At the end of her shift, Shiloh turns over her clipboard to Ivy.

"Wonderful." The old woman flips through Shiloh's notes from behind her desk in the little office off the stockroom. Other than the desk and chair, there isn't much room for anything else but a trash bin and a safe.

Shiloh's eyes round as she considers what's locked inside. Visions of money stacks and jewels circle in her head.

"You did well today. I'm proud of you."

"Uh . . . thanks?" Her gaze swerves back to Ivy.

Ivy smiles warmly. She puts her elbows on the desk. "How are things?"

She frowns. "What do you mean?"

"With your uncle. Everything going well?"

"Um, yeah." She fidgets with the cord in her hoodie, tugging one string then the other until the hood shrivels into a tight ball of material behind her head.

"I imagine it must be tough being away from home."

"Not really."

Ivy frowns. "You don't miss your mother?"

"I do," she admits in a flat, monotone voice, her heart aching for the mom Harmony was before she got into drugs. But she can't reflect on that now, remembering she needs to stick to the story she and Lucas invented. "I meant I visit Uncle Lucas all the time. This isn't the first time I've been away from home."

"Really?"

"Why just last month we went camping in Zion—"

"Last month?" Ivy interjects.

Shiloh's stomach bottoms out at her gaffe. "Last year." She laughs it off. "We went to Zion last year."

"I thought you hadn't been. That you two are going this summer."

Shiloh shuffles her feet. Ivy heard that? She remembers telling that story to one customer yesterday while wrapping a sandwich but didn't think it was while Ivy was there. Obviously she screwed up.

A nervous chuckle. "You're right. We are. This summer. Going there. Is there anything else you need me to do? Because if not . . ." She jabs a thumb over her shoulder at the door behind her, anxious to leave before she digs herself into a ditch. "I'm going to go."

Ivy shakes her head, her expression curious.

Shiloh doesn't wait around for her to poke more holes into her stories. *Shoot.* She needs to learn to not say more than she needs to, or she'll screw up this whole arrangement. Pushing hard through the glass storefront door, Shiloh rounds the corner of the building to the stairs for the apartment and runs smack into somebody.

"Oh." A woman gasps. Her purse drops to the ground.

"Sorry." Shiloh ducks to retrieve the purse. From habit, her hand dives into the bag. She pockets the woman's wallet and gives her the purse, avoiding her face.

"Thanks." The woman juggles a small duffel bag, sleeping bag, and pillow to take the purse.

"No prob." Eyes averted, Shiloh turns to leave. Her sneaker lands on the bottom concrete step when the woman says, "Are you Shiloh?"

The skin behind Shiloh's ears tightens at the sound of her name. She turns, her heart taking a leap. It's the same woman from yesterday. "You ordered a turkey and cheddar on sourdough," Shiloh says, recovering quickly. She's feared Ellis would catch up. He's probably the one pressuring her mom to email her to come home. She wouldn't put it past him to send someone after her to bring her back. Ellis needs to be in control. She got away from him, and that's a blow to his ego.

The woman smiles. "Yeah, I did. Good memory."

"Nah. I only made five sandwiches yesterday. Yours was my first."

"You just started to work here?"

"Mm-hmm. Yesterday." Shiloh rolls her lips over her teeth so she doesn't say more.

"Interesting." The woman tilts her head, looking at Shiloh curiously for a beat. She thrusts out an arm, her purse dangling on her elbow. "I'm Zea."

She shakes her hand. "What's with all the stuff."

"I'm moving in. Got the empty apartment behind you. Don't tell anyone." She leans in close. "But I'm kind of nervous."

"Why?"

"I'm a city girl. Never lived in the country before."

Shiloh glances around. "I wouldn't call this place the country."

"Okay, the desert, then."

"Sick." She wants to ask Zea why she came. Who would want to move here? But the longer she chats, the greater the risk she'll say something she shouldn't. She's also itching to leave before Zea realizes she lifted her wallet. She backs up the stairs. "See you around, I guess."

"Yes. Tonight. At dinner. Ivy invited us."

"Awesome." Shiloh grins stiffly, calculating how she'll return the wallet before then. If she'd known the woman was going to be their neighbor, she wouldn't have taken it. Maybe. Probably. Because Lucas would go ballistic, and for a reason she can't explain, she doesn't want to screw up around him. He'll make her leave. But she also wants to count Zea's cash. The wallet feels loaded. Zea probably wouldn't miss the few bills Shiloh kept for herself.

She jogs upstairs, feeling Zea's eyes burning through her back. When she reaches the top, she glances back. Zea is smiling up at her.

"Creepy," Shiloh mutters, and hurries to Lucas's apartment.

Inside her room she flops onto the bed and opens the wallet. "Holy shit." She whistles. It's loaded with cash, but that's not all. Shiloh counts six different ID cards, all from different states, each with a different name. But only one ID is tucked in the pocket behind the clear plastic cover, the ID Shiloh suspects is the woman's legit identification.

Whoever moved in behind them is not Zea Dawson. Shiloh will bet the $261 she pockets into her jeans the new neighbor's real name is Sophie Renau.

Who is she? Why did she lie about her name? And why does she have so many IDs?

Like recognizes like, and Shiloh quickly sums up she isn't the only thief in their midst. This woman could be conning them. She could be extorting Ivy, that sweet old lady. Other than the building, Ivy doesn't have much else. So what is Zea's endgame?

Only one place to start looking.

Shiloh puts the wallet back together and goes searching for Lucas's laptop.

26

"She's a bounty hunter!" Shiloh exclaims the second Lucas steps foot in his apartment at the end of the workday. She's standing at the kitchen island with his laptop open. Anxious horror sucks the color from her face.

"What are you talking about?" His eyes ping-pong from her to his laptop as he struggles to make sense of Shiloh's fear and what it could mean for him.

"Zea Dawson. That woman moving into the apartment behind us. The same one who ordered a sandwich yesterday and was all up in my business about my black eye."

"She was what?" Shiloh hadn't told him that. Closing the door, he crosses the room to her, swearing at himself. He knew there was something about Zea, and he kept making excuses.

"She thought you hit me."

"And what did you tell her?" He empties his pockets from habit, his eyes never wavering from Shiloh. He'd thought Zea was a drifter when he rung up her order, possibly an undercover cop when they spoke earlier. Nosy, eager for conversation, overly neighborly, and packing light. Yet he'd still written off his suspicions because he'd seen something of himself in her. He thought she was running from her past, too. How could he have been so wrong?

"Girl fight. Anyway"—Shiloh swoops her arms to the side—"the point is: Zea isn't Zea. She's using a fake name, and she has six of them. I think her real one is Sophie Renau. Most of her credit cards are in that name."

"How do you know this?" Her mouth flatlines, and her gaze skitters away like a mouse scurrying for cover. His palms start to sweat. "Shiloh, what did you do?"

"It's habit, I swear. I didn't mean to."

"Shiloh," he warns, dreading her answer. She's going to get them into trouble if they aren't already.

She tosses up her hands. "I stole her wallet, okay?"

His stomach drops into his boots. "You did *what*?" If this woman is what Shiloh says she is, she'll notify the police as soon as she realizes her wallet is missing. That is if she wasn't sent by them in the first place. "Are you trying to bring the cops to us?" The patrol car could be on its way this very moment. Blistering-hot panic sears his limbs. His worst nightmare is coming true.

"I know. It was stupid," she whines with a dramatic flourish of her hands. They fling in the air. "But look at these." Her hand arcs over the counter.

Lucas tears his eyes from her and looks. Six IDs, all with their neighbor's face, each a different name and state, just as Shiloh said. Beside them a brown wallet thick with cards and cash.

His brow quirks. "You didn't take the money."

She grimaces. "I put it back."

"All of it?"

"Enough."

"Hell, Shiloh." His fingers trowel through his hair, taking in the IDs, wondering what it all means. Who the hell is this woman? "Tell me what you know," he says, and mentally starts tallying what to pack and how quickly he can leave. He isn't even locked behind bars yet, and he's already terrified.

"The only name, the one with the most credit cards, which is also the one that got any search hits, is Sophie Renau. That proves she lives in Redondo Beach, same address as the one on her driver's license, and that she's a bounty hunter."

"Show me." He tries not to hyperventilate.

She turns the laptop toward him. A deck of browser windows fill the screen. With mounting alarm, he clicks through the windows and skims the short articles about the fugitives she's apprehended. One of them was only last week, a guy in Temecula accused of domestic violence against his wife who'd missed his court date. While she was bringing him into the station, the fugitive's brother, the one who'd put up his house as collateral, attacked the accused, and Sophie had been caught in the middle. She took the punch. The scuffle occurred outside the police station and attracted enough attention to make the local section of the paper.

"I bet Ellis sent her. She's here for me." Shiloh bounces on her toes, as edgy as him. But she's not the one with the warrant. Genuine fear pulls at her face. Her hands tug the strings on her hoodie. "I told her my name. She knows who I am. I bet she's called Ellis already to tell him she's found me. He's probably on his way here right now." Her gaze swerves to the window by the front door. With the curtains wide open, they can see the parking lot below and road beyond. He doesn't notice anything out of the ordinary, but that's not to say the cops weren't on their way.

Panic breathes down his neck, pushing his back to the wall.

"She's not here for you." She's here for him. He killed his father in Carlsbad, less than two hours from Redondo Beach. Right in the middle of her territory. She probably works the entirety of Southern California, especially if the pay is good. How did she find him?

"How do you know?" Her eyes jump between him and the door. He gathers up his wallet and keys. A change of clothes and cash is all he needs. That'll cover him until he lands on his feet. Shiloh smacks her palms on the counter to get his attention and repeats in a shrill voice, "How do you know?"

"I just do," he snaps. She flinches, but he's too worked up to apologize. "Assuming Ellis sent her because he didn't know where you are, he'd hire someone by him in New Mexico. He'd also hire a PI, not a bounty hunter. They chase criminals. You have nothing to worry about." Though *he* does.

He takes off down the hall.

She follows him to his room. "Why's she here, then? Where are you going?" she asks when he shoves clothes into a duffel. He changes his shirt and yanks a lightweight jacket off a hanger.

"I take that back. She could be after you now."

Her face drains of color. "What do you mean?"

"You stole her wallet. Where were you when you swiped it? What were you doing?"

"I . . . uh . . . It was at the bottom of the steps outside. I ran into her on accident when she was carrying her stuff in, and she dropped her purse. It was open so I took it."

"Did you pick up her purse or did she?"

"I did. I gave it to her." She tugs hard on a hoodie string until the other end disappears into the folds of fabric.

"Put the wallet back. She needs to find it." If they're lucky, she hasn't noticed the wallet is missing yet and hasn't reported the theft. If he's lucky, she hasn't notified the police she's located him. He needs a jump on them, to put some distance between him and this bounty hunter before she has a chance to bring him in.

"How am I supposed to do that? 'Hi, Zea. Welcome to the neighborhood. Here's your wallet. Sorry I stole it. Borrowed some cash. Hope you don't mind.'" She gives him double thumbs-up. "Yeah, no. Don't think that'll go over."

He moves past her to the front room. "Drop it near the bottom of the stairs. She'll think it fell out when she dropped her purse." He reaches for the door.

"Wait a second, are you leaving?"

"Heading out," he says, allowing her to think he'll be back. If she doesn't know he's left for good, she can't tell anyone he has. They won't come looking for him. They'll be waiting here instead.

"You can't leave me." She looks around wildly. "Take me with you."

"I'm going to the tavern," he lies, but can tell she's conflicted. She doesn't know whether to believe him.

"You promised I could stay with you. Wait. I'll get my stuff." She runs to her room.

"Sorry, kiddo," he says to the apartment, adrenaline shooting through him. This is one trip he's riding solo.

27

Shiloh quickly stuffs her few belongings into the backpack and rushes back to the front room, but Lucas is gone. Outside, she hears his truck, tires spitting gravel. She races to the window and parts the curtain just in time to see him speed off.

He left her.

Just when she was starting to trust him.

Just when she was beginning to lean on him.

The curtain falls back into place, and she retreats from the window, frantically looking around the apartment, her heart clamoring. Nausea boils and bubbles in her stomach, the acidic taste rising into her throat. What is she supposed to do now? Where is she supposed to go? She chews her bottom lip, hoping he was telling the truth and hasn't left for good.

Please, please, please, don't be gone.

She can't stay here by herself. Ivy will call the police, thinking Lucas abandoned her. They'll send her home.

He did leave you! her inner voice screams.

Someone knocks on the door. Shiloh gasps, clapping a hand over her mouth.

"Shiloh? It's Zea, your neighbor. We met earlier?"

Oh shit, oh shit, oh shit.

She's here for the wallet. Shiloh's gaze leaps to the counter, the contents of Zea's billfold spread across the surface.

"We saw Lucas leave. Ivy's wondering if you're coming to dinner."

Shiloh didn't know anything about dinner. She tiptoes toward the window to peer through the curtain. Zea's silhouette blends with the other shadows.

"Shiloh, I know you're in there. I can hear you."

A sound of distress rumbles in her throat. She holds her breath and doesn't move.

Zea knocks again. "Shiloh, open the door. Please? Ivy's worried."

Shiloh scrambles for something to say that'll convince her to leave. Lucas may think Zea is here for him, but Shiloh isn't entirely convinced. If Zea saw Lucas leave, wouldn't she chase after him? She might be a bounty hunter, but she could also be a PI. With that many IDs, she could be anything. Ellis threatened her mom's life if Shiloh ever went to the police. If he at all suspects she has, Shiloh knows he'd hunt her down. She's convinced Zea's distracting her until Ellis arrives.

Fear coats her spine in ice. She needs to get rid of Zea, and Shiloh needs to leave town, and fast.

She parts the curtain. "What do you want?"

Zea smiles, but her grin quickly fades when she notices Shiloh's distress. "Are you all right?"

"Of course, why wouldn't I be?" She tries her best to sound normal, but it's hard with her heart pounding in her head.

"Well . . . you guys were coming to dinner, and it seems Lucas left."

"It's a free country."

"Doesn't mean you're stuck in the apartment. Why don't you come over and eat with Ivy and me? Better yet, open the door. We can talk."

"Lucas told me not to." A necessary lie.

Zea's eyes widen to moon size. "He told you that?" She glances behind her down the road.

Shiloh curses herself. Zea already thinks Lucas clocked her. Now she'll never leave her alone.

The knob jiggles, and Shiloh lurches back, her gaze flying to the door. "Did he tell you to bolt the door, too?"

"You need to leave," Shiloh calls out to her.

"Just tell me where Lucas went."

Nerves shoot down her arm. "Why?"

Zea sighs, and Shiloh senses she's testing the woman's patience.

"Ivy's upset you're missing dinner. Are you sure you're all right? He hasn't hurt you, has he?"

Shiloh pulls the hoodie low over her forehead, wishing she could hide. "I'm fine. Lucas just went to the tavern. He'll be back in a few hours." She wants to believe that, but he packed a duffel. Her stomach clenches, the nausea thickening as she considers how meaningless she is to him if he did in fact leave.

A long pause.

"I'll be next door if you need me. Come over if you get hungry."

"Sure, no prob." Shiloh holds her breath until Zea retreats and Ivy's door closes. She almost collapses to the floor with relief, but rushes to the counter and puts Zea's wallet back together. She can't wait around to see if Lucas returns. She needs to leave now, which means she needs money and a phone. The phone is downstairs, but the cash in Zea's wallet is a good start.

She pockets the cash, keeping it for good this time, and goes to Lucas's room for the cash she saw stashed in his boot when she went searching for his laptop earlier. Why he didn't take it is beyond her, but he left, so now it's hers, as is the laptop. She adds both to her packed backpack.

Scooping up the spare set of keys to the Dusty Pantry, Shiloh drops her bag on the couch and peers out the window through the crack in the curtains. The balcony is clear. If she's going to do this, now's her chance, while Ivy entertains Zea.

Carefully, she unbolts and opens the door, cringing when the hinges squeak. She pauses to listen, her breath already coming fast. Ivy's laugh followed by Zea's steady voice reaches her through Ivy's open window. Quietly, she steps out onto the balcony, closing the door behind her under the cover of their voices, and drops to her hands and knees. She crawls past Ivy's apartment under her window, breathing only when she reaches the stairs where she gets to her feet and slowly goes down one step at a time. At the bottom, she drops Zea's wallet like Lucas suggested and kicks it under the staircase. Then she lets herself into the pantry through the rear entrance.

Inside, she uses the phone in Ivy's office and calls Finn.

"Pick up, pick up, pick up," she pleads to the room when the phone rings. Just as she's about the cut the call and redial, he picks up.

"Shy? That you?"

Her relief is as sweet as cotton candy. "Yes."

"Didn't expect to hear from you so soon." He sounds bored and uninterested. He doesn't like that she chose staying here over him.

"I need you to come get me right now," she rushes to explain.

He huffs with impatience. "Seriously, Shy—"

"Finn! I'm in trouble. This woman showed up today. She's like a bounty hunter or investigator or something. Ellis sent her."

"What?" Now she has his attention.

"Lucas took off. Finn, I'm scared."

"Don't be scared, baby. I promised you I wouldn't let Ellis hurt you again."

She's counting on that promise with her life. "He could already be on his way here. You have to come tonight."

He swears profusely; then his end of the line goes quiet.

"Finn?" The phone trembles her hands.

"I'm coming." Shiloh hears a door close and keys rattle. He shouts something indistinguishable to someone else.

"How long before you get here?" Her eyes nervously dart about the office.

"Few hours. Hang tight."

She prays she has that long. "I'll be ready."

She ends the call, her gaze settling on the safe. Ivy's trusting. She's also forgetful. She couldn't even remember where she'd seen Shiloh before, and it was in her own damn store.

Shiloh jerks open the center desk drawer, betting she'll find the safe's combo written on a sticky. Sure enough, she does. Second drawer down on the left. She spins the safe's dial, biting her lip when the lock unlatches to quell her guilt. She always felt guilty when she stole, but until now, she hasn't had a choice. She had to survive. But between Zea's cash and Lucas's money, she doesn't need more. Though she'll take whatever extra to make life easier once she moves in with Finn.

There isn't much cash in the safe, several hundred dollars at most, she guesses without taking the time to count it out. But she pockets the money and closes the safe. Then she raids the Pantry's candy and cosmetics before she heads upstairs. Ivy's door swings open just as Shiloh reaches the second-floor balcony. Zea stops abruptly upon seeing Shiloh. She's holding a plate of food and a bottle.

"Oh." Zea sounds as surprised as she looks. "Hello. Were you coming over to eat?"

Shiloh shakes her head, guilt knotting her throat. She jams both hands into the hoodie's kangaroo pocket to hide her loot.

Zea shows her the plate. "I was bringing you dinner. Ivy insisted."

She cautiously approaches the woman and takes the plate with one hand, using it to cover the stash hidden in her sweatshirt. "Thanks," she mumbles, looking at the food so she doesn't have to make eye contact, afraid Zea will suspect exactly what she's been doing. Meatloaf. It smells amazing. Something else homemade she's never eaten. Her stomach growls, and she wonders if she'll have time to eat before Finn arrives. Will she be able to hold the food down despite her worry Ellis makes it here before him?

"This, too." Zea shows her the bottle. "I brought this tonight for you."

She had? Shiloh's gaze lifts to the woman, finding it hard to hate her for ratting her out to Ellis. Her smile is bright and warm. If she didn't know she had six identities and worked for her mom's boyfriend, Shiloh would say the gift was genuine rather than an attempt to win over Shiloh's trust. Still, she takes the bottle. "I've never had Italian soda before."

"It's good. I work with a lot of kids like you. They love it."

Whatever that means. Shiloh frowns with unease.

Zea rushes to Lucas's apartment. "Let me get the door for you." Before Shiloh can object, she throws open the door Shiloh left unlocked. Shiloh thinks of the backpack she left on the couch loaded with Zea's and Lucas's cash, his laptop. She feels the weight of Ivy's cash and the makeup and candy she stole from the Pantry and starts to sweat.

Zea steps aside as Shiloh warily enters Lucas's apartment. "Want some company?" Zea asks with enthusiasm.

That's the last thing she wants. She turns to tell Zea she has a stomachache and just wants to go to bed when a car enters the parking lot. A tall woman with long brunette hair brushed to a sheen unfolds from the compact sedan. Thin body decked in flared jeans and a tube top, she wears sunglasses that cover half her face.

"What's with the shades?" Zea mutters under her breath, watching the stranger. Shiloh's mouth quirks with humor. The woman does look ridiculous. The sun set almost an hour ago.

Sliding the shades onto her head, the woman looks up at them. "Who are you?"

Shiloh creeps forward to get a better look. Zea approaches the rail. "I'd ask the same of you."

"Where's Lucas?" She leans to the side to see past Shiloh and into the apartment.

"He's not here," Zea answers.

The woman's eyes narrow as she peers at her. "Are you his new piece? You don't seem his type."

Shiloh covers a laugh. She can't help it. Just yesterday she'd asked Lucas if he wanted to do Zea because Lucas seemed totally interested. Of course, that was before they knew who and what she is.

Zea rolls her eyes, unfazed. "I'm the new neighbor."

Ivy appears from her apartment. She grasps the rail, yelling down to the woman, "Go back to your husband, Faye. Lucas doesn't need your kind of trouble."

Faye's face flames red hot, and Shiloh can't tell if the woman's angry or embarrassed. Faye flicks down her sunglasses where they drop onto her nose, and she sinks back into her car. "Tell him my husband is out of town," she hollers up through the open window. "He got a last-minute job. I need to talk to him about the other night."

"Who, your husband?" Ivy asks. "Why don't you call him? Or are you afraid he'll find out you're cheatin' on him. Again," she adds after pausing for effect.

Zea's mouth falls open, and Shiloh's eyes go wide. They share a look.

"I need to talk to *Lucas*. Now tell him to call me. I've been trying to reach him all day."

"If he isn't answering, he doesn't want to talk to you."

"Just tell him I dropped by, old woman." Faye revs her engine. The car squeals from the parking lot, the rear tires spinning in her haste to leave.

"I went to her and Rafe's wedding fifteen years ago. Even then, her eyes wandered, as did his hands. I don't think there was one bridesmaid he didn't make a pass at that night. Honestly, I'm surprised they're still married." Ivy faces Shiloh. "Get inside and lock the door in case she comes back. I don't think Lucas was dumb enough to give her a key, but he's a man, and men don't always think with the head on their shoulders."

"Ivy!" Zea exclaims, appalled. Shiloh stares at Ivy, stunned and a little grossed out.

"Stick a chair under the knob, honey. Her husband is crazier than her. He gave Lucas that shiner he's been carrying."

Zea looks at the landlady. "Really?" She frowns, and Shiloh wants to smart off. See? It wasn't her who punched him.

Taking Ivy up on her advice, she scoots into the apartment and bolts the door.

28

The Fly By Tavern on the edge of Reefer City looks like a set out of *Top Gun*. With its dark-wood paneling, pool tables to the side, dart boards on the other, the place is a time capsule. Van Morrison plays on a jukebox in the corner. Vinyl booths line the wall, the bench seats deep red and cracked with age and use. The place is popular with tourists, what with the air force base nearby and alien knickknacks on display. It might be exactly where Lucas lied to Shiloh he'd be to throw Zea off his trail. Give him time to escape. But it's right where he ended up.

He should be over a hundred miles from here by now. Instead he made it twenty and veered into the parking lot in a panic. He'd left behind over five grand in cash and his laptop in his haste to get away.

For an hour he sat in his truck, baffled he could have forgotten something so important as he deliberated why he was running and where he was running to until he finally ventured inside.

He still doesn't have answers or a plan.

Settling at the bar, he orders a Corona with a lime slice and a shot of Cuervo and sees exactly how this night will go down: him wasted and passing out in his truck.

Unless he drives home drunk to seek out the blade in his nightstand. Him and his ever-present death wish.

Or Zea locates him first and takes him into custody.

Thoughts of the bounty hunter have him circling back to why he stopped here in the first place. And the answer is clear to him. He wasn't forgetful. He was intentional. He'd left the cash and laptop on purpose so he'd have a reason to go back.

And since he's being honest with himself, he doesn't want to run. He doesn't want to abandon Shiloh either. Quite simply, he doesn't want to leave California City.

He came here to die but somehow built himself a new life. Made connections. Befriended people he's starting to care for. Does care for, he amends. He found a new home.

Then he met a runaway, lost like him. He wants to make a positive difference in her life, guide her in the right direction as Ivy said he could. Shiloh's another Lily.

His second chance.

Murderers don't deserve second chances.

He also doesn't deserve Lily's forgiveness. Though he craves it deeply. He wants to believe he is the person Ivy and Shiloh see him as: a good man.

He wants absolution.

The bartender is a gruff old man with faded military tats and wiry gray arm hair. He serves Lucas his drinks, then leaves him alone to tangle with his demons, retreating to the far side of the bar where another veteran is seated nursing a Miller Lite. They pick up their conversation where they left off when Lucas entered the bar.

Lucas looks blankly at the order in front of him. Who is he kidding? He's not a role model. He can't return to Shiloh, and he can't go see his sisters, not with a possible prison sentence hanging over his head. He murdered their father. He isn't good.

You're used goods, Carson. Morris's voice is a sinister whisper in his ear.

He tosses back his shot and guzzles half his beer to wash down the bile the memories of his last day in juvenile detention always induce. His tattoo draws his gaze when he lifts the bottle to his mouth, and he's reminded that he's weak. A coward. He couldn't go through with the attempt on his life the one time he tried because it was the only way he believed he could shut up Morris Stanton's taunts in his head.

He's weak because he couldn't defend himself that day Morris and his gang cornered him in the detention center's mess hall. Every day Lucas sees that weak kid he was at sixteen, restrained on the ground while a meaty hand pressed his skull against the scuffed linoleum and someone else stuffed a humid, sweaty sock into his mouth so he couldn't shout for help. More hands stripping him of his clothes. Hands, hands everywhere. To this day he sees himself as the same loser who spent his middle and high school years conditioning for football and studying martial arts but couldn't fend off five untrained guys.

No, he is not a good man.

He's a coward drowning in liquid courage who never had the strength to stand up for himself. To go after what he wants.

He's also tired of running. Tired of bearing the weight of his secrets. So he drinks, and drinks. Because the only place for guys like him is hell.

A beer shy of a six-pack in and a half-dozen shots later, Zea enters the bar. He senses her before he sees her, the air going still upon her arrival, like the millisecond of absolute silence before the sound barrier is broken. She settles on the stool beside him. He's been expecting her, almost relieved to see her. It means he doesn't have to run anymore. He may even stop feeling guilty about his mistakes and give himself permission to grieve over the time lost with Lily and the injustices done to him. But his pulse speeds up, and he starts to sweat all the same.

"'Bout time you got here." He tips back what's left of his beer, knowing it's the end of the road for him, and flags the bartender.

She hums, glancing at him, but doesn't say anything further.

"How was dinner?" he asks conversationally, as if a criminal having a drink with his bounty hunter is completely normal. Inside, he's a perfect storm of fear and resignation. It's high time he faced his past, but doing so scares the hell out of him. So does the inevitable: prison.

But he's so damn tired of trying to stay one step ahead of his shame and remorse and the law. He's just exhausted.

"Great. The meatloaf was huge." She flattens her hands on the bar top, drawing his gaze. Her nails are blunt, smoothly filed, and her fingers long and sleek, almost too delicate for how tough and strong he suspects she is. He has the inexplicable urge to trace her fingers with his, then lay his hand over hers. Will her skin warm his palm? Will she let him hold her hand? And why does he have such a pressing need to touch her when others repulse him?

"Does Ivy always cook like that? Enough for an army?"

He lifts his head to meet her eyes and frowns. He didn't notice before her eyes were such a soft brown. She repeats the question. He clears his throat, trying to focus. "Yep. Nobody starves on her watch." Ivy was the mother he never had. He hopes she finds a buyer for the property and can take that cruise around the world she's been wanting.

He wishes he could buy the building from her, to have something to nurture and reshape that he can call his own.

The bartender approaches. "Another round?"

Lucas nods and tilts his head toward Zea, or Sophie. Whatever her name is. The bartender looks at her.

"Soda water and lime, please," she says.

"Coming right up." He pats the wood surface, then pulls a beer from the fridge behind him and gives it to Lucas after popping the top. Then he pours a shot of Cuervo, which Lucas tosses back before Sophie takes the first sip of her drink.

He slides the empty shot glass across the bar. "How long do I have before the police arrive?"

She spares him a glance. "Excuse me?"

No more secrets. He's through. "I know your name isn't Zea. You're Sophie Renau, and you're a bounty hunter."

She blinks in surprise but recovers quickly. Biting into her bottom lip, she pushes her glass aside. "I wondered what happened to my wallet. When did you steal it?"

He smirks, unwilling to be baited into throwing Shiloh under the bus. "You'll probably find it under the steps at the apartment." Her eyes narrow, and he tips back a mouthful of beer, holding her gaze. "So how much time do I have?"

"You think I'm after you? That why you ran?"

"Isn't that why you're here?"

She swings her stool around to face him, her elbow on the bar. "I'm not here for the reason you probably think I am."

He frowns at that. "You're not taking me in? I don't understand."

"Truth for a truth?" Her low voice rolls over him, and his gaze drops to her lips.

"Hit me," he says, staring at her mouth, the alcohol impairing his thoughts. His finger twitches. He wants to trace her pouty bottom lip.

"I know there is a warrant for your arrest for several traffic violations from last September."

He forces air out his nose and leans back, waiting for the rest. When she doesn't say more, he asks, "And?"

"And you spent time in juvie during high school."

His gaze flips up to hers. That can't be all.

"To answer the question you're probably thinking, no, I haven't notified the police of your whereabouts."

That isn't what he's thinking, not at this exact moment. He murdered his father. The accident happened on a major road and should have been caught on CCTV. His hands were bloody. His blood would be at the scene. There should be a warrant for his arrest for first-degree murder.

"What can you tell me about the girl with you?" she asks, oblivious to his inner turmoil.

"Shiloh?" Her interest in the girl baffles him. Sophie/Zea must have missed something if she looked up his records. Then it smashes into him. She isn't here for him. Shiloh was right. Sophie's after her.

"She's not your concern." A tingling sensation spreads down his arms. He never should have left her alone.

"I know she isn't your niece. She looked pretty roughed up when I met her." Shiloh's black eye and the scratches on her face and neck.

"You think I hit her?" Disgust sours his tongue.

"I don't know what to think. That's why I'm asking."

"What's your fascination with her?"

Sophie's expression softens when she notices how fired up he's getting. Without taking her eyes from him, she lays her arm on the bar top. Lucas's gaze dips to read the script tattooed on her forearm. *I have swept away your offenses like a cloud, your sins like the morning mist. Isaiah 44:22.*

Like him, she wants redemption. He meets her eyes and studies her in a new light. Their souls are kindred. Drifters aching over a past they can't let go of. But what does hers have to do with Shiloh?

"Explain."

"I used to work for a network that places homeless and runaway kids into homes."

"Foster care?"

Her eyes skirt away. "Something like that. The network vets its angels—that's what we call the people who open their homes for these kids—but not well enough in my book. This one girl, Alma, she was twelve when she ran away from home. Her stepfather sexually abused her. I placed her into one of our homes with a woman we thought we knew. She was a longtime angel. But unbeknownst to us, she had a new boyfriend, someone we hadn't vetted. Someone with a record. He got to Alma, and he . . ." She clears her throat. "He used her, and he killed her. It's my fault. I placed her in that house. I put her in the exact situation she ran from when I promised I'd protect her."

"And now you seek redemption through Shiloh?" Her cheeks darken, and Lucas tilts his head toward her tattoo, understanding dawning. He, too, has been seeking redemption through Shiloh. If he could protect her, he could make up for failing his sister. Seeing someone else do the same shows him how fucked up his reasoning is. But it doesn't change his mind. Shiloh still needs him.

"Shiloh's safe with me, if that's what you're asking." He finishes his beer, the urge to get back to his apartment to check on her pushing him to leave before history repeats itself and he loses Shiloh, too. Even though he knows she can't stay with him in the long run, he shouldn't have left her on her own. He shouldn't have left her the way he did by lying to her. But his fear and cowardice had gotten the best of him.

"Who hurt her?" Sophie presses.

He doesn't want Sophie to see him the way he suspects she does, as a predator. So he tells her. "She ran away from home and was living in a homeless encampment. A couple of guys attacked her. I pulled her out." He slaps bills on the counter, urgent to return home, and swipes up his keys. "If the cops aren't coming for me, we're done here. If you're here for Shiloh, forget about it. I'm taking care of her. Go home to wherever you came from. Look for your redemption elsewhere," he says, his anger rising, more upset with himself that he was using Shiloh to fix himself than he is at Sophie.

He goes to stand and stumbles off the stool.

"Oh!" Sophie grabs his arm before he faceplants. Lightheaded, he feels the room spin. Damn, he's drunker than he thought. He shakes her off and leaves the bar.

She follows him out as he weaves toward his truck. "You're harboring a runaway, Lucas. Have you checked if her parents are looking for her? If the authorities think you're holding her against her will, they will arrest you."

"Let them try," he flings over his shoulder. He won't let them take her home unless that's what Shiloh wants. He promised to protect her.

"Not that it's any of your business, but she doesn't have a father, and her mother is a drug addict whose live-in boyfriend sexually assaulted her."

Sophie pales.

"Sounds familiar, doesn't it?"

"I admit it hits home." She visibly swallows. "At least call CPS. They'll put her in foster care. She'll be safe from him. You have to trust the system."

He stops abruptly and goes utterly still. Given his experience, that was the wrong thing to say to him. He pivots, seeing red, and gets in her face. "Trust the system?" Her eyes widen, and she holds up her hands to warn him off, but he can't see past his fury. "Trust the *fucking* system? Are you out of your mind? The system is broken. The *system* let me take the fall while my *friends*"—he spits the word with distaste and ire, alcohol loosening his tongue—"including the jackass who brought the gun with him, who loaded it, got off. You want a truth for a truth? Well, I got a doozy for you. The system put me in a hellhole that allowed a gang of kids to get away with rape. The system paid off my parents and buried it. I left that place wondering what the fuck I did to deserve any of it. I was left wondering what the fuck to do with my life because no one, not a single person—especially not my mother or my waste of a father—did anything to help me get over it. I was left feeling like a worthless pile of shit. That *I* was to blame for what happened to me in there. Do you know how that feels? Do you?"

She shakes her head, her gaze cutting from his face to his hands, which flex at his sides. It occurs to him how menacing he must seem, and he backs off. He puts a foot of space between them, and after a beat, he admits, defeated, "To this day I wonder what I did wrong. The system doesn't give a fuck, Sophie. So, neither do I."

He's breathing heavily when he finishes. He can't believe he confessed, to a stranger, no less. He's never shared that much. Even his sisters don't know what happened to him in juvenile detention or why he was released to the hospital three days before the end of his sentence.

He rolls his shoulders, feeling gross and dirty. Ill. Why does he still feel their hands on him?

Morris Stanton was one of his bunkmates, already a repeat offender at seventeen. And he'd made several attempts at sexual advances during Lucas's sentence, but Lucas fended him off. Except once, three nights before his release.

The detention center was overcrowded, the guards overtaxed. A fight had broken out in the common room while Lucas was on kitchen-cleanup duty. Morris and his gang found him there. And while the guards were occupied breaking up the fight, they took advantage. By the time the fight was resolved and someone could respond to Lucas's assault, he was unconscious on the floor. A guard found him curled in a fetal position, bloodied and broken.

Lucas wanted his father to file charges. But Dwight insisted he forget about what happened and worked with the detention center's attorneys to bury the incident and seal the records else Lucas further tarnish the family's reputation. He was ordered to never speak of it again. It would be his secret, his burden to bear. Be a man. Suck it up and handle it. Dwight said he probably had it coming, anyway. Lucas was prone to instigating fights.

Sophie stares at him in open-mouthed horror. "Jesus, Lucas. I—I didn't know."

"You wouldn't. The records are sealed." Ashamed, he averts his face. He can't look at her. But he's drunk. If he's lucky he won't remember this in the morning. "Arrest me if you want for keeping that girl safe. But she's better off with me than where she came from."

29

Lucas turns back to his truck, anxious to apologize to Shiloh for abandoning her, and pinches the key fob. The truck disarms with a beep and flash of its lights.

"You shouldn't drive," Sophie says, dogging him.

"Try and stop me."

"If you insist."

He reaches for the door, and a blur of movement appears in his peripheral vision. She grabs the wrist of the hand holding his keys and wrenches his arm behind his back, straining his shoulder. Her boot connects with the back of his knee. Pain shoots up his leg as his knee buckles and he drops to his shin. She plucks the keys from his hand.

A laugh, low and dark, builds in his chest. "Didn't see that coming." Then he moves without warning.

He swings his leg, catching her behind an ankle and throwing her off balance. She lands hard on her back, and he winces. "Ouch. That looks like it hurt."

"You're an asshole," she wheezes, the wind knocked out of her.

"You wouldn't be the first to call me that." He gets to his feet, weaving slightly, and holds out a hand, feeling bad that he hurt her.

"I was only trying to save you from killing yourself or someone else."

His mood sobers. "I know."

Their eyes meet and hers soften. She takes his hand, her fingers warm and delicate in his. Lethal, too, he bets, so he doesn't try anything ill-advised like dropping her. He hauls her up, reluctantly letting go, odd for him, and she dusts off her jeans.

"So, what do I call you?" he asks, looking at his palm where their skin touched, amazed he doesn't feel repulsed.

"Since the cat's out of the bag, Sophie."

Good. That's how he already thinks of her.

"How much money are you making off me?" he asks, conflicted over who she's after, him or Shiloh.

She glances away. "None."

He frowns. That doesn't make sense to him. Convinced she missed it, that there is a warrant on him for first-degree murder, he wonders what her motivation is. Why is she here? Why is she renting for just a week? Why is she so neighborly and inquisitive? Her dog-and-pony show couldn't be solely for one girl.

She starts walking toward her nondescript Honda, breaking off his train of thought. "I'll drive," she announces.

"We aren't taking your piece-of-shit car."

Sophie turns on her heel, walking back to him. "My car isn't a piece of shit. It's a great car."

He throws her a flat look. "You can drive, but we're taking my truck."

"We are not—"

He cuts her a look, and she stops. Her blouse flutters in the slight breeze, and he catches her scent, something citrusy. He feels a curling in his groin, and his gaze drops to the hint of cleavage at the opening of her blouse. Hunger roars to life. Drawn to her in a way he can't explain and has never felt with anyone before, he wants to devour her. He wants her to touch him. Can he withstand it like he was able to when he held her hand? He aches to test that theory. He aches for a connection, something less fleeting than a one-night stand.

He draws his arm around her waist and yanks her flush against him, smiling with blessed relief when his body doesn't revolt. He buries his face in the curve of her neck and inhales with force. The scent of her is tantalizing, rippling through him with warmth.

"What are you doing?"

"You smell good." His throat vibrates with a groan, and his mouth coasts up her neck to skim the shell of her ear. *Touch me*, he wants to beg. "Why are you here?" he whispers instead.

She's immobile, rigid in his arms. But she's not pushing him away. He kisses the skin below her ear, the contact whisper light, and her body goes pliant. Then her hands are on him, fingers burying in his hair, and he wants to shout with triumph. He can feel. He can savor. Her mouth is on his skin, and he trembles at the sensation, nerve endings firing. She peppers him with kisses, and he treasures each one. His cheek, his collarbone, nipping and biting, and arousal shoots to his center. He wants to bellow with pleasure, such a rare and precious gift for him, as his teeth graze her neck. This woman is a stranger to him. She could very well be the one who turns him in to be put away for life. But right now, she's his everything. She's set him on fucking fire. His fingers slip under her shirt, eager to explore.

"Oh, no, you don't." She pushes at his chest. "I've heard about you."

Her words are a bucket of ice water on his head. He backs up, shaking off the fog of arousal and awe. "What do you mean?"

"Your girlfriend came by," Sophie says, chest heaving, her face flushed with arousal. He hopes it's arousal. Though her eyes are bright with ire. "Faye. Lovely woman."

"She's not my girlfriend."

"That's not the impression she gave us."

He runs a hand over his head. Faye is the last person he wants to talk about. "She isn't my anything. She's . . . was . . . a thing. But you . . ." He looks her up and down, a grin spreading, the alcohol distracting him. "Truck's got a nice back seat."

"You've got to be kidding me." She rolls her eyes with flair. "Get in the truck. The *front* seat."

He laughs, shaking his head as he settles in the passenger seat. Sophie goes to her car first. He assumes to get her purse or something. But she gets into his truck carrying a holstered pistol.

Blood empties from his head. "You plan on shooting me?" He told her he wasn't going to run.

She looks appalled. "Of course not. I can't leave it overnight in my car."

He stares at the weapon, recalling the feel of cold metal on his palm once a long time ago. He swore he'd never touch another gun.

"It's loaded, but I'm licensed. After what you told me, I wanted you to know."

She assumes he isn't comfortable around guns.

"I'm cool. I won't freak out on you." But he doesn't like them.

Sophie tucks the pistol under her seat and presses the ignition button. "Buckle up."

He leans his head against the window. "Where are you taking me?"

"Home."

"But the warrant—"

"I'm not dragging you in for a traffic ticket."

"Not that one."

She glances at him, a frown marring her smooth forehead. "I don't know what you're talking about."

"The one—" He abruptly stops before he incriminates himself.

"What?"

"Never mind."

They sit in silence for a few miles as he runs through the sequence of events the night Dwight died over and over again. Tracking his father down. Confronting him in his hotel room. Their fight. His father knocking him over the head with a trash bin. Sprinting down ten flights of stairs. Chasing him across town. Running lights, speeding, and driving recklessly. Then a big blank hole in his head until flashes of memory. Climbing down the ravine. His father unconscious in his car. Wrapping the seat belt around his neck, suffocating him. Then he's back in his truck staring at his bloody, cut-up hands. Why isn't there a warrant?

Sophie glances at him. Then glances at him again, pulling him out of the past.

He shifts uneasily in the seat. "What?"

"Back there in the parking lot . . ."

He interrupts with a sigh. "Sorry about that." He wants to blame the alcohol for lowering his inhibitions, but he'd be lying. He wanted to touch her, and for a moment there when she reciprocated, he felt a spark. But he should have asked her first.

"It's all right. Unexpected, but not . . ." She shakes her head.

He looks at her curiously. "Not what?"

"Never mind."

"Not what, Sophie?" He leans toward her, liking the feel of her name on his tongue much better than Zea.

"It was not bad," she says, her gaze forward. She's clearly uncomfortable with her reaction to him.

He stares at her. "So it wasn't just me. You felt something, too."

"You don't have to be so blunt about it." She's quiet for a moment. "Yes, I felt something." Pause. "Something good. I like you, Lucas."

Stunned, he stares at her. Then he smiles ridiculously. Alcohol is making him loopy. "You like me."

She glares at him. "Wipe that smug look off your face. We didn't even kiss. Dammit, Lucas." She smacks the steering wheel several times. "You've put me in a tough spot. And don't ask me to explain," she quickly adds, shaking a finger at him.

His grin easing, he frowns, wondering what she means.

"It wasn't supposed to go this way. I'm so screwed."

He starts to ask her why when she turns into the Dusty Pantry's parking lot and abruptly stops. A van is parked at the base of the staircase to the second-floor apartments, its motor running. His gaze narrows on the two guys waiting inside the van. A guy with a scruffy beard sits behind the wheel, and another guy, lanky with boy-band hair, gets out of the vehicle at the sight of Shiloh rushing down the stairs.

"Finn!" she squeals and launches into the guy's arms.

A growl emanates from Lucas's throat.

Sophie parks the truck. "Do you know them?"

"Some guy she met online." And by the looks of him, he's much older than the nineteen years he told Shiloh he is.

Knew it. Lucas exits the truck before he processes what he's doing. He strides over to the trio. "Where do you think you're going?"

Shiloh looks at him, startled. "Lucas!"

Finn lowers Shiloh and tucks her behind him. He extends a hand toward Lucas. "Hey, man. Thanks for taking care of my Shy Girl."

"She isn't your girl, and you're not taking her." He pushes Finn aside to get to Shiloh, stunned at how afraid he is for her but too livid to process it in real time. Doesn't she realize the risk she's taking running off with a guy she's never met in person? A guy much older than her?

Shiloh retreats from Lucas, backing up toward the van. "You can't make me stay. You left me."

"I'm back, and yes I can make you stay." He reaches for her wrist.

Finn shoves him back as Shiloh yells. "You can't tell me what to do. You're not my dad."

"Listen, I know I said you could leave anytime, but you don't know this guy. You have no idea what you're getting yourself into. He could be worse than Ellis. Or what about those assholes from the other night? Have you forgotten what Bob and Barton wanted to do with you?" Fear unlike anything he's felt fuels his words. And for a second there, it's not Shiloh he sees. It's Lily. It's not Shiloh he's talking about, but Lily.

"Lucas."

He registers Sophie's voice, but he doesn't react.

Shiloh's face has gone sickly pale at the mention of the men who attacked her.

Finn flips him off. "Fuck you, man."

Lucas points a finger at him. "You, shut up."

"Lucas," Sophie says louder.

Finn must have seen something in Lucas's expression warning him to back off. He shows his hands. "Hey, man, we're cool."

"Finn, get in the van," Shiloh yells, splitting her wide-eyed gaze between Lucas and Sophie, who's now beside him. "You're with her?" Betrayal slackens her mouth in disbelief. "How could you?"

"Gotta jam, dude," says the guy behind the wheel. "I don't want to miss Mulvey."

"Do not get in that van, Shiloh," he orders, scared for her.

"Lucas." This time Sophie speaks his name gently and cautiously touches his arm.

He flinches, but she shakes her head in warning.

"Give me the keys." He'll follow them across the state if he must.

Sophie shakes her head. "You're drunk."

"I can't let her go."

"You can't force her to stay either."

He knows she's right. He could face charges of unlawful confinement. He has no legal say over her. But it doesn't diminish his fear or discount his worry. It doesn't change his mind on the matter either.

"Shiloh, don't," he pleads. He won't be able to keep her safe. If anything happens to her, if Finn does anything to her, or if Ellis catches up to her, it will be his fault. He was the one who left her. He abandoned her, just like he had Lily. He broke her trust when he left.

Shiloh settles into the van's middle seat, her gaze forward, her mouth a firm line of resolve. With a wary glance at Lucas, Finn shuts the side door. Lucas and Sophie watch them leave in a cloud of desert dust.

"Do you know where he's taking her?" she asks.

"Holly-fucking-wood."

"Do you have his address or phone number?"

He shakes his head and holds out his hand. "If you're not taking me in, we're done. Give me my keys."

She stares him down.

"I'm not going to drive. I'm going to bed." To sleep off the alcohol so he can go after her in the morning.

She drops his keys in his palm, and he stomps up the stairs. It isn't until he reaches his door that he's aware she followed him up to his apartment.

30

Beck guns the van, and Shiloh watches Lucas out the back window. When she can no longer see him, she turns forward and stares straight ahead. He left her to fend for herself and brought back the very woman she's running from. Is he helping Zea bring her in to the police? Goes to show she can't trust anyone.

Except Finn. He finally came through for her.

She looks at the guy sitting beside her. He's taller and skinnier than he seemed on video. Hotter, too. His hair is finger-combed off his face. A short, scruffy beard covers his jaw, circles his mouth. His eyes glitter in the dark, reflecting the dashboard lights, the dark pupil large enough for her to drown in. She's been crushing hard on him for months, and he's finally here.

Nerves quiver in her stomach. They have a lot to talk about, but she kind of wants to know what it would be like to kiss him.

He throws his arm over the seat back, turning to look out the rear window, which brings him closer to her. She can smell his cologne, and butterflies tickle her stomach. His black shirt with the name of a band she's never heard of stretches tight across his torso. "Shit, that guy was whacked."

Then he shifts, pulling up a leg so that he fully faces her. He grins, teeth flashing, eyes crinkling in the corners like candy wrappers until his mouth softens into a bemused smile. Those glittery eyes move over her, soaking her in from head to toe.

"Shy Girl, in the flesh." Exactly what she was thinking about him.

She smiles and dips her chin, feeling shy. She pokes his thigh. "Hi."

He laughs and taps her nose. "You're cute." He cocks his head. "You look younger than I thought."

Dread swells. She fears he'll discover the truth before they've left the city limits. "It's the dark." She picks at an invisible speck of dirt on her jeans.

"Must be," he murmurs. His hand cups her jaw, coaxing her face up. His palm is warm on her skin, his fingertips calloused from playing his instrument. His thumb caresses the swell of her cheek. "Still fucking gorgeous."

Her heart thuds at the compliment, but before she can fully appreciate his words, he's on her. His lips land on hers, his tongue invading her mouth, trapping a gasp in her throat. The coarse bristles of his beard scratch her chin, a sensation she doesn't enjoy. It reminds her of Ellis.

His fingers touch her jaw, skim down her neck, and graze her breast. Alarm sends her butterflies into a frenzy. She pushes his shoulders.

"What?" He lifts his head with a lazy half smile, the same one that made her heart thump with anticipation when they'd videochat. Tonight she only feels doubt and confusion and nerves. One minute she has a job and a place to sleep. Next minute Lucas bails, and she's running before Ellis can catch up to her. Everything's happening too fast.

Her gaze slides to the back of Beck's head. "Not here."

"Ah. My bad. I got carried away."

He's under the impression she wants privacy when she's nervous and inexperienced.

"You just smell so good." He buries his face in her neck and sucks on her skin.

She smells like Lucas's sandalwood soap. And she might be fifteen, but Finn's not going to give her a hickey. She pushes him away, and he chuckles, shifting so that he faces front. He drapes his arm over her shoulders and pulls her into his side. His nearness makes her uneasy, but she doesn't move or he'll think she's being difficult. Then he won't let her live at his place.

"Beck," Finn says to the driver. "Shiloh. Shiloh, Beck. This guy"—he slaps Beck's shoulder—"is the best front singer you'll ever hear. The dude's got pipes."

Beck catches her gaze in the rearview mirror. Just around his eyes alone, he looks older than Finn. "Nice to finally meet you. Finn hasn't shut up about you."

"Hi," is all she can manage. She didn't realize she'd be so out of her element. These guys are way out of her league. And she almost, almost asks Beck to pull over and let her out. But she needs to put as many miles between her and Ellis as she can.

Beck lights a joint and takes a hit. He passes it to Finn, who inhales deeply, holding in the smoke for a couple of beats before exhaling long and steadily. He holds it out for Shiloh. She shakes her head. The smell makes her ill and reminds her of Ellis. He owns a vape and smoke shop and always smells like weed.

"Suit yourself," Finn says, taking another hit.

They settle in for the drive back to Hollywood. Beck asks Shiloh a few questions about why she left New Mexico. She doesn't go into the messy business of Ellis and her mom, and Finn sums it up with a "Her home was shit, dude. Drop it." For the rest of the trip, Shiloh is pretty quiet, listening while Finn and Beck hash out their favorite gigs as they finish the joint and light another. She thinks of Lucas, disappointed and sad he betrayed her, missing the safety she felt being with him, however fleeting. And for a heartbeat, she worries Ivy and Lucas will report her for stealing. But that thought doesn't stick around for long because by the time they reach the strip, Shiloh is as relaxed as a wet noodle from secondhand smoke and can't think much about anything. Beck parks in a loading zone in front of single windowless building painted in matte black. Band posters cover the front. Behind a roped off section, people line up, angling to get inside.

She grabs his wrist when he throws open the van's side door. "I thought we were going to your apartment."

"Later, Shy. We want to catch Mulvey's last set."

She bites her lip. She won't be able to get in.

He tugs her with him when he gets out. "You're gonna love them."

Despite the line curving around the building, Finn pulls her along as he and Beck walk to the front where two burly bouncers watch the door.

Beck tosses one of the guys his keys.

The guy catches them and throws them right back. "I'm not a valet."

Beck laughs. "Find me if you need me to move it."

"Nah, I'll just call a tow truck."

Shiloh's eyes widen, and Finn squeezes her hand. "He's kidding. Aldo's one of our biggest fans. Beck and him kick the shit like this all the time."

Her mouth opens on a silent oh as Finn leads her inside.

"Whoa, there." Aldo grasps her shoulder. "ID please."

"She's cool, man." Aldo's thick eyebrow arches, and Finn sighs. "She's with us."

"Still, ID." Aldo holds out his hand.

Finn nudges her backpack. "Come on, show him. Band's about to go on." He sounds impatient.

The only ID Shiloh has on her is her high school ID. She lifts her chin. "I'm eighteen."

Noticing they didn't follow him inside, Beck returns. "What's the holdup?"

"Shy got carded."

"Get on with it and let's go," says Beck.

Aldo crosses his arms over a heavily muscled chest. His bicep bulges when he points a finger at the line. "They look eighteen. You, sweetheart, do not. No ID, no admittance."

Beck takes a good look at her for the first time. "How old did you say you are?"

"Eighteen." But even to her, her voice sounds unconvincing.

"I call bullshit."

Finn punches Beck's shoulder. "Shut up." He faces Shiloh. "Give him your ID, and let's go."

"I don't have it."

"What?"

"I don't have it. I lost it."

"Bullshit." Beck coughs into his fist.

Finn tilts his head, studying her. Doubt shadows his expression. "You *are* eighteen, right?"

All three—Aldo, Beck, and Finn—tower over her. They stare at her, their glares intimidating, and she loses her nerve. She shakes her head.

"How old are you?" Finn asks.

"Fifteen," she whispers, and Finn has to ask her to repeat her age because he couldn't hear her over the noise. The band has started to play. "Fifteen," she yells.

"Fuck." Beck pivots only to turn back. "You can't tap that," he tells Finn.

"No shit," Finn says, his eyes on her. His face slackens with betrayal. "You told me you were eighteen."

"Yeah, well, you said you were nineteen."

Beck barks with laughter. "He told you that?" He laughs again. "He's fucking twenty-five. Smooth, dude."

Shiloh's jaw comes unhinged at the ten-year age gap.

Beck knocks the back of his hand against Finn's chest. "Come on, dude." He disappears into the dark mouth of the Grotto.

Finn holds up both hands and backs up inside with a slow shake of his head.

"Where are you going?" she asks with mounting panic.

"Sorry, Shy Girl. I can't be with you." He turns around and disappears inside.

Shiloh stands there in a daze. Did he dump her?

"Want me to call your mommy to come get you?"

Taken aback, Shiloh glares at Aldo. "Fuck you."

He throws his head back with a burst of laughter. Then he drags his stool over and pats the seat. "The band's only playing for another hour. The guys won't be long. You can wait here with me."

As if he's her babysitter.

No, thank you.

Shiloh doesn't give him the courtesy of a reply. Arms crossed tightly over her chest, she turns in a circle. It was foolish to call Finn and come here. Now what's she supposed to do? Where can she go? Girls in line laugh at her. The bouncer calls her over again. He's laughing, too. Her throat starts to close up. She feels like she can't breathe. Everyone's pointing and laughing and gawking, and she has nowhere to go. Panicking, she slips around the building to hide.

31

Lucas wakes up with the mother of hangovers. He slowly eases from bed. Feet on the floor, he drops his face in his hands and leans over, waiting for his stomach to settle, and not just from the alcohol. He's sick with nerves, terrified for Shiloh. He blacked out after Lily ran away, and he blacked out before he chased his father in his truck. But this time he remembers everything. Not even the laughable number of shots he tossed back will let him forget he lost Shiloh.

He needs to find her and ensure she's safe.

Someone bangs on the door, and his heart lurches into his throat. He jackknifes from bed, glancing at the clock. Six a.m. Why is he still here and not behind bars?

Memories from the previous night light up. There's a warrant for his arrest, but not for what he thought, which doesn't make sense to him. Neither does Zea. Sophie, rather, or whatever her name is. Who is she?

More banging. "I know you're in there, Lucas. Open up, or I'll bust this door down."

Sophie. Shit.

He looks down at his naked body and wonders if he undressed in front of her. There's a glass of water on his nightstand and two aspirin. He'd never have left those there for himself. Pushing off the bed, he pops the pills and downs the water. The room spins, and he stops short of hurling when he takes several deep breaths. He pulls on athletic shorts and pushes his arms into a shirt on his way to the door.

"Lucas!"

He jerks it open, and she jumps at the suddenness of it. "You never answered my question last night."

She blinks. "Good morning to you, too." She moves past him into the apartment.

He shuts the door. "Two questions, actually."

"Here, for you." She gives him a coffee in a disposable cup. She sips from her own.

"Where'd you get these?" They left her car at the tavern, and the keys to his truck are on the counter, so she didn't use it to go get coffee.

"Toya made them for us." Their neighbor next door to Sophie and behind Ivy's apartment. "Her espresso machine is badass. Did you know she's a retired barista?"

"Are you always in your neighbors' business?" He drinks the coffee, and his stomach turns over. He sets it aside.

"You're a bucket of sunshine in the morning. Do you know where Finn lives? I asked you last night, but I'm not sure if you remember."

"Uh-uh." He wags a finger in her face. "Who sent you, and why are you here?"

"I need a ride to my car."

"You know that's not what I'm asking."

Her mouth flatlines. "I told you. Don't ask me to explain. I'm already in enough trouble."

He grinds his teeth. What is she hiding? Who's she protecting?

His eyes narrow, and she holds her gaze, even lifts her chin. He swears. He doesn't have time for her games. Shiloh is out there, possibly alone and hurt. He made a mistake when he didn't go after Lily. His sister spent her life running from Ryder Jensen. He tried to kill her. What if Ellis is Shiloh's Ryder? What if Finn is? Shiloh could be just one of many underage girls he preys on through that half-baked app.

He isn't going to make that mistake again. He's going after her.

"Answer me this," he says pointedly to Sophie. "Do I need to worry about you calling the cops on me?"

191

"Depends on what you have planned."

"I'm going to find Shiloh, then I'm bringing her here." He heads for the bathroom.

"You can't force—"

He shuts the door in her face.

After a quick shower, he towels off and returns to his room. He pulls on jeans and a shirt and goes to retrieve his boots when he notices the envelope of cash is missing. "Fuck." He shoves on his boots as he jerks open the dresser drawer where his laptop should be. "Fuck, fuck, fuck." He slams the drawer and strides into Shiloh's room. The bed is a mess, the sheets balled at the foot of the bed, the pillow on the floor. He tears off the sheet and shakes it out. Nothing. "Fuck!"

Sophie appears in the doorway. "What's wrong?"

"She took it." He looks under the mattress, livid not because she stole from him. Rather, with the cash and laptop, she could be anywhere now. She only needed Finn for a ride. She's young, naive, vulnerable, and alone in a big city. And he has no way to reach her. No way to help her.

"What did she take?" Sophie asks.

"My laptop." He rakes fingers through his hair, looking up at the ceiling. "My cash. She took everything."

"How much?"

"Five grand."

"You need to report her."

He swings around to face her. "Are you kidding me?"

"It's theft, Lucas. Enough that it's a felony."

"Do you remember anything of what I told you last night?" he asks. She can haul him to jail, but he'll never go out of his way to contact the police, especially on Shiloh. They'll send her to juvenile detention. He'd never expose her to what happened to him.

"I'm surprised you do."

He scowls and her eyes soften.

"I'm sorry for what happened to you. Those guys should have been tried and convicted. But—"

"I don't need your pity," he interrupts. He swipes up his keys and wallet and heads for the door.

"I'm coming with you." She rushes after him. They get in his truck, and he guns it for the highway.

"I'm contacting the police if you won't. We need to find out if she's been reported as missing," she says when they're on the road. "They'll put an APB out for her. We also need to get CPS involved."

"No." His grip tightens on the steering wheel. "Let me handle this."

"They need to be made aware that her situation back home isn't safe."

"They'll just stick her in foster care, where another jackass like Ellis will take advantage of her."

"You don't know that," Sophie argues.

"Neither do you," he snaps. "And you're not coming with me."

"Why? I have experience with runaways."

He shakes his head hard. "Did you see the way she looked at you last night? She thinks Ellis sent you to find her."

Sophie grabs the handle when Lucas speeds through a tight turn. "I didn't know that."

"Did he?"

"Send me? No."

That answers one of his questions.

"How do you intend to find her?" she asks.

"Don't know, but Lily is out there. I have to try."

"Lily?"

Shit. He's losing it. He grinds his jaw and takes a beat to regain his focus as he turns into the tavern's parking lot.

"What are you doing?"

"You said you needed a lift to your car."

"I'm going with you. The police—"

193

"There will be no police. I'm not an animal, Sophie. I'm trying to be good. But if you don't get out of my truck . . . Please. I have to do this. I have to know she's okay."

Sophie's eyes swing between his, holding his gaze until she sighs, resigned. "I wasn't hired to chase a bounty."

He focuses on what she didn't say. "Who hired you?"

She gets out of the truck and looks up the road, her expression conflicted.

"*Who* hired you?" he presses.

She meets his eyes. "Log on to your cloud account. You should be able to track Shiloh through your laptop." Then she shuts the door.

He stares at Sophie through the window. That's how she found him.

He doesn't ask how she hacked into his account or how she came by his email address in the first place. He doesn't press why she's here, only that he now knows for sure she's here because of him. But for some reason, she's become distracted with Shiloh.

He should ask what she plans to do next, but the clock is ticking.

He floors the truck for the highway.

———

Lucas coasts up and down Sunset Boulevard waiting for a ping, growing antsier by the hour. Shiloh hasn't turned on his laptop since she left California City. He's low on gas, hungry, and terrified for her. Ivy's called him twice. He didn't show up for work. Sophie is probably tracking him, too. But they can wait. Shiloh's his priority.

He refreshes the map on his phone again, and like magic, a laptop icon appears as if it's been there all along.

Air bursts from his lungs with his relief.

He enlarges the map. She's about a mile from him. "Thank Christ." He tosses the phone onto the seat beside him and makes a U-turn toward Shiloh.

The building he arrives at a few minutes later is nothing to shout about from its slate-gray, windowless exterior. The posters plastered on the front tell him it's a dance club or rock grotto, the latter more likely given Finn's in a band. She's not out front, so he assumes she's inside, and turns into the driveway adjacent to the building to park in back.

He takes a few breaths, preparing what to say after last night's confrontation, promising himself he'll assess the situation first before he jumps to conclusions. If she's not in distress, and she doesn't want to stay with him, he'll leave. But if Finn is keeping her against her will . . . If he's laid a hand on her . . . Memories of his father holding Lily at gunpoint clash with his imaginings of Ryder strangling her, which contort into Bob and Barton attacking Shiloh and the fear on her face when she thought Ellis sent Sophie for her. Lucas grinds his jaw, his hands squeezing the steering wheel.

He eases his truck around the corner of the building and slams the brakes. Seated with her back to the wall, his laptop in her lap, is Shiloh. He gapes at her, almost disbelieving she's here. That it was this easy to find her. She's alive and she's whole. The exact thoughts that raced through his mind when Olivia had left the message that she and Josh found Lily.

Shiloh looks up, her eyes huge. "What are you doing here?"

"Looking for you." His voice is strained through a throat tight with emotion. Relief and something else. Regret? Could he have found Lily this easily if he'd tried?

"How'd you . . . ?" Her gaze drops to the laptop. "Oh." She frowns. "But I just turned it on."

"I arrived several hours ago. I've been driving around." He puts the truck in park and gets out, his movements slow so he doesn't spook her. He was drunk last night and a bit out of his mind when she last saw him. "I was worried about you. I wanted to check you were safe, that Finn—" He glances around. "Where is he?"

Shiloh doesn't answer. She stares at him for one beat. Two. She puts the laptop aside and launches at him. He stumbles back against the truck. Her hug is fierce and unexpected. More surprising, he doesn't flinch. That's the second person with whom he's been able to tolerate physical contact without mentally preparing himself beforehand, and he briefly speculates whether things are changing in him because he finally confessed his assault. His secret is out in the open. He talked it out. Or in his case with Sophie, he yelled it. It isn't a cure, but it's a start. And he wonders if it'll get easier the more he shares, and the more he lets people in. Because his assault isn't his only secret.

"I'm so glad you're here." Shiloh bursts into tears, pulling him back into the moment.

Lucas can't remember the last time he held Lily when she cried. But he holds on to Shiloh, needing the reassurance that she's okay as much as she does. He pats her back and lets her soak his shirt. He wants to believe he's making up for when he abandoned Lily when she needed him. But that isn't entirely true. Finding Shiloh, and her relief that he did, shows him he can be a good guy. He made the right decision by coming here. It's also helped him realize he doesn't just want the life he started to build in California City and to feel a connection to others. He doesn't just want a second chance with his sisters, with Shiloh. With life. He wants to fight for it. He wants to be in control of who he is.

But he's let his past—the assault, his suicide attempt, his apathy—define him for so long, he just doesn't know where to start.

Shiloh's sobs recede, and she steps back, turning her face in embarrassment as she wipes off her tears and snot. Then she glowers at him. "You left me."

Alone and unprotected, the way she was in the encampment.

"I know. I realize that now. I'm sorry."

"I was so mad you. You promised I could stay with you."

"I know. If I could change what I did, I would. But I'm here now."

Her mouth pinches, and she glances away before turning back to stare at the center of his chest. "You were right. Finn's a dick." Her rib cage widens, and nostrils flare with a sharp, deep inhale.

He frowns, leaning down to catch her eyes. "Shiloh, where is he?"

"Home, I guess."

"You guess?" he repeats, incredulous.

"He and Beck were here last night to watch a band; then they took off."

"He left without you?" She nods. "How long have you been here?"

She chews her lip. "Since last night."

"Last night?" His blood pressure spikes. "You slept here, in the parking lot?"

"I didn't sleep." Her eyes shift left and right to encompass the lot. She was too scared to fall asleep.

Lucas can't believe Finn abandoned a fifteen-year-old girl, when it occurs to him that might be why he did. "How old is he?"

She pulls at her sweatshirt. She can't look at him.

He dips his head again to see her face. "Shiloh?"

She huffs and looks past him. "Twenty-five."

"Twenty-*what*?"

She meets his gaze. Fire burns behind her eyes. "You heard me, now shut up. I made a mistake. I never should have come."

"Why are you still here, then? You took my cash. You could have gotten a hotel."

"I'm fifteen, remember?" Underage, she wouldn't have many options if she tried to book a room. None that were suitable for an unaccompanied minor.

"You could have used the money to get a cab anywhere you wanted to go. You have enough."

She tugs the drawstring in her hoodie and visibly swallows. He knows guilt when he sees it. "You couldn't spend it."

"Yours or Ivy's."

He balks. "Where'd you get her money?"

Her gaze skirts away. "I stole more from Ivy's safe."

"Jesus, Shiloh." Though he's got to hand it to her. She is resourceful. He laughs. He can't help it. He's too relieved he found her to care what she took.

"It's not funny." She grimaces.

"No, it's not. And you're going to return it." Before Ivy notices it's missing. She'll report it.

"Good, because I don't want it." She buries her fists into her kangaroo pocket. She squints up at him against the sun that's moved behind his head. "So what happens now?"

"Now we get something to eat." He hasn't eaten all day, and she must be hungry, too.

"Then what?"

"That's up to you."

32

"Here you go, one All American Burger and fries." The waitress deposits Shiloh's order in front of her. Lucas sits in the booth across from her at the Bob's Big Boy in Burbank slathering extra ketchup onto his bacon cheeseburger.

"Anything else I can get you?"

Lucas catches Shiloh's eye, and she shakes her head.

"We're good," he says.

"Enjoy, then." The waitress leaves for another table.

"Dig in." Lucas lifts his burger and takes an enormous bite.

Shiloh peeks under the bun on hers at the dressing inside. The burger is huge. It smells amazing. The chocolate shake she's been drinking is the best one she's tasted. She's so relieved Lucas came for her that she can't describe her feelings, and she's grateful he brought her here to eat. But she's suddenly not hungry.

Her backpack rests beside her, weighed down by a stolen laptop, over $5,000 in cash, and her guilt. She shouldn't have trusted Finn when she knew he was unreliable. But she was desperate to get to Hollywood. Now that she's here and realizes how sorely unprepared she was, she just wants to leave. She feels terrible that she repeatedly stole from Ivy when the woman hasn't been anything but nice to her. And it was wrong of her to take Lucas's cash and laptop. She wants to return to California City with him, but what's to stop him from taking off again? Without a guardian, she runs the risk of being sent home or getting lost within the system. Or worse, getting kidnapped and trafficked. Someone eventually will turn her in or sell her off.

But most of all, she misses her mom.

She wishes she could go home, but she doesn't see how, not with Ellis around.

Lucas chews a bite and looks at her over his half-eaten burger. "Aren't you going to eat?"

She picks up a fry and nibbles on the end. It tastes bland without ketchup, and she doesn't feel like reaching across the table for the bottle. She drops the fry on the plate.

Lucas frowns. "What's wrong? Food not good?"

"It's okay." Delicious, she'd bet. It's been years since she had a diner burger. She was five when her mom took her for a late lunch after visiting a museum. They used to spend time together before she got into drugs. Then Ellis came along, and they didn't do anything together at all.

"How was the shake?"

The best. She almost finished it. "Fine."

"The burger? Have you tried it yet?"

She shakes her head.

"Want ketchup with those fries?" He grabs the bottle.

"No, thanks." Her shoulders droop.

Lucas puts down his burger and wipes his hands with a paper napkin. He crumples the napkin, tossing it aside, and wipes his hands on his jeans, glancing around and looking uncomfortable. Then he clears his throat and leans his arms on the table. "Talk to me. What gives?"

"Nothing." She mopes. She can tell it was difficult for him to ask and that he doesn't really want to talk. She's not in the mood either.

"Bullshit."

"Stop bugging me," she says, annoyed.

"Shiloh—"

She stares at her plate. "I don't want to talk." She's too embarrassed, making one naive decision after another ever since she left home.

"Something is obviously bothering—"

She lifts her head. "Why'd you leave?"

As soon as she says it, she realizes that's what bothers her most. Almost as much as the fact that she can't return home. She really thought Lucas was different from the other men she's met. He promised he'd help her. He said she could stay with him if she wanted. Then he took off.

Lucas lets out a long sigh, leaning away from the table. He presses his back into the seat back and stares out the window. Down the road is Warner Bros. Studio. They drove past on the way here and Shiloh told him that's the studio producing the *Tabby's Squirrel* movie. Lucas went still. After that, he got very quiet until they arrived here and sat down.

But he turns to her now, his expression resigned. "I thought Sophie was after me."

She frowns. "Sophie? You mean Zea?"

He nods. "You were right. Her real name is Sophie Renau."

"She's here for you?"

He frowns, his gaze turning inward. "Apparently not."

Her heart starts beating very fast. "Then she's after me. Ellis sent her."

"No."

"She tell you that?" She doesn't know whether to believe him.

"Yes. Bounty hunters chase criminals with warrants, not fifteen-year-old runaways. Unless you got a warrant?" He gives her a look.

Her eyes widen. She shakes her head hard. She doesn't. But he does; otherwise, he wouldn't have left her. She remembers how he reacted when she told him Sophie was a bounty hunter, how wild his eyes were.

"Why would a bounty hunter be after you? What did you do?" There is something hard and untamed about Lucas, but she can't imagine him murdering someone. At least not intentionally or unless they deserved it. She thinks of what he did to Bob and Barton.

Lucas drags his hands down his face. They drop into his lap. His lips purse, and it looks like he's biting the inside of his mouth before his mouth pops open. He exhales heavily. "I've done a lot of things."

Her eyes grow large. "Like what?" she asks, intrigued. If she was smarter, she'd be scared, but if he was going to hurt her, he would have done so already. He's had plenty of opportunities.

He shakes his head.

"Come on, tell me." When he doesn't, she pouts. "Then tell me why you thought Sophie was after you."

"That's the one thing we're not talking about."

"Well . . ." She chews her lip, thinking. If she can get him talking, she won't have to talk about herself. Her life is too depressing, and she finds his much more interesting. He's a mystery to her. And if she's going to live at his place, that is, if she's still welcome, she wants to know more about him. "Sophie's a bounty hunter. If you thought she was after you, that means you have a warrant. But since she isn't, you don't?"

"Not for what I thought."

"I don't understand."

"Neither do I." The lines between his brows deepen. "Guess things didn't happen as I remember them."

"Meaning?"

He slowly shakes his head. His elbow on the table, he turns toward the window again, his fingers absently tapping his mouth. Her gaze snags on the rigid scar under his tattoo. She loves the intricate vine. One day she'll get her own tattoo. But it's the scar that compels her to ask, "What happened?" His eyes swing to her, and she juts her chin at the scar. "Your arm? Why'd you do it?"

He lowers his arm to the table and rubs a hand over the tattoo. "I was in a bad spot."

Like her friend Jace. He didn't see any escape from his mom's abuse until he decided he wouldn't let what she said define him. That he was better than how she saw him. Every day is still a battle, but so far he's managed to overcome his struggles. She owes him a phone call. She

202

told him she'd reach out when she made it to Hollywood. He must be worried.

She picks up another fry only to stop when it's halfway to her mouth, registering that Lucas is talking.

"I was arrested when I was sixteen while trying to buy beer. My friend brought a gun. I didn't know he had it, but when he pulled it out, I grabbed it from him, thinking he was going to shoot someone, and it went off. I almost killed the guy working there."

The fry hovers near her mouth. "Holy shit."

"Long story short, I spent six months in juvie. Something . . ." He takes a beat. "Something happened while I was there. I was . . ." He swallows roughly, agitatedly rubbing his palms up and down his thighs. "I was assaulted."

Shiloh slowly puts down the fry and sits up straighter.

"When I got home, my headspace was shit. I tried to kill myself."

"Did it hurt?"

He gives her a blank stare, then a bark of emotionless laughter. "Yeah, it hurt. Like hell."

Her heartbeat slows. There's an ache in her throat. "Then what happened?"

He sighs, weary, and Shiloh notices the exhaustion pulling at his face. "My mom found me and slowed the bleeding. Then the ambulance took me to the hospital."

He stops talking, and Shiloh is quiet for a stretch, processing what he went through. She has an idea of what his recovery must have been like, having witnessed Jace's. "I'm sorry for what happened." All of it. The arrest, the attack, the suicide attempt.

"Why? It wasn't your fault."

"Yours either."

His mouth flattens, and the tension in his face bleeds out. "I'm starting to realize that." He holds her gaze for a few beats; then the corner of his mouth curves up.

Shiloh smiles back. Then she picks up her burger and crams it into her mouth, taking the biggest bite ever. Lucas watches her with a bemused smile, shaking his head. "What?" she asks, mouth full.

"Nothing. You remind me of someone."

That's the second time he's said that to her.

She puts down the burger and wipes her mouth. "Who?"

His nostrils flare. "Lily, my sister. Though I guess she goes by Jenna Mason now."

Shiloh's mouth falls open. One beat, two. Then she smacks the table. "I knew it." She points a finger at him. "Knew it, knew it, knew it."

"Shush." He bounces his hand for her to lower her voice as he looks around.

"Omigosh," she loudly whispers, clapping her cheeks. "Jenna Mason is your sister. That is sick. You have to introduce us. I want to meet her. I have so many questions."

Lucas is shaking his head, and he looks kind of sad.

Her hands flop into her lap. "What?" Then she remembers the article she read, the one she told him about. Jenna Mason hasn't seen her brother since she ran away fourteen years ago. Her chest deflates. "Why haven't you called her? It's been so long. Don't you want to see her?"

"Every day." He absently scratches a fingernail on the table.

"Then call her."

"I can't."

"Can't or won't?"

He scowls at her.

"You're scared."

"By all means, beat around the bush. Subtlety is not one of your strong suits."

She shrugs. "When I want something, I go for it." And right now she wants to talk about his sister.

"I envy that about you." He pulls out his wallet, inching toward the seat edge, but Shiloh isn't ready to go. This is Jenna Mason they're talking about, her idol. And she senses something terrible must have happened between them. But the article she read left her with the impression Jenna misses her brother, too.

"I'm scared," she admits. Lucas stops fiddling with his wallet and looks up at her. "I'm scared to go home. I know I need to. Eventually. It really hurt when my mom didn't believe me, but it doesn't mean I never want to see her again."

Lucas leaves the wallet on the table and leans back. His face slackens and his mouth parts. His shoulders drop, and his hands fall listlessly into his lap, and what Shiloh witnesses is a man who's been carrying a lifetime of regret and guilt and shame finally set down his burden at his feet. "I was there the night my sister ran away. I saw everything. My dad, the gun, Wes. I was living in the apartment above my parents' garage, and Lily was shouting for me to come help. It was foggy. I knew she couldn't see me, but I was already there. Watching. I didn't help her."

"Why not?"

He shrugs. "Don't know. No . . . I do. I've been telling myself I didn't care. I was still hating on myself and the world, you know, because of juvie. But really, I was scared."

He visibly swallows, and she can tell it was difficult for him to admit. But it still doesn't explain why he hasn't reached out to her. Unless . . .

"You're still afraid."

His eyes snap to hers.

"Of Jenna. Lily to you. You're afraid of what she'll say if she finds out you were there." His mouth pulls into a taut line. "You have to tell her, and you have to apologize."

"Uh-uh." He shakes his head hard. "Won't change anything." She suspects he thinks the truth will make things worse between them. But it might ease his guilt.

"You don't know that."

He doesn't say anything.

"I hate that my mom didn't believe me about Ellis. But I miss her, and I'd forgive her in a heartbeat if she apologized."

"Thanks for the pep talk, Dr. Bloom." Shiloh snorts, and his face sobers. "This is different. She lived a life on the run because of me. I didn't stop her or go after her. She won't forgive me," he admits in a low voice.

"Only one way to find out." She waits for him to look at her before her smile explodes. Her chest inflates with excitement.

"What?" he asks, wary.

"Tomorrow's Saturday. Jenna will be signing at the Grove." He frowns, and she rolls her eyes. "You know, *Tabby's Squirrel*. Big promo event before the movie release. Jenna's here in LA. It's going to be huge."

"Oh, hell no."

She pulls her trump card. "You promised what we did next would be up to me."

He glowers. "That's blackmail."

And she isn't ashamed one bit. She grins uncontrollably. She's going to meet Jenna.

33

Lucas sits alone in a hotel room, staring at the minibar. He wants to open it and power his way through the shot-size bottles. Seven should do. Enough to make him feel numb so he stops stressing over tomorrow. But he worries about Shiloh in the adjoining room. She's his responsibility, at least until they get where she wants to go. And he'll only add to her unease if he's hungover tomorrow and reeks of alcohol.

Sitting on the bed, knee jiggling, he roughly pulls at his fingers to distract him from the monster clawing up his throat, tempting him. *What's one drink?* He hears the TV in the next room. From the sound of it, Shiloh's flipping through channels. Where he's nervous and agitated, she's excited. She could barely contain herself in the car when he reluctantly agreed to go tomorrow. He took her to Target for clothes so she could wear something other than that sweatshirt that could probably walk on its own by now. She picked four outfits; she couldn't decide. Lucas bought them all. And through the entire shopping spree, she talked endlessly of Lily and her own plans to study video animation.

Shiloh's right, though, about Lily. He wants to apologize, has known the day would come when he'd have to summon the courage to do so. Olivia once told him she wished the three of them could be close like they were as kids, before their family imploded. That won't happen unless he reconciles his guilt. Tomorrow's event is that opportunity.

And he's nervous as hell about it.

How does he start? What does he say? Will Lily even want to talk with him? Will she ever want to see him again once she knows the truth?

Why is he so damn thirsty?

He lurches for the fridge door, only to throw himself back on the bed. "Fuck." He shovels his hair. His phone buzzes. He lunges across the bed for the distraction. "Hello?"

"Lucas, it's Ivy. I've been trying to reach you all day."

He knows. He's seen her calls come in. He left a message this morning that he had family business to take care of and wouldn't be able to open the market for her. Little had he known then how true his excuse would be.

"I'm here. Don't know when I'll be back, though." That depends on the kid in the next room.

"Zea told me about Shiloh. I've been worried. Did you find her?"

Damn Sophie. He swears under his breath. He hadn't mentioned Shiloh for that exact reason. He didn't want her to worry. But apparently Sophie did, and she neglected to let Ivy in on her real name.

"I found her. She's fine."

"I'm so relieved."

"Listen, Ivy." He grips the back of his neck, looking at the carpeting. "I'm not sure when we'll be back. I know I've left you in a bind—"

"It's family," she interrupts. "You take all the time you need."

"Thank you." The impulse to tell her he wants to buy the building sits on his tongue like a rider waiting for the bus. He realizes now that he never gave up on his dreams to design and build. They've just been waiting for him to go after what he wants. But he can't make promises when his future is still unknown. He has to find out about Dwight and what the police suspect. Either Sophie is wrong about her information, or his mind is messing with him.

He sighs, resigned. "We'll talk when I get back. 'Night, Ivy."

He ends the call and listens. Shiloh's room has gone eerily quiet.

Did she leave? Has Sophie found them? He's been wondering if she'd follow, but he hasn't seen or heard from her, which makes him just as nervous.

Come to think of it, maybe they should skip tomorrow's event and head back now before she gets the wrong idea about him with Shiloh. But he needs to get Shiloh's situation squared away before Sophie convinces the cops he's kidnapped her.

Shooting off the bed to check on Shiloh, he hears her adjoining door unlock and open. Then she knocks. "Lucas?"

He hurriedly unlatches and opens his door. "You okay?"

She looks up at him with big eyes. "I want to go home. My home," she clarifies.

"Now?"

"No, tomorrow, after the book event. You're not getting out of introducing me to your sister." She jabs a finger at him.

"Shiloh, I can't—" He shakes his head. He'll take her anywhere but home. "What about Ellis? You aren't safe with your mom."

"I know. That's why I want you to take me. If you're there, he won't try anything. And you can help me convince her she's better off without him."

"I don't know." He's shaking his head, having his doubts. With his background, he's the last person anyone will listen to. He's a stranger to her mom. Practically one to Shiloh. Ellis will see him as a threat. Who knows what he'll do? He could have a weapon Shiloh isn't aware of, and he might not be afraid to use it. Lucas would much rather take her straight to his place, where he knows she'll be safe, and he tells her so. They can call her mom from there.

"I have to see her in person. For once I want her to look me in the eye and choose me, not him. And I want her to promise she'll stop using. If she doesn't, then, well, I'll tell her I'm moving to California City with you. That you've given me a job, and I'll finish high school there. That is, if I'm still welcome."

Of course she is, but as with Ivy, he can't make promises. Until he straightens his own issues, he doesn't know what commitments he can make.

There's also another not so tiny issue.

"It won't work." Her mom will call the police on him if he takes in Shiloh without her permission. He's already crossing that line.

"How do we know if we don't try?"

He groans his annoyance. He doesn't.

"You know I'm right."

He knocks his forehead against the door. "Yes, I do." They won't know what her mom will say or do unless they try. And Shiloh's well-being is worth that try. The same goes with Lily. He can't control how she'll react when he confesses what he did. But he can no longer put off making that first step. He has to try, even at the risk she'll never want to see him again.

As for him and Shiloh, he already knows her mother will never allow her to live with him, not with his record and lack of parenting experience. Not that Harmony's one to talk. But he might be able to convince one of his sisters to look after her. Because he can't leave her in New Mexico where Ellis has access to her.

"All right. We'll go see Lily tomorrow; then I'll take you home."

34

Lily's book signing is outside at the Grove, an upscale shopping plaza, and the turnout is insane. People mill about, waiting for a chance to meet the author Jenna Mason.

Lily.

His baby sister.

A stage has been set up front with two armchairs where a guy named Felix, an editor with *Comic Sonic* magazine, will interview Lily. From what he researched of the event last night, the interview will be live streamed on YouTube. Off to the side is a table stacked with books for Lily to sign afterward. Lifesize banners of her quirky characters frame the stage. Music blasts from the speakers surrounding the make-shift arena. He overheard one kid tell his mom it's the theme song to Lily's upcoming movie. Shiloh mentioned a second trailer dropped last night. She saw it while flipping through the TV in her hotel room.

Lucas takes it all in. There must be several hundred kids here, along with another few hundred parents. So many people. Laughing and shouting and singing along. How do they know the words already? Some kids are in cosplay dressed as Lily's characters. Others wave books and merchandise for her to sign. Pop Figures and stuffed animals. Lego boxes and shirts.

This is nuts.

So is his idea, he realizes, having second thoughts as he notes the number of media and security present. His idea to apologize to Lily here about ranks up there with the one that landed him in juvie all those years ago. This isn't the time or place. If he hadn't promised Shiloh she could meet her, he'd leave. He's still tempted to take off.

The afternoon sun beats down on him. Sweat drenches his forehead and pools in the curve of his lower back. He's melting, and his mouth is as dry as the desert he lives in. He hasn't had a drink in thirty-six hours, and he's feeling it. He's anxious and jittery. And he's about to see his sister for the first time in fourteen years. God willing, she'll forgive him.

Beside him, Shiloh appears just as overwhelmed. She hugs Lily's books he bought her upon their arrival that she plans to get signed. "Can we get closer?"

They need to if he wants the chance to introduce Shiloh and Lily. "Yeah, come on." He leads her toward the stage where he's seen VIPs enter backstage. The area is cordoned off with tape and manned by a burly security guard in black and a well-dressed woman with an iPad. Arms crossed over a meaty chest, the guard moves into Lucas's path as he and Shiloh approach.

"I need to get back there," Lucas says.

"Name?" The well-dressed woman taps her iPad.

He won't be on the list. "Lily . . . er, Jenna. She's my sister."

Her mouth pinches and brows lift above thick-framed glasses. "Name?"

"Lucas Carson. I'm her brother."

She scrolls down a list on her screen. "Sorry. I don't see you on here."

"She's not expecting me. Tell her I'm here." It'll probably shock the hell out of her, but what else is he to do short of leaving and reaching out to her another day? He might never get the chance again.

The security guard snorts. "You and every nut who wants a selfie with her."

The woman tucks the iPad under her arm. "Uh-huh. She's busy."

With growing irritation, Lucas scans the area behind the guard. He's hot and hates crowds. The energy's making him itch, and his body wants to twitch like an addict. "Just get my fucking sister," he snaps, his anxiety getting the better of him when he doesn't see her anywhere back there.

The security guard gets in his face. "You need to leave."

"Back off," Lucas warns at the guard encroaching on his personal space. Then he sees Olivia. Relief washes over him. "Liv," he shouts, and then again when she doesn't hear him at first, "Livy!"

Olivia glances over her shoulder, searching.

"Livy," he yells again, waving. He should have known his older sister would be here, too.

Olivia sees him, and her mouth falls open. "Lucas." She rushes over, squeezing between the guard and the petite gatekeeper, and pulls Lucas into a hug. "Oh, my god. We've been looking for you. We've been so worried. Where've you been?"

"Around," he says, hugging her back. Until this moment, he didn't realize how much he's missed her. It was wrong of him to leave her out of the blue like he did. But after the loss of Dwight, he didn't want to kill himself and chance Olivia being the one to find him. He thought he was protecting her.

She leans back and cups his face, his shoulders. Looks him over from head to toe. "I've missed you." Tears flood her eyes, and she punches him in the arm. Hard. "Fuck you for scaring me like that. You could have called. Why didn't you text me back? I thought you . . . I thought you died."

"I'm sorry." His smile is strained as his chest caves in with regret. No, she didn't. She thought he'd offed himself. He'd left so he wouldn't hurt her and ended up doing so anyway.

"We need to talk." She glares at him.

"Later, I promise." They have a lot to discuss, a lot to catch up on. But he puts a pin in that conversation. He needs to take care of Shiloh first.

"Where's Lily?" he asks. He'll introduce them, then go.

"Backstage, getting ready. Can you believe this?" She throws out her arm to encompass their surroundings.

"Pretty outrageous."

"I'm so proud of her. She's amazing, truly incredible. You're going to love her." She grabs his hand. "Josh is here. He'll be excited to see you."

"And Lily?" he asks when she motions to the guard to let him pass.

She turns back to him, and her expression turns serious. "She'll—" She stops, noticing Shiloh for the first time. "Who's this?"

"She wants to meet Lily."

"I'm Shiloh."

"Hi," Olivia says. A crease appears between her brows when she looks back at Lucas.

"Shiloh, this is my older sister, Olivia."

"You're Jenna's sister, too?" Shiloh's grin expands to epic proportion. "That's sick. I'm such a big fan. I want to be an animator just like her."

"Oh. That's . . . nice." Olivia splits her attention between him and Shiloh, cautiously curious. Lucas erratically taps his thigh. Olivia could ruin his plan in a heartbeat. He's a screwup in her eyes. They weren't on good terms when he left. The last time she saw him, he'd just returned from seeing their father. She was the closest to Dwight and had just learned he'd died in a car accident. Lucas didn't confirm he'd hastened his death with a seat belt, but she suspected he was involved.

"Do you mind if I go sit over there?" Shiloh asks him. She points at an empty seat in the first row. "They're about to start."

"Don't you want to meet her?"

"She can't now," Olivia says. "Lily's busy."

"Sure, go ahead," he says to Shiloh, frustrated it doesn't look like they'll be leaving anytime soon. "Meet me here afterward."

"Who is that?" Olivia asks when Shiloh's out of earshot.

"She was homeless. I saved her from a couple of guys trying to rape her."

Her complexion turns ruddy. "Where are her parents?"

His jaw flexes.

Her eyes widen. "Lucas, please tell me you aren't doing anything illegal," she hisses under her breath.

"It's a long story." She glares at him. "I'm handling it." He can't meet her eyes.

"Which scares the shit out of me." She grabs his wrist and drags him away from the security guard and pretty door monitor, instantly making him feel like he's ten years old again. She stops near the outskirts of the stage. A curtain blocks them from the crew, but they're still visible to the audience, and he can still see Shiloh. She whirls on him. "There's a warrant out for your arrest."

"Why do you think I ran?" he states, calmer than he's feeling.

"But to risk getting caught with an unaccompanied minor? Look around you. This is the worst place you could have come to. Why are you always doing shit that gets you into trouble?"

It isn't intentional.

He loves Olivia, but he doesn't want to get into it with her right now. With each passing second the crowd's cheers crescendo. He swears the music is getting louder. Press fill the back rows. Cameras are everywhere. His determination starts to waver.

"Why are you here?" she shouts above the noise.

He runs a hand over his head and grips his hair. "I owe Lily an apology."

"You owe us both apologies."

"I do, but for different reasons."

"Explain."

He starts to, but the crowd claps. Feet stomp. Someone rushes onto the stage dressed as an old woman with exaggerated glasses and frazzled white hair. Someone else in a giant gray-squirrel costume leaps onstage from the opposite side. The characters wave at the audience. They cheer. Kids scream. Lucas sweats.

Then the music cuts out, and a woman announces, "Hello and welcome."

Olivia leans in close. "Do not leave. We're talking when this is over." She folds her arms and turns toward the stage.

Lucas swears at himself and considers bailing. But he'd only let Shiloh down again. And that isn't an option he'll consider. He's let too many people down in his life, including himself. He'll just have to convince Olivia, too, that he believes what he's doing for Shiloh is right.

The woman onstage introduces herself as Camille Fleming, Lily's publisher and the sponsor for today's lavish event. She couldn't be more excited to see the success behind not one, but two *Tabby's Squirrel* books. And she's even more excited for the movie, which the critics have already hailed as this summer's animated blockbuster. The crowd roars again.

Camille waits out their screams before reciting the interviewer's bullet-point list of achievements. Then she throws her arm toward stage left. "Please welcome Felix Donohue with *Comic Sonic.*"

A short, wiry man with thinning hair, baggy khakis, and a neon-blue shirt with a *Tabby's Squirrel* screen print runs onstage. He dances with the life-size characters and hugs Camille before she walks off stage. He turns to the crowd and fist pumps the air. The audience roars.

"This is a circus," Olivia shouts in awe.

Lucas can only nod. His heart pounds, his body growing tense in anticipation of Lily's appearance. He's waited years to see her.

Felix is good, uproariously funny. He's a presence on the stage, rousing the audience until they're cheering for Lily at a decibel that stings his eardrums.

"Here she is, kids. The magic behind the pen. The dreamer behind the paintbrush. The one. The only. The incredibly talented . . . *Jenna Mason!*" He screams her name, turning stage right where Lucas and Olivia watch from below, stupefied by the theatrics.

Hands clap, feet stomp, and there she is. Lily.

His heart drums in his ribs.

She's shorter than Olivia, but just as beautiful, dressed simply in jeans and Chucks like the ones Shiloh has. She wears the same *Tabby's Squirrel* shirt as Felix, but in highlighter green. She's dressed for the kids, and she's so completely Lily.

His chest tightens, trapping his breath. His eyes feel like ice picks are stabbing them, they burn so badly. "It's Lily." His voice is rough, gravelly with disbelief. Olivia briefly grabs his arm and leans her head against his shoulder to acknowledge the intensity of what he must be feeling. He glances quickly at her before turning his attention back to Lily in utter shock that she's there and he's here when he never believed he'd have the courage to see her again. Ever.

Beside him, Olivia claps with exuberance. She cups her hands to her mouth and lets rip an earsplitting whistle, capturing Lily's attention. Lily waves at Olivia, then shifts her gaze to him. Her expression falters. Her hand stills in the air. Her eyes widen, and he sees the moment she recognizes him. She stumbles.

"Whoa." Felix grabs her elbow so she doesn't topple over, and he chuckles. "You fall, and that giant squirrel over there will accuse me of tripping you and tackle me."

The giant squirrel shakes his fists, and everyone laughs, including Lily, although uneasily. She glances back at him one more time, her shock finely etched on her face, before giving her full attention to her fans.

35

Shiloh can't believe she's here, that Jenna Mason is right there, less than twenty feet from her. They're breathing the same air, existing in the same space. *Oh, my god!* She jumps up and down with the crowd.

Shiloh's never been to a concert, let alone sat in the front row. But she imagines it would feel something like this. Loud, electric, and colorful. The crowd's energy dances along her arms. Her scalp tingles from it. Jenna's fans adore her.

Ever since she came out about her true identity, that of Lily Carson, and why she'd been in hiding, Jenna Mason's popularity soared. People empathized with her. And her publicist worked her story from every positive angle, especially one that now resonates with Shiloh because of her own experience: Jenna is the voice for every abused teenage runaway.

Giddy, nervous, and excited beyond comprehension, Shiloh lets herself get caught up with the crowd. She's going to listen to the interview, then Lucas will introduce them, then Shiloh will ask her every burning question she's had about animation since she watched her first *Tabby's Squirrel* video short.

Shiloh has followed Jenna's career since the beginning. She grew up watching her YouTube videos, where plenty of nights she waited with bated breath for the next hilarious clip of quirky characters to drop. Jenna's stories were a slice of sunshine in Shiloh's gloomy existence. She made Shiloh laugh when all she wanted to do was cry, her mom having spun out, leaving Shiloh to fend for herself. Jenna's characters made her feel a little less alone, and Shiloh hopes to do the same. Out there, somewhere, there's a young girl fending for herself who will grow up watching Shiloh's videos.

Jenna waves at the audience, and Shiloh waves back with her books. Grateful Lucas brought her, she catches his attention. He's still talking with his older sister, but he waves back. She then turns her attention to the stage. Jenna and Felix are sitting down. They pick up their microphones.

"Can you believe this?" Felix starts.

Jenna takes in the crowd. "No, I can't. If you told me eight months ago this would be my life, I wouldn't have believed you."

"You have quite the story. You've had quite the life," he says, hinting at her past. "A very successful YouTube channel with millions of hits. Two books in less than a year, and now a movie."

"Coming out this summer."

"*Tabby's Squirrel: Lost in the Park.* Quite a year it's been."

"It sure has."

"In more ways than one."

A shadow falls over her face. "Yes, that's true."

Felix leans forward. His voice lowers, a ploy to hold the audience captive. "Tell us how it started," he asks, diving straight in.

Jenna chews her bottom lip, her gaze sliding to stage right toward Lucas and their older sister. Shiloh holds her breath, wondering if she'll talk about what happened the night she ran away.

"Doodles," she says.

"Doodles?" Felix lurches back at the unexpected, simplistic answer. His movements are exaggerated, a performance itself.

"Doodles in a notebook." Jenna grins with a shrug. "An idea. A dream. And a fat squirrel nesting in the tree outside my window when I was a little girl," she explains, to which the giant squirrel onstage does a jig. The audience laughs on cue.

Under Felix's intense and charismatic questioning, a lively conversation evolves. Shiloh is transfixed, oblivious to the passing time when she feels a hand on her knee. Startled, she looks down. Crouched beside her so she isn't in the way of anyone's view, is Sophie.

"I'm so glad I found you."

She blinks, uncomprehending how Sophie can be here. Why she's here. Lucas said she was back at Ivy's. "What are you doing here?"

Commotion behind her draws her attention. She glances around. Police block the end of each aisle. A couple march up the center aisle. Several more toward stage right, toward Lucas.

Her heart pounds in her ears. She rises on shaking legs.

Sophie isn't here for her.

She spins back to her. "You called the cops on him."

"I had no choice. Your mom's been looking for you. She filed a missing person report. The police, your friends, they've all been looking for you. They started a hashtag-find-Shiloh campaign. Your mom was on the local news pleading for your safe return."

That doesn't make sense. When she ran, her mom was barely coherent enough to know the difference between day and night.

Shiloh glares accusatorily at her. "Ellis sent you, didn't he?"

Sophie shakes her head, but Shiloh barely notices. Four officers have surrounded Lucas.

"He'll be fine. They only want to talk with him. They're just asking him to go with them to the station."

They aren't asking. One officer has his cuffs out. Another has his hand on his holstered pistol. Lucas won't go easily. He hates cops.

An officer grabs at Lucas's wrist, and Lucas jerks his arm out of reach. He also hates to be touched. He looks wild and scared. He starts yelling at the cops.

Panic consumes Shiloh. "Lucas," she shouts and runs toward him. "Leave him alone," she screams at the cops at the same time Sophie grabs her arm, drawing her back. She turns on Sophie. "What are you doing? Let me go. They're going to hurt him."

"He'll be fine. This'll be over before you know it."

But the scene has already caught the audience's attention. People in the middle and back rows stand to see what's happening. The press swivel their cameras from the stage to Lucas. Jenna notices the commotion and halts Felix's questioning. He turns to look behind him, asking into the microphone, "What's going on over there?" If anyone wasn't looking or yet aware of the police activity below stage right, they are now.

A cop hollers for Lucas to get on his knees. Olivia yells over the noise for them to leave him alone. Jenna gets up from her seat and strides across the stage.

"Let me go." Shiloh tugs her wrist, but Sophie's grasp is steadfast. "They're going to hurt him. He doesn't like people touching him."

Sophie's gaze shoots to Lucas as if she's just now seeing how this will unfold. Her grasp loosens enough for Shiloh to slip free. Shiloh shoots over to Lucas, calling out to him. They can't take him away. He's the only person who can help with her mom. He's the only one who'll ensure her safety. The only man she can trust. The first one who's come close to being anything like a father to her.

Two officers grab his arms and hold him in place. The officer with his hand on his holstered pistol stands before Lucas, ready to aim it at him if Lucas makes a move that would endanger the audience or himself.

"Don't hurt him. Don't hurt him," Shiloh shrieks.

Lucas's head jerks toward her. Their gazes meet, and his face falls. Tension bleeds out of him. "I'm sorry," he says, and drops to his knees, giving up the fight. "It wasn't supposed to be like this."

36

They come at Lucas from all sides. He should have seen them, but he'd been spellbound watching Lily onstage. He should have anticipated they'd catch up to him, but he didn't want to break his promise to Shiloh, not when he's broken so many promises.

The officer in front of him informs him that he's under arrest for the kidnapping, trafficking, and unlawful harboring of a minor.

"What?" he balks, his stomach dropping to his feet. Where in the universe did they get the idea he was selling Shiloh? Disgust coats his tongue. His heart pounds violently in his chest. He can feel it against his ribs. "That's bullshit," he bellows.

"You have the right to remain—"

Lucas doesn't hear him over the clamor in his head. He barely registers the officer behind him ordering him to put his hands behind his back. When he doesn't, an officer to his side makes a grab for his wrist. He jerks his arm from him.

"Don't touch me." Instinct has him backing away. He bumps into an officer and is pushed forward. He feels their hands on him, and his vision darkens along the edges. He's not at the Grove. He's back in the juvenile-detention mess hall. These aren't the police ordering him to surrender. They're Morris and his gang. Lucas starts to rage.

"Lucas!"

Somewhere in his brain he picks up Shiloh's voice. His head jerks in her direction.

"Leave him alone," she screams, running toward him. Then he sees her, Sophie. She brought the police. He knew she wouldn't have waited for him to return and explain, but he hoped she would have given him the chance. He's such a fool. He should know not to put his faith in anyone. It always backfires on him.

Sophie grabs Shiloh's arm, drawing her away from him, and Lucas wants to strangle the woman for touching her.

The cops wrestle him to hold still as one attempts to cuff him. But all Lucas can feel are their hands. Hands, hands, everywhere, and his skin starts to crawl. His blood begins to boil. He yells at them to back off, which only pisses them off.

Beside him the audience rises like a wave to watch him. He feels the cameras on him. Then he hears Felix over the speaker ask what's going on, and he knows Lily can see everything from her vantage onstage. Nausea floods his stomach, and his limbs weaken with utter humiliation. He's so incredibly sorry she's witnessing this. That he's the cause of any embarrassment and humiliation she has to be feeling. He's ruining her event.

A cop gets in his face. "On your knees."

"Leave him alone," Olivia yells, and his eyes burn like blisters with unshed tears. Lily strides across the stage toward him, her expression muddled from confusion and accusation, and he's absolutely mortified. Once again, he's failed her.

Shiloh slips free of Sophie's grasp and shoots over toward him. "Lucas! Lucas!" His heart cracking, he wants to shout for Sophie to take her away. He doesn't want her to see him like this. But the officers on his sides grab his arms, yanking them behind his back. His shoulders burn with the force. He grimaces.

"Don't hurt him. Don't hurt him."

He jerks his head toward Shiloh. Their gazes meet, and the fear he sees in hers pierces his chest. He's failed her, too. He's such a disappointment. "I'm sorry." His body slackens, and he drops to his knees. "It wasn't supposed to be like this."

"No!" Shiloh screams. She starts to cry. Sophie grabs her from behind and tries to drag her away. Shiloh cries harder, fighting Sophie.

His need to protect her instinctual, Lucas struggles against the cops restraining him.

"Don't fight, Luc," Olivia yells. She pushes people aside to get to him. The officer who was behind him rushes over to restrain her. "Get your hands off me." She dodges him, retrieving her phone. "I'm calling my attorney, Luc. I'll take care of you. I've got you."

He wants to believe she can, but the law has screwed him over before.

"This is your fault. Your fault," Shiloh wails at Sophie. Tears plummet down her cheeks. Lucas squeezes his eyes. He can't bear that he's the cause of her agony.

"What's happening?" Lily asks from the stage, and her voice almost kills him until he hears, "You. What did you do?"

Thinking she's asking him, he braves facing her. Though no amount of apologizing will ever make up for what he's done to her here. He's ruined her event. He's made a mockery of their family. But Lily isn't looking at him. She's glaring at Sophie.

"I'm sorry, Jenna. I didn't have a choice."

Olivia swings her head in their direction. Her mouth falls open. Lucas watches them. What is going on here?

"You are so wrong about that," Lily says, coming off the stage. Her expression is outraged. "This is not what we hired you to do."

Her words smack him in the face. His head snaps back. *What the fuck?* They know Sophie? His gaze whips between Sophie and his sisters as he scrambles to catch up with what's happening around him, and the sickening feeling of betrayal slides in. His sisters hired Sophie to what, arrest him?

"She called the cops?" Olivia points in shock at Sophie with her phone and it careens into him. She's just as baffled.

"You weren't supposed to interact or intercede," Lily accuses.

"I know, I can explain," Sophie pleads. She tries to move Shiloh away, but Shiloh won't budge.

"That explains why she never returned our calls," Olivia says.

The police force him to the ground, pressing his cheek into the concrete. Memories lash his mind like a leather whip slicing his back. It takes everything in him not to go berserk and create more of a scene than he already has. He bites down on the cries of agony filling his throat. Shiloh will remember this for the rest of her life. She'll never trust men again. "I'm sorry. I'm sorry," he repeats over and over, glancing from her then to Lily when she comes into his line of sight. His face crumples. None of them should have to see him like this. Weak and broken, vibrating with shame and rage. After years apart from his sister, he's manhandled to the ground in front of a live audience.

Shiloh wails for him, and he silently cries for her. They'll send her back to Ellis, and Lucas will be locked up. He won't be able to help her.

An officer plants a knee in Lucas's back, and he finally feels the cold metal of the cuffs as they are locked tightly on his wrists. He grimaces with pain and humiliation. "I'm sorry," he cries, looking from Lily, to Olivia, then to Shiloh. "I'm sorry."

The cop pulls hard on the cuffs to check they're secure, further straining Lucas's shoulders, and he bellows.

"You're hurting him," Shiloh wails. "Stop hurting him."

"That's my brother," Lily shouts, shoving the stage crew aside as she tries to reach him. "Leave him alone."

He's hauled to his feet, and he levels his gaze with Lily. Tears glisten along the rims of her hazel eyes. God, it pains him he may never see her face again. "I'm sorry," he says, for abandoning her when she needed him. For not being the brother she deserves. Then he looks at Shiloh, his expression ravaged. "I'm sorry." For breaking his promise. For not being able to protect her.

"He's good," she cries to the police. "He's a good man. He didn't do anything wrong. I'm fine, see?" She pounds her chest. "I wanted to stay with him. I don't want to go home. Don't take him." She looks from Olivia to Lily then to Sophie, but it seems no one is listening to her. "Don't let them take him away. He's a good man. He's good. He's good." She sobs, and Lucas's heart cracks wide open for her. He never thought himself capable, he never imagined himself worthy of someone coming to his defense so passionately. But in the worst moment of his life, as a father would a daughter, he couldn't love someone more.

"I'm sorry," he tells her one last time. Then the officers take him away.

37

Lucas is escorted down a wide, sterile hallway, handcuffed and dressed in a drab cement-hued jumpsuit. He was told someone was here to see him. His attorney, Lee Bailey, just left, and he fears Lily's the one waiting for him. Jail is the last place he wants to have his first conversation with her. He doesn't even want to see her until he clears his name, assuming that's a possibility.

Frankly, he's surprised he's allowed visitors. He hasn't been arraigned yet.

Officer Toth opens a door to a windowless room and moves aside for Lucas to enter. Seated across the table facing him is Olivia. He doesn't realize how tense he was until he sees her and his shoulders relax.

"Ten minutes," Toth says, and points at a camera in the corner. "We can see you. Don't try anything futile." He leaves the room. The metal door bangs behind him, echoing in the small room.

"What are you doing here?" he asks his sister.

"Are you cuffed?" she asks, appalled.

He lifts his hands. "Flight risk."

"Are you serious?" She sneers.

He settles in the seat across from her, dropping his hands onto the table. The cuffs clatter on the metal surface. "Good to see you, prince-*sis*," he says at an attempt for levity. Though nothing about his situation is funny. The charges against him aren't for murder, but they are serious and carry a hefty sentence.

She scowls at him. "Cut the crap. I really hate you right now." Her bottom lip quivers, and she looks away. She inhales a shaky breath, and he wants to reach across the table for her hand, but he doesn't dare touch her. She's angry with him and has every right to be. When she turns back, she says, "What were you thinking, running off with that girl?"

Anger bunches the muscles in his arms. "I wasn't running off with her," he says, coming to Shiloh's and his defense. "She got into some trouble, and I was helping her. I was going to bring her home."

"Then why the hell were you at the Grove?"

He wants to tell her he was there to apologize to Lily, but that's a bigger conversation for another day, and with his other sister. The corner of his mouth lifts. "Would you believe Shiloh's a big fan? She asked me to take her."

"Well, it was irresponsible on your part, especially with your warrant. Speaking of which, why are you still here? I thought you posted bail."

He sighs. "For the traffic violations. Arraignment's day after tomorrow for the other stuff."

Olivia shakes her head. "You caused quite the scene," she says, bitter.

He looks at his cuffed wrists. His palms shake. "I know. I'm sorry." There's so much he regrets.

"It made the news. You were on *Entertainment Tonight* and *TMZ*. We all were."

He sags in the chair, his hands dropping into his lap, defeated. What a mess he made. "Shit, Liv. Tell Lily I'm sorry."

"Tell her yourself."

His pulse rate spikes. "Do not let her come here. I don't want her to see me like this."

"Why? Because it's so much worse than getting taken down by four cops in front of a thousand people?"

228

He clenches his jaw.

Olivia covers her face and swears into her hands. "Sorry. I didn't come here to argue," she says, dragging her hands through her hair. She holds her waves from her face.

"Why are you here?"

She shoots him an incredulous glare. "For you, of course."

"Me?"

"Is it so hard to believe we care about you?"

For him, yes. He gives her a blank look, waiting for her to elaborate.

"I needed to see for myself that you're okay. Lee got me ten minutes with you. I've been worried sick about you." She lets go of her hair, and he notices her hands are shaking. His chest concaves, feeling hollow.

"I'm sorry for running out on you," he says, bothered he's the cause of her upset. "I left you to handle Dad's death on your own."

"Yeah, that was a real shit thing to do. Why did you?"

He glances over his shoulder at the door before leaning over the table and lowering his voice. "I don't understand it, Liv. I swear there should be a warrant for my arrest for Dad, that I'd been caught on traffic cams. It was me. I—"

Olivia claps a hand over his mouth. "Shush. Stop right there," she orders in a harsh whisper. Her gaze darts to the camera then back to him. "I don't want to hear it."

He nods gently, and she releases her hand. Keeping her head close to his, she says, "I suspected that was why you took off. You were acting weird that night. I knew something was up, especially when you wouldn't tell me what happened to him. I read the accident and autopsy reports. It wasn't you, Luc. It was all Dad. He was drunk. His alcohol level was way above the limit, and he was speeding."

"Because I was chasing him."

"He got in his car and chose to drive."

"But I strangled him with the seat belt," he says under his breath through gritted teeth.

"How? You didn't even get out of your truck."

He lurches upward. "Yeah, I did." That, he specifically remembers. He'd been sitting in his truck on the side of the road with blood on his hand. Then he got out of the truck and saw his father's demolished car in the ravine. As to whether he went down to look, that's where his memories get cloudy.

"I mean you did, but you didn't go down to Dad's car. The police report says you got out, looked around, then got back in and drove off. The only blood on the scene was Dad's."

A glimmer of hope flares, but he quickly douses it.

"Then why isn't that the way I remember it?" It doesn't make sense to him.

She shrugs. "I don't know. Were you high?"

He shakes his head. "Just my anxiety pills."

"You're still on clonazepam?"

He nods. "Was."

"Maybe you were hallucinating. My therapist has me on the same meds. I read that's one of the side effects. Rare, but possible. You were pretty stressed out."

And he is prone to blackouts.

He stares at her. The answer couldn't be that simple. Nothing in his life has been that easy. "I wasn't hallu—"

"I don't know what happened to you, or what you saw, only that you didn't do it. Now, shut up about it. What I don't get is why you think you did it in the first place. Dad was an asshole, I understand that now. But did you want to kill him?" Her eyes are bright with her pain. She'd been close to their father their entire life. Olivia took it hard when she learned their father murdered Lily's biological father.

"Mom asked me to."

Her mouth falls open. "She what?"

He scratches his palm with his jaw stubble. The cuffs rattle. "Not directly. She was afraid of Dad. She thought he was going to kill her, that's the impression she gave me. She insinuated she wanted me to take care of him."

A gasp of disgust. "That woman was manipulating you. She used you like she always has with us."

The venom in her voice stuns him. "What are you talking about?" Then he remembers the article he read about Lily in *Luxe Avenue*. Lily hadn't seen their mom either. "Where's mom?"

"You need to ask Lily."

His eyes narrow. He doesn't like the sound of that. "Tell me."

"Lucas, you've missed a lot. There's so much you don't know."

She pulls at the ends of her hair, and something catches the light. His chest tightens. "Like that ring on your finger?"

She holds her hand out to look at her ring.

"Blaze?" he asks, and she nods. "I'm happy for you." He's pleased they reconciled. They belong together. Lucas has thought that since they were kids and spent their summers at the lake with the Whitmans.

"I'll catch you up later." Her gaze swings to the door. "Listen, time's almost up. Stop worrying about Dad. You didn't do it, and leaving me to deal with the burial and the police was totally uncool, but I get it. Right now, you need to focus on getting your charges dropped. Lee thinks Shiloh's mom has a weak case. Let's hope he's right."

At the mention of Shiloh's name, his head lifts. "How is she?" He's been frightened on her behalf.

"You shouldn't even be asking after her." Lucas glares, and she rolls her head. "Fine. From what I've heard, she's fine. Sophie's gone to check on her."

She's the last person short of Ellis who should be anywhere near Shiloh. So much had been going on at the time he was arrested that he almost forgot what he'd overheard. "You know Sophie's a bounty hunter. Did you hire her to find me?"

"Lily did. She—"

The door swings open. Officer Toth fills the doorway. "Time's up, Carson."

38

Shiloh jams a knife into the toaster to wrangle free the sliced bagel she forced into the slot. She's home, and Ellis is gone. When her mom realized Shiloh ran away, she filed a missing person report and a restraining order the same day. Harmony says she isn't using anymore, and in her quest to make it up to Shiloh, she cleaned the apartment from floor to ceiling as soon as the police sent word that they'd located her daughter and were bringing her home.

Shiloh can't recall the last time their place has been this clean, or if it ever was.

She's relieved but worried, happy yet sad, hopeful but wary, and grateful yet bitter.

Hair bundled in a topknot, she wears athletic shorts and a thick hoodie. She wipes butter grease off her fingertips on her sweatshirt, which makes her think of the sweatshirt she'd worn two weeks straight and threw away in the hotel room after Lucas bought her clothes at Target. They told her he was arrested for kidnapping, trafficking, and unlawful confinement of a minor. Her mom believes he planned to sell her for sex. Shiloh told the police Lucas saved her from an assault, and that she was with him willingly. She ran away from home because her mom was an addict and her live-in boyfriend attacked her. Shiloh chose to stay with Lucas. It wasn't the other way around. She even wrote a ten-page statement detailing why she ran and why Lucas had taken her to the Grove. She wanted to go. Jenna Mason was her idol.

When she asked after him, they told her Lucas was still in jail, the charges pending. She hasn't heard anything in two days.

She again tries to free her bagel, roughly stabbing the bread with a knife.

"You'll electrocute yourself."

"Like you care." She glances at her mom over her shoulder. Harmony is wrapped in a terry robe. Her hair is brushed and eyes are clear. Yet Shiloh can't help holding her breath. This isn't the first time her mom has quit using on her own, but it never lasts long. Her resistance will eventually fade. Shiloh fears now that she's home and Harmony's no longer working closely with the police to find her, her mom will revert to her old habits of drugs and men.

The bagel slice pops free and pinwheels across the counter, leaving burnt crumbs in its wake. Shiloh catches her breakfast before it drops into the sink. Then she dusts the crumbs off the counter. Might as well keep this place clean as long as possible.

"I care," her mom says softly behind her.

Shiloh turns to face her. "Why didn't you believe me about Ellis?" She's been home two days, and her mom has yet to apologize. He would have raped her if she hadn't kneed him and ran. But by that time, his hands had already been all over her, leaving her sickened with the memories.

Her mom's mouth turns down. She twists the robe's sash. "I should have, and I'm sorry."

And there it is.

Shiloh waits for the apology to sink in, to make up for the hurt her mom caused. She told Lucas she wanted him to take her home to her mom, but she wanted her mom's apology more. That she'd forgive her mom in a heartbeat if for once her mom put her first, before the men and drugs.

But she can't force herself to believe everything will suddenly be better. Whatever she intended to say to absolve her mom is stuck behind her ribs. She rubs her chest bone because the pressure is causing aches.

She's heard her mother apologize before, and nothing changes.

Tears flood her eyes.

Turning back to the counter, she butters the bagel slice with a shaky hand.

"It won't happen again."

She's heard that before, too. What makes this time any different?

Shiloh pulls a sleeve over her palm and dries her eyes before putting the bagel on a plate and pouring a glass of orange juice. She takes both to the table.

Her mom settles into the chair across from her and reaches for her hand. "Ellis won't bother you again."

"A restraining order won't keep him away," Shiloh mutters around a mouth full of food, pulling her hand away. For that to happen, her mom would have to call the police when he returns, and she fears he will. He sweet-talked and threatened Harmony once before. It's only a matter of time before he tries again. He's a man who likes to be in control.

"I'm also pressing charges against that man who kidnapped you."

Her bagel plunks on the plate. "He didn't kidnap me. I ran away from you."

"He took you to LA."

"Because I was already in Hollywood. Finn dumped me, and Lucas came to get me. He was worried about me. I asked him to take me to the Grove before he brought me here. God." She cries with frustration. "Have you listened to anything I've told you?" Her mom also read the report she wrote. But nothing has swayed her. "You're using Lucas to make up for what you did. Charging him won't change the fact you let your boyfriend touch me and you didn't believe me."

Her mom flinches.

"I'm trying to protect you now."

"You're going after the wrong guy. Lucas rescued me when two guys were attacking me. And when a guy I thought that I could trust ditched me in Hollywood, he's the one that came to help me. Not you. It's never been you. You always put the next high and your guys above me. How am I supposed to believe this time is any different than before?"

"That man has a record. There was already a warrant for his arrest. He was dangerous."

"I felt safer with him than I ever did in my own house."

Her mom releases a shuddering breath. "You don't mean that."

Someone knocks loudly on the front door, and Shiloh jumps in her seat.

Her mom twists in her chair to look toward the door. "Expecting anyone?"

Nerves skitter down her arms as her thoughts go directly to Ellis. She shakes her head. "You?"

"No." Her mom peeks through the peephole. "It's that woman who notified the police about you."

"Who?" Shiloh moves cautiously toward her mom.

Harmony unbolts and opens the door.

"Is Shiloh home?" a woman asks.

"She is." Her mom opens the door wider to reveal Sophie and another woman.

"You." Shiloh sneers. She's the one who called the cops on Lucas. Shiloh has never been as humiliated as she was to be escorted from the Grove to a waiting police car, where she was taken to the hospital and examined before meeting up with her mom. She can only imagine how Lucas must have felt. They were both on the news that night. Shiloh will never live that down when she returns to school.

"Lucas is a good guy, and you screwed him over," she accuses Sophie.

"I know. I made a mistake. That's why I'm here. Can we come in and talk?"

Shiloh crosses her arms and scowls.

"Yes, please do. I haven't had the chance to properly thank you for returning Shiloh to me." Her mom shows the two women inside. They both wear pantsuits. Sophie is taller, and the other woman has a file and paper pad.

"Thank you," Sophie says. "This is my friend Nichele Gat. She's a social worker with child protection services."

Her mom's face drains of color. "I don't think it's necessary for her to have come."

"We've received reports of abuse and neglect," Nichele says. "I have to investigate whether those claims are true." She turns to Shiloh. "Is there a place we can speak privately?"

Shiloh swallows roughly. Her heart beats furiously.

Her mom snatches her hand with both of hers and holds it to her chest. "You can't take my daughter from me."

"Ms. Bloom, I'm here in the interest of your daughter. I only want to assess the safety of her environment. Surely you want what's best for her."

Shiloh looks nervously from the social worker to her mom. She, too, is afraid. There's the possibility she'll be sent to live in a strange house with a new family. But it's only temporary, and this is her chance for her mom to go away to get the help she needs. Shiloh's also tired of being the parent in their little family of two.

"It's all right, Mom."

"I'm so sorry, Shiloh." Her mom tears up. "I should have been a better mom."

"You will be. We'll get through this. Together." Shiloh squeezes her mom's hand and kisses her cheek. Her mom was right. Things will be better now. Then she looks at Nichele. "We can talk in the kitchen."

Sophie smiles reassuringly at her, then says to her mom, "While they're talking, can we discuss Lucas? I think there's been a misunderstanding."

39

Lucas sits on the narrow cot in his cell with his knees spread and face in his palms. Tremors ripple through him. Sweat coats his skin. His head feels like a chisel's picking away at his brain.

And it's not solely from being dry for several days.

He's locked in a windowless cell, and this afternoon is his arraignment for the kidnapping and unlawful harboring of Shiloh. The DA is requesting his bail to be set higher than he could ever afford. His attorney believes the case is weak and doubts it'll make it to trial. Lee's confidence still doesn't prevent Lucas from having a full-fledged panic attack.

He breathes in, then out. In. Out.

He tries to keep his mind off his impending imprisonment by mulling over yesterday's conversation with Olivia. He has so many questions about their parents. And he has yet to apologize to Lily, not just for when she ran away, but also for ruining her event. He wonders if he'll get the chance. He'll accept his fate if he gets time, and he'll deal with that. At first he didn't want to face her while he was in jail, but now that he's had time to think, he realizes he doesn't want to be put away without talking with her first. She deserves to hear the truth from him about what happened the night she ran.

Then there's Shiloh. Nobody is telling him anything about her. Did she make it home safely? Is Ellis still living there? He shivers violently at the thought and wonders who is protecting her.

Squeezing his eyes shut, he counts back from ten. Nine . . . eight . . . seven.

A metal door slams, and heavy footsteps approach. Keys jangle outside his cell. He lifts his head and watches Officer Toth unlock and slide open the barred door. "It's your lucky day, Carson. You're free to go."

He blinks, straightening his back. "What do you mean?"

"Charges have been dropped."

He feels a jolt through his body. "Which ones?"

"All of them."

"You serious?" He eases off the cot, hesitant to believe what he's hearing.

"Come on, let's get you processed. There's a lady waiting to take you home."

In a daze, Lucas follows Officer Toth. He changes into his street clothes and signs some paperwork; then he's released to go. Lucas walks outside, squinting up at the sun, soaking in its blessed heat. He inhales deeply, absorbing the sounds and smells of the city. Cars on the freeway and a plane flying overhead. The distinct scent that comes with LA smog: smoke and eggs. The taste of freedom.

Lucas heads down the steps for his ride, fully expecting to see Olivia waiting for him. But across the lot, leaning against her piece-of-shit Honda, is the woman who had him arrested.

Sophie's his ride?

He doesn't know whether to strangle her or thank her. But something tells him she's behind his charges being dropped.

Arms folded over her chest, she doesn't move as he warily approaches. He stops a few feet in front of her. He doesn't smile.

She pushes away from the car. "I was wrong about you, and I am sorry."

He squints at her. "You did what you thought was right." And she was thinking of Shiloh. He can't fault her for that.

"I let my personal issues influence my judgment. That was unprofessional of me."

238

His mouth tightens; then after a beat he says, "Olivia told me Lily hired you."

"She did. Both of your sisters, actually, and I never should have gotten involved with you, Shiloh, Ivy, anyone for that matter. They asked me to locate you and report back when I found you."

But she'd rented an apartment from Ivy to get closer to him. "Why didn't you?" He recalls Olivia telling Lily that Sophie hadn't been returning their calls.

She twists a stud in her ear. "Remember that story I told you about Alma, the girl I placed with an angel?"

He nods.

"I saw you that night when you brought Shiloh home. I thought . . . I knew there was a warrant for your arrest and that you've had a troubling history with the law, and even though I know Jenna and had just met Olivia, I didn't know you. I needed to get close to see for myself what was going on. I wasn't comfortable leaving while she was with you, especially after I saw her black eye and the scratches on her face. If something happened to her . . ."

"I get it." She didn't trust him, and she'd blame herself for not doing something about it.

"I didn't expect the police to arrest you. I reached out to Shiloh's mom and was there to bring her home. Anyway, it was a mess. Jenna's never going to forgive me, and for what it's worth, I'm sorry. I read Shiloh's report. You tried to tell me, and I wasn't listening. But I understand now you were only helping her."

"She'd been traumatized enough as it was. I wasn't going to let anyone else hurt her. How is she?" He's been dying to find out.

"She's home."

"Ellis?"

"Out of the picture. Her mom filed a restraining order."

He exhales, relieved. Pressing a palm to his eye, he turns away as he collects himself. He'd been so afraid for her.

"I had a lovely chat with Harmony. She really does want to do right by Shiloh. She's checking into a rehabilitation facility, and Shiloh will be staying with me for a while. I thought maybe, if my apartment is still available after she finishes the school year, Ivy could extend my lease through the summer."

A smile pulls at his mouth. "I think that can be arranged."

Sophie grins back. She tosses up her keys and catches them. "How'd you like a ride to your truck?"

His truck is in impound. "Thanks. I appreciate that."

She rounds the front of her car to the driver's side, and he reaches for the passenger door when he remembers what he's been wanting to ask her. "How do you know Lily?"

"She's like a sister to me. My mom, Murielle, took her in when she ran away. I helped her create a new identity. She's Jenna Mason because of me."

Lucas stares at her. There it is, what he's always wondered about when he feared the worst for his sister. Lily hadn't been alone. She had help. And by the sound of it, she found a new family.

He glances away, eyes stinging. "Sun's sure bright out here." His voice catches, and he clears his throat. "My attorney send you?"

"No, but he knows I'm here."

He pauses. "*You* got the charges dropped?"

She smiles brilliantly. "Shiloh did. That girl went to bat for you. Convinced her mom, the police, and her social worker you were the best thing that happened to her."

Lucas's throat abruptly tightens. Joy spreads through his body, giving lightness to his limbs. So this is what it feels like to be worthy.

"Thank you," he says, breathless.

"Don't thank me. You can thank Shiloh when you see her this summer."

40

Lucas rests his oar over his lap. Crisp, cool air cuts across the bay, the water a myriad of blue and green gems reflecting the sun. Underneath him, his kayak leisurely bobs in the water. He inhales the musty scent of algae and tastes salt on his tongue. He's missed his morning rows, but not enough to consider Seaside Cove home, not anymore.

Home is in the desert with an old lady who bakes lasagna, a teen who gives him lip, and a woman whose mysteries he has yet to unravel. Something he looks forward to.

Unzipping a jacket pocket, he takes out the switchblade Mr. Whitman gifted him when he was ten. He gave one to each of them—Blaze, Olivia, Tyler, him, and later Lily when she was old enough. A reward for passing his impromptu survival lessons during summers at the Whitmans' lake house.

The blade once reminded him of the happiest moments of his life. He loved those summers, tackling Olivia and farting in her face. Tipping Blaze in the canoe. Letting everyone think he got lost in the woods. He chuckles at the memories. Until he remembers he used the blade on his arm. He didn't think he could ever be happy or hopeful again. Now the blade only reminds him of when he lost the will to live, and how he let what happened to him in juvenile detention and the months following taunt him for years.

He chucks the switchblade hard.

It lands in the water fifty yards from him, gone forever.

A smile pulls at his face. He picks up his oar and coasts back to shore, feeling a ton lighter than he did when he took his kayak out at dawn.

When he nears their dock, Olivia and Lily are waiting for him. They huddle under a shared blanket, sipping coffee from the café up the road, and the sight of them together without the chaos of a thousand people surrounding them breaks his stride. It's been a week since he's been released. He hasn't spoken to Lily or seen her since that day at the Grove. Olivia's coordinated this morning's meetup. He's nervous, regretful, and unsure. How will Lily react after all he's done to her?

When he hits sand and rocks, he gets out, sloshing through the water as he drags his kayak to dry land. Lily puts down her coffee and throws herself into his arms before he can fully straighten. They almost topple over. Bracing his legs, he hugs her back, burying his face in her hair. He cradles her head, and the words tumble out. "I'm sorry. I'm sorry." He apologizes over and over for the Grove and the embarrassment he caused her.

Her head shakes under his hand. Moisture soaks his neck from her tears.

Olivia joins them, wrapping her arms around them both, and it almost shatters him. To feel their love. To feel connected with them. To be touched and to not balk. He'd be on his knees if Olivia wasn't holding them up. They're a tripod. He should have known with one of them missing, the others would collapse. Lily ran away, and he and Olivia fell apart. Like Ruby, Titian, and Dahlia, Olivia's superhero siblings in her graphic novels, they're stronger together. A force to be reckoned with.

They could have been a solid front against their parents had they only stuck together. He'll always regret he hadn't come through for them.

"No regrets," Olivia harshly whispers into their huddle as if she's reading his thoughts. "No apologies. We're together now. That's what matters."

She's the first to break their embrace. Lucas pinches the wetness from his eyes, and Lily wipes hers with her shirtsleeve, laughing into the material. "I'm a mess."

He offers her a hesitant yet hopeful smile when their eyes meet.

Olivia gives him a coffee and retrieves the blanket. "Come, we have a lot to discuss."

They take their coffees to the back deck of the house he learned earlier he's now one-third owner of. Olivia explained their mother left the same day he did with no explanation. When an envelope arrived with the deed and three bank-account numbers, one in each of their names, she realized Charlotte wasn't coming back. Olivia hasn't told him much else about their mom, only asking that he be patient and wait for Lily. She reminded him again a lot has happened in the last eight months.

Lucas doesn't like the sound of that.

They settle on chairs facing each other, his sisters bundled in blankets to ward off the chill. He removes his thin water-resistant jacket and pulls on a thick sweatshirt. Then he takes the lid off his coffee only to pause when he realizes what he's doing. Only a week ago he would have spiked it, starting his day off with something strong. Sometimes he'd skip the coffee and go straight for the tequila.

He sets the lid and cup aside and turns to his sisters. "I start AA tomorrow," he says, and immediately chokes up. He's nervous about what he wants to share, his mind resisting. One last-ditch effort to protect himself.

Olivia rests a hand on his knee. "It's okay. We're listening."

Lucas puts down his coffee and picks up a rock, rolling it between his hands, clearing his throat. "I started drinking in high school. You know that. Dad was always on my case. I couldn't take the pressure. I partied to let off steam."

He rolls the rock over his palms and meets Lily's gaze. "I heard you yelling for me that night." She inhales sharply. "I was there . . . at the dock. I saw everything."

"The night Dad . . . ?" She can't finish. Her throat ripples.

He nods. "After the gun fired and Dad told you to run, you ran right past me."

"I didn't see you." Her voice is disbelievingly small.

"And you didn't help her?" Olivia looks stunned.

He shakes his head. "I couldn't."

"Why not?" Lily asks.

He forces himself to look at her, to face the pain and accusation that clearly shows in her expression. The truth is always the hardest to admit, but he does. "At the time, I told myself I didn't care. I didn't care about you, or Dad, or Wes. Anybody. But the real reason is that I was scared. I was weak, and afraid, and . . . I was a fucking coward." He clenches his hands. The rock bites into his right palm.

There's a long beat of silence with Olivia and Lily just watching him, waiting for him to continue. But he's locking up.

He feels a hand on his. Lily gently uncurls his fingers and tosses the rock. She cradles his palm. "It's okay, Luc. This is a safe space."

"You can tell us," Olivia speaks gently.

A tear slips down his cheek, shocking him. He didn't realize he was crying.

"I don't know where to start." His voice is a hoarse whisper.

"How about the beginning?" Lily suggests.

He nods and takes a shuddering breath. "All I wanted was to play football in college and build skyscrapers. I could have done it. I'd be doing it now. If not for the drinking." He looks up at the blue sky, his voice going distant. "Tanner and Reg were cool guys. We'd known each other since I was, what . . . nine, ten?"

"You partied more when you were around them."

He nods. Olivia remembers the bonfires on the beach during high school. She had to pick him up a few times because he was too drunk to drive.

244

"Tanner always brought the beer. He'd raid his dad's fridge. Reg and I would pick him up, and if there wasn't a party happening, we'd make our own.

"The night I was arrested, Tanner didn't have any beer when we picked him up. His dad found out he'd been skimming his supply and locked the fridge. The old man literally wrapped that thing with a chain and padlock. They fought. Tanner scored a shiner, but he said he was going to get his dad back. That he has it coming to him. We had no idea what he meant. All we cared about was that it was Saturday, and we didn't have beer.

"Reg had heard this friend of ours Johnny bought alcohol at the minimart without getting carded. We figured it was worth a shot. The worst that could happen is we'd get carded and we'd leave empty handed.

"We get to the market, we each grab a six-pack, and take it to the front. I didn't recognize the guy at the register. He was new. Gary was his name. I'll never forget it. He asked for our IDs.

"Next . . ." He drags in a breath. "Everything happened so fast."

Lily squeezes his hand, reminding him they are there for him.

"I look over at Tanner to ask what we should do. Play it up or leave? But he's pointing a gun at Gary. It was the most surreal thing I'd ever seen. Tanner holding a gun . . . my mind couldn't grasp that. I was like, where the fuck did it come from. The idiot had stolen his dad's gun. That's what he meant by getting his dad back.

"I don't know why I did what I did. I wasn't thinking. Maybe I thought Tanner was going to shoot the guy. I grabbed the gun from him, and it went off. The bullet blew through the window and shattered Reg's windshield. Tanner and Reg split." He snaps his fingers. "Don't know why I didn't. I froze. I couldn't move. Next thing I know, this Gary guy is tackling me. He held me down until the police arrived. Tanner and Reg got off with a week in detention and community service. I got six months."

"Those assholes," Olivia mutters.

He takes a breath. Lily blots her tears. "I remember that," she says. "Not the details. Mom wouldn't tell us. But I remember when you were gone those months. You missed most of the school year."

"What happened in detention?" Olivia asks.

He knows she's always wanted to know. He didn't return home the same kid he was when he left.

He picks at his thumbnail. "There was this kid there, Morris. They had six of us in a room, and he was one of my bunkmates. He'd been in for a couple of years already and had fifteen years to serve on top once he aged out. He was in for rape and murder charges. A real peach, that guy. He and a fellow gang member lured a couple of teen girls into a public bathroom, raped them, then shot one of them in the back. It was part of their induction ceremony to get initiated into their gang.

"Morris was a show-off. He was rowdy and loud. He was also angrier than shit and had a dangerous drive to control everything around him. I heard rumors he'd raped a few guys while inside. I didn't think much of it. I was going to do my time, get out, and get my life back.

"Morris would make passes at me and insinuate shit he wanted to do to me. I ignored him best I could, until I couldn't. A few weeks before my release date, someone tripped me in the mess hall. I was on cleanup, and the dirty trays I was carrying dropped in Morris's lap. It made quite the mess, and he made my last weeks there hell."

Lily makes a pained noise in the back of her throat. Olivia squeezes her empty paper cup until it folds.

"He and his guys harassed me in the mess hall. They ganged up on me in the yard. I was so paranoid I couldn't sleep. I just wanted to get the hell out.

"Three nights before my release, a fight broke out in the common room while I was still cleaning in the mess hall. Morris came in with four of his guys. The guards were busy breaking up the fight. They were distracted, and I knew nobody would come for me. But I fought." Pause. "I fought real hard."

Memories crawl up his throat like a disease. But he plows forward, needing to get everything out in the open. He can't let what happened to him fester further. "They pinned me down, stripped me, and Morris . . . Morris, the fucker . . ." He rubs his forearm. "He raped me."

His body shudders with the admission. This is the first time he's said those exact words, in that order, and in reference to him. Until now, there's always been a part of him in denial about what exactly it was that happened to him.

"Luc." Olivia swears, and before he sees her move, Lily is out of her seat and kneeling in front of him. She grasps both his hands. "I'm so sorry," she says through tears. "So, so sorry that happened to you."

Olivia scoots her chair closer and draws her arm over his shoulders. He clings to his sisters as he lets go of the pain and suffering he's borne for over a decade, and he just cries. He hates that he was violated. But he hates more how long he's let that one incident dictate his life.

When he feels he can talk without choking up, he says, "Give me a sec, guys."

"There's more?" Lily shares a tortured glance with Olivia.

"I need to finish this." Get it all out. "When I got home, I thought I'd be okay. I thought I could forget what happened and move on. But Mom and Dad didn't want to hear any of it. They wouldn't press charges, and I wasn't to speak a word of it. I'd embarrassed the family enough with my arrest. They wanted me to pretend nothing happened. But it ate at me. Every time I closed my eyes, I saw them. I could feel their hands on me. They were always there. I couldn't make them go away, and the only way I knew how to stop it was to kill myself." He shows them his scar. "But I couldn't go through with it," he whispers harshly. "I was so afraid you'd find me, Lily, that I couldn't do it. I tried to stop the bleeding on my own, and when that didn't work, I shouted for Mom."

Lily cries outright. Olivia's face crumples with the weight of her devastation. Overcome, she buries her face against his shoulder.

"Mom took me to the hospital, where they stitched me up and sent me home with a referral to a therapist. She never made an appointment. I told myself if she didn't care, neither did I. So I stopped caring. I didn't care about you, or you." He looks at them both. "I didn't even care about myself."

Tears cascade down Lily's face. He catches one with his thumb, and her eyes, more green than hazel behind the moisture, meet his. "I'm sorry I didn't help you with Dad. If I could go back in time and change that, I would in a heartbeat."

"I believe you," she says, rapidly nodding.

"I know St. John is your father. Mom told me Dad killed him. She said he was coming unhinged and was afraid he would hurt her. After hearing that, and knowing what he'd done to you and what he didn't do for me, I wanted to kill him. I . . ." He looks at his palms, remembering the blood after beating up his father. "Olivia says the video doesn't show me leaving the road, but I remember strangling him with the seat belt."

"But you didn't," Lily says, vehement. He looks at her in confusion. "Olivia told me what you said to her. You didn't do it, Luc, so stop beating yourself up about it."

"But I saw—"

"It wasn't real," she argues.

"You probably wanted to so badly that you hallucinated doing so," Olivia says.

"Or it's a false memory," Lily points out, looking between him and Olivia. "Our minds trick us when we're under duress. That night I ran? I came back looking for Wes. He'd hit his head, and I found him bleeding and totally out of it. I thought I'd shot him and was so relieved to find him alive. But he was confused and disoriented, and he attacked me. I was able to fight him off, but he hit his head and died on impact. Dad saw it and convinced me that it wasn't self-defense. He said I'd murdered my best friend, and for years I believed that. In fact, I manufactured memories that I did."

"Dad's dead through no fault but his own. We don't blame you, so don't blame yourself."

"Easier said than done." He thinks of the domino effect. If he hadn't shown up at the hotel, he wouldn't have given his father a reason to run. Indirectly, Lucas is the cause, and that's something he'll have to contend with for the rest of his life.

As for what he believed he did to his father, what he possibly only imagined, he's probably way past time to seek professional help.

"Since you brought up Dad, there's something else you need to know." Lily shares a look with Olivia.

Lucas frowns. "What?"

"Dad didn't kill Benton," Olivia says.

He blinks. "Then who did?"

"Mom."

His head swings to Lily. "What?"

"I overheard her and Dwight arguing. That's why I left. Mom literally shoved me out the door. They were afraid I'd tell the police."

Lucas stares at her, speechless. His mom murdered Lily's father. He knows she's coldhearted, but damn. "That's messed up." Downright cold blooded. He can't even begin to unpack that.

"She told me it was Dad." And he'd believed her. "You guys are serious?"

They nod.

"I had a hard time wrapping my head around it, too, when Lily told me," Olivia confesses.

"Not possible." He shakes his head, recalling the day he left to go after his father. His mother's fear was tangible.

"She's a manipulator, Lucas. You know that."

He sits back and rubs his hands on his thighs. "This is going to take time to digest."

"We think she left because I'm back," Lily explains. "She didn't have to go. I don't have anything on her other than a conversation I overheard fourteen years ago, which wouldn't be admissible in court, and she can easily deny it. The worst thing the three of us can do to her is cease contact."

"Seems like she's done that to us already," Lucas says.

Olivia picks at her fingers. "I might be able to do one better than that."

"How so?" Lily asks.

"I have the murder weapon."

"What?" Lucas and Lily exclaim in unison.

"I think I do. Benton was stabbed. And if memory serves, Mom was cooking dinner when she went looking for Dad that night. She took the chef's knife with her."

"Stop." Lily grabs her arm. "You saw her murder him?"

"I've had a recurring nightmare my entire life. My therapist thinks it's a memory, and it's become clearer since we've been working together. I followed Mom to the beach." She takes a beat as they gape at her. "I also have their old knife set. Blaze held on to it when I wanted to get rid of it. I didn't like them in my house. I've since turned them over to the authorities. Not sure if they can do anything with them. It's been over thirty years. But they have them. Gave them a statement, too. I also tipped off Benton's widow in Texas. She can work with the police to reopen the case if there's enough new evidence. But they did issue a BOLO to bring Mom in for questioning."

"Holy shit." Lucas can only shake his head.

"You've been busy," Lily says.

Lucas rubs his jaw. "This is our mom we're talking about. You're telling me she's the murderer."

"I know this is a lot. It's not easy on any of us," Olivia points out. "I love her. I probably always will. But she lied to us, Lucas. She lied to Benton's wife, the police. Everyone. She took a man's life. Our sister's dad. I can't let her get away with that, not after the way she played us against each other. And she's been doing it our entire lives."

"I know. I just meant this is our mom. We came from that."

"It doesn't mean we're anything like her," Lily says. "Took me a long time to realize I'm not like her either. None of us are."

"She's right, Luc. We're better than our parents. Their poison ends with us. We have that power. Our kids will never have to deal with what we experienced." She grasps his hand. Her palm is warm in his, her skin smooth against his calluses. "We'll help you however you want. Just say the word. But this time we're sticking together." She glances at Lily for confirmation.

"Every step. And Lucas." Lily grasps his free hand. "You have nothing for me to forgive. But if you want to hear it, I forgive you. I turned out okay. Better than okay. I have an amazing son and the best fiancé who loves me to the moon and back. My career . . . wow, I don't know where to begin except to say that if I hadn't run away, I doubt I'd have achieved what I have today. Being on my own forced me to succeed. I had no choice."

"You're a celebrity."

"There is that." Lily laughs, but her forgiveness means more to him than she might ever realize. It flows over him and sinks in, washing away years of guilt and regret like a spring rain cleansing the ground of dust and oils, bringing new life. He feels lighter, free of the burden he's carried half his life, and above everything, awed. Spilling his secrets has been one of the most difficult things he's done. He didn't know how his sisters would react. Would they hate him? Shun him? No. They opened their arms for him. Their acceptance of him, their understanding of what he's endured and the mistakes he's made, and their love despite it all, have rocked him to his core. He doesn't regret taking this long to share everything with them, and he can't regret having not reached out to them sooner. He wasn't ready. But going forward, he won't keep such closely guarded secrets about himself. He sees now how destructive that can be, how bottling up guilt and shame and regret can fester until it dictates how he behaves and reacts. How he lives. And does he ever want to live.

Olivia smiles tenderly. "You were a shit as a kid, Luc, but we love you."

He chuckles, his laugh waterlogged. He has a long road to recovery, today being only the first step. But it's one in the right direction, and he won't be traveling alone.

Rising to his feet, he pulls his sisters up with him and bear-hugs them, dropping kisses on their heads. After refusing to feel anything for so many years, he can't describe how good it is to have them back. To have their forgiveness. To start forgiving himself. To allow himself to touch and be touched. To feel.

"What next?" Lily asks when they break apart.

Lucas looks over the water. "I love the bay, but I need to move."

"Where to?"

"California City. I want to put an offer on a multiuse building. It's got apartments and a market." And he's installing a security camera first thing. Just the thought of returning brightens his mood, which tells him it's the right thing for him. "It'll be good for me."

"Good, because we want to sell this house," Olivia announces.

Fine with him.

"Think Mom will be upset we're selling?" he asks.

"She doesn't care. She's probably left the country," Lily says. He agrees. He wouldn't put it past their mom to escape somewhere they wouldn't extradite her back to the States.

"Actually, she hasn't. We found her."

"What do you mean 'we'?" Lily asks.

"Don't be mad, but I hired Sophie to locate her."

Lucas looks at Olivia. "Where the hell is she?"

41

Charlotte studies Alexander Stingel's painting on the wall, *Lust*, her pièce de résistance during last night's exhibit. The half-shrouded woman done in vibrant violet and crimson is as seductive as she is mysterious. The artist's lover. Her almond-shaped jade-green eye, the one that is visible, holds a secret. Slightly parted lips breathe words for the artist's ears only, leaving the admirer to wonder what she's whispering. Flaxen hair spilling over a shoulder like a golden river covers a naked breast, aroused and perfectly upturned. She envies the woman. To be young again, desirable. If she hadn't sold the piece, she'd consider keeping it for her own collection, adding it to the one she'd inherited from her mother, hidden away from her husband until recently. As for the rest of Alexander's canvases, she'll have everything sold by the end of the month. She's that good, and Alexander will be that much wealthier and more famous thanks to her.

In the few short months her gallery's been open, she's found flipping art worth tens of thousands more electrifying than the years she spent flipping million-dollar homes. Wining and dining art enthusiasts and their pocketbooks, matching buyers with the perfect pieces she has in her possession or can acquire on their behalf. The chase is what satisfies her, not the actual deal. It's what drove her to amass millions selling real estate, which she safely tucked away from her husband, Dwight. That miserable wretch would have spent her hard-earned cash before the ink dried on the sellers' contracts.

Countless times Charlotte has wished she could go back in time and bitch-slap some sense into her younger self. Wake up and smell the pocket fuzz in Dwight's Kmart-brand khakis. The guy had no money, didn't come from money, and didn't know how to keep it when he got his hands on it. No wonder her father, Gilbert Dayton, wrote her out of his will. She would have, too, if their roles had been reversed. His failed attempts at running for Congress aside, Dwight was an embarrassment to the family. He embarrassed her.

Her mother, Val, thankfully took pity on her after she'd divorced Charlotte's father and he passed. Charlotte inherited an ungodly sum from her, basically setting her up for several lifetimes. She'd never wanted for anything except this one thing: her own fine-art gallery. A dream she's had since she was a child and her father slammed it down. Within five years' time, she predicts she'll have locations in Paris, Florence, Sao Paulo, and Singapore, the art capitals of the world.

Granted, she's a little late to the art scene, given her age and thin book of connections, but nothing has stopped her before, and starting from scratch only makes her that much thirstier. She built her real estate empire from nothing but a license. She can do it again with art, so long as she doesn't make more mistakes.

Marrying Dwight had been a mistake. Killing Benton St. John was inexcusable. She hadn't planned that. But what's done is done. She can't take either back.

"Charlotte, I'm heading out."

Charlotte pulls herself from the lure of *Lust* to see her assistant thrust her arms into her Fendi sweater, a knockoff. The stitching's wrong. Wafer thin, Priscilla towers in her Valentino pumps. The girl weighs less than Charlotte's tote and lives in a rundown flat in Hell's Kitchen she shares with three other women, and takes modeling classes in the evenings. She aspires to walk the runway for Dior and Versace, as do all the other brainless twits she's hired. They're beautiful girls, which counts for something. She can't have ugly engaging with her clients.

"Would you like me to lock up for you?" Priscilla touches up her lipstick, a deep, dreadful rouge.

"Thank you, no." She's expecting someone, a buyer who wishes to remain anonymous. His representative is due shortly to handle the transaction for *Lust's* companion painting, *Betrayal*. Alexander painted his lover lying on her side, nude, her back to the viewer. A male hand rests on the sensual curve of her hip, his fingers depressing the flesh, pulling her into him. Veins line the back of the hand. His bent leg protrudes between hers. It's left up to the admirer as to whom the hand belongs, the artist or another man. The piece is even more arousing than its counterpart.

"Have a good night, then." With that, Priscilla departs, and Charlotte is alone.

She retreats upstairs to her office, a glass box stabilized with cables and balanced on beams. From her desk, she can see every corner of the gallery. She loves everything about her space, the blond-hickory planks and the buttery soft walls. The way the light from the setting sun spills across the floor. She especially loves that Dwight will never set foot in this gallery. The only downside is she'll never see her children again. But she did her best raising them and taught them the skills to survive. The world is bloodthirsty. To succeed, they need to play just as mercilessly.

At the top of the stairs, Charlotte hears a noise, heels treading on hardwood. A woman stands where she just was. Her back to Charlotte, she studies Alexander's painting.

Her 7:00 p.m. She's early, but no matter. A sale is a sale, and Charlotte intends to close the deal tonight.

Returning to the gallery floor, she manufactures her best smile and approaches the woman with the confidence of one who's in control. "Beautiful painting, isn't it? Alexander Stingel is one of my most gifted artists. His paintings don't just capture light. They reflect and absorb. He's a true master with color."

The woman turns to Charlotte. She doesn't smile. "Hi, Mom."

"Olivia." Charlotte can't hide her shock. "What are you doing here?" She hasn't been hiding, not really. But she never told them where she landed. Didn't plan to either.

A smile appears, and it isn't warm. It's brittle with betrayal and disappointment. "We have an appointment."

Unless she's hosting an exhibit that's open to the public, visits to her gallery are by appointment only. She serves a very exclusive clientele and doesn't want lookie-loo tourists off the street tarnishing a reputation she's been working meticulously to build. The art world is ruthless. She must play by their rules and make her own if she wants any credibility in this industry.

Then it hits her. There is no seven-o'clock appointment. There will be no sale. "When did you get in? You should have called."

"Would you have invited me in if I didn't have an appointment?"

Charlotte smiles through pursed lips. Olivia wouldn't have been able to walk in. There's a keypad on the door. The only reason Priscilla left it unlocked was because Charlotte was expecting her buyer's representative. Which was a ruse, and that twit of an assistant who set up the appointment fell for it.

"I didn't think so." Olivia returns her attention to the painting, and Charlotte maps out her profile, memorizes the slope of her nose and curve of her chin. Why is she here? She gave her children the house and more than enough money to satisfy their urge to seek her out. Enough that should have clued them in she was done being their mother. Took her several decades to admit, but Charlotte was never cut out to be a parent.

Olivia's tongue darts across her lips. She is beautiful, her daughter. Her oldest and her favorite. Brunette hair cascades to her midback. High boots hug her calves as does her dress with the three-quarter sleeves. Why Olivia didn't take up modeling, she doesn't understand. She's more gorgeous than Priscilla and her flimsy roommates. Instead, Olivia took up smoking, sketching cartoons, and falling in love with a man who doesn't know how to brush his own hair. Theodore Blaze Whitman was never good enough for her daughter. His father was a letdown in bed.

Another mistake.

She has so many of them.

Charlotte crosses her arms and studies Alexander's painting alongside Olivia. "What do you make of it?"

"She's beautiful. Alluring. Who is she?"

"The artist's girlfriend."

"And the man, the artist?"

"That is the question."

Olivia wraps her arms around herself. "I've got another one for you." She turns to her with raised brows. "Why?"

That's a loaded question.

Why did she leave Seaside Cove? Why did she manipulate and lie to her children? Why did she kill Lily's father? If she felt any remorse, or had any doubt they could prove her guilt, she wouldn't be here living out in the open. Olivia never would have found her. Simply, Charlotte doesn't give a fuck what her children think. Don't they get that?

"You'd never understand." Olivia didn't grow up having to prove herself to her father over and over again just to get an inkling of his attention. A sliver of acknowledgment. No, Dwight coddled her. Made her soft and ridiculously naive.

"Try me."

"I don't have answers. Not the ones you want." They wouldn't change anything. They won't bring Benton St. John back or the years she lost with Lily. They won't stop her from lying. Her father taught her well. She has no plans to change if it gets her what she wants, and that's this. The gallery and a lifestyle running in the circles of the wealthy and privileged. The life she was destined to live.

Olivia holds her gaze, and Charlotte feels her own gaze wavering. Her daughter's arms fall along her sides. Her hands tense, and a finger taps her thigh. Charlotte wonders if she still craves a smoke, that need to hold something in your hand. Ah, the rush of nicotine. A disgusting habit.

Olivia inhales sharply and makes an announcement. "We're selling the house."

She didn't expect that. Her house is beautiful, with its elegant architecture and desirable location. She hated leaving it more than her children. But Dwight lived there. The carpet and linens reeked of him. "It was a gift."

"We don't want it."

"The taxes?" They'll be obscene.

"The price of no one wanting to live there. Too many bad memories under that roof."

Olivia's eyes glow like hard emeralds, and Charlotte rubs her hands together. "By *we* do you mean . . ."

"Lily. Yes."

A mix of nerves and longing flows through her. "You've seen her? How is she?" she asks before she stops herself. She left Seaside Cove to avoid Lily's return. The daughter she insisted on keeping to spite Dwight and his infidelities is more than the child she paid to run away. She's a reminder of the night Dwight forced her hand, and she took Benton's life. Looking at Lily is like staring down the mouth of her ill deeds. But the mother in her can't deny it means something to know she's alive. That she's healthy and thriving.

No, she never forgot her daughter. Not a single day went by that she didn't wonder how Lily was coping on her own. Surely that counts for something. She isn't a total monster.

Soft footsteps approach. "She's good. Fantastic, no thanks to you and Dwight."

That voice. Charlotte turns to take in the woman behind her. "Lily." Lips trembling, she reaches to cradle her daughter's face only to hesitate at the fury burning in her eyes. "Lily, darling," she whispers, hands shaking. "My little angel." Though she isn't so little anymore. Lily is a grown woman, and by the look of her, Charlotte's daughter despises her. "I always knew you were a survivor."

Lily's mouth curves into a tight smile. "Better than believing I'm a murderer like you and Dwight convinced me I was."

"Show a little respect." Charlotte crosses herself. "He's your father."

"No, he isn't."

Charlotte's spine straightens. Her hands fold at her waist. "He raised you."

Lily snorts her derision and looks over Charlotte's shoulder. "Have you told her yet about Jean St. John?"

"I was just getting to that," Olivia says.

Ice pours into Charlotte's veins. But she doesn't move, not even a glimmer of a reaction that shows how Jean's name sends a bolt of fear into her. Benton's widow remarried and moved to Texas ten years ago, but kept her house in Seaside Cove, which Charlotte only recently sold on her behalf less than a year ago. It was the least she could do after killing her husband.

She takes a breath, telling herself to keep it together. "What about Jean?"

"She's trying to reopen Benton's case."

Charlotte weaves slightly. She imagines her face has become as pale as the walls behind her. "Why would she do that?"

Lily shrugs. "Some new evidence has come to light."

"You have nothing on me. You can't prove anything."

"Dad didn't get rid of the knife," Olivia says. "He gifted the set to me with the house. He'd stored them in the attic."

Charlotte stares at Olivia with stunned contempt. "Why, that worthless piece of shit. Your father was a dumbass."

Olivia tilts her head, looking sidelong at her mother. "Finally, she shows her true colors."

"You've always known who and what I am, Olivia. Stop being naive."

"Tell her about your dream," Lily says.

"What dream? That ludicrous nightmare you had as a child?" Charlotte sounds horrible even to her own ears. But Olivia is putting her in a poor position, backing her into a corner with claws out and teeth bared.

Olivia folds her arms. "I still have it. And according to my therapist—who's great, by the way. You should consider seeing one for yourself."

"A lot of good that would do." Lily rolls her eyes.

"My therapist is convinced it's a repressed memory. I was there, Mom. I saw you murder Benton."

Her posture stiffens in appalled disbelief. "You were a child. Nobody will believe anything you say."

"I guess we'll have to wait and find out."

"You'd betray your own mother? How dare you. After everything I've given you."

"She was trying to buy our silence, that's what all the money was for." Lily folds her arms, leans her weight on one hip. "Shame on you, Mother dear."

"I think I've heard enough." Olivia jerks her head at Lily, motioning for the door. She leans in and kisses Charlotte's cheek. "Goodbye, Mom."

Charlotte reaches for her, but Olivia's arm slips through her fingers. "You can't go. You can't tell me this and leave. Who do you think you are?"

"Mom."

Lily draws her attention. Her daughter's hazel eyes glisten. Benton's eyes. They mock her. Charlotte's skin tingles all over, and she starts to sweat. What is wrong with her? She doesn't sweat. She's better than them. They have nothing on her. They can't prosecute her. They can't prove anything.

Lily gives her an envelope of cash. "Five thousand. Same amount you gave me."

Charlotte almost laughs. "You expect me to run?"

Lily lifts her brows. "Isn't that what you're doing already?"

"I walked away from you. There's a difference."

"If you say so."

Her skin feels tight, heated. Her blouse clings to her back. This is too much. Her daughters will ruin her. Her breath shortens. They need to leave, and she needs to get out of here.

She turns and bumps into a wall.

Not a wall. Her son.

"Hello, Mother."

She gasps, dragging her gaze from his wide chest up to his hard face. Her heart bangs in her rib cage like a persistent neighbor knocking on her door, screaming at her to get out of her burning house.

"Lucas, darling. You're here, too?" Forcing a smile, she cups his face. His stubble is rough on her skin. He clenches his teeth, and she feels his jaw flex in her palms.

He removes her hands, his gaze angling toward the windows. Two uniformed police officers stand outside the glass door. Panic flares inside her.

"They're waiting on us. We asked them to let us talk to you first." Her gaze swerves to the rear exit, and he says, "They're back there, too."

"You can't have me arrested." Appalled, she shoves his chest.

"They just want to bring you in for questioning."

"This is my gallery," she shrieks. "My place of work. My reputation."

"I don't think you have a choice. They will arrest you if you resist."

She wants to smack the smirk off his face.

His eyes narrow. "You lied to me. You manipulated me."

True. She did plant the seed for him to murder his father.

Charlotte tugs her cuffs and pushes back her shoulders. "Then some dignity, please."

"You don't deserve it." But he concedes and tilts his head toward her office.

"Thank you." She releases a relieved breath and looks at each of her children, memorizing their faces the moment they betrayed her.

They watch her as if she's a depraved maniac. Don't they know? She's not the crazy one. That was their father. He made her this way. They should be thanking her, ungrateful leeches. If she weren't so peeved, she'd demand their respect. She'd take back her house and leave them with nothing.

She retreats upstairs to her office, overhearing Lily ask, "Do you think they have enough evidence to file charges?"

"Not sure," Lucas says. "But it's worth watching her squirm."

Charlotte lifts her chin. Inside her office, she pours three fingers of bourbon and tosses it back without a wince. Through the glass walls, she looks down at her children. *Her children.* She gave them her home, her money. Their lives. And what have they given her? A knife in the back. Spoiled little brats.

Lucas waits on the threshold, holding open the door for his sisters to leave and for the police to come in. He looks up at her, and they make eye contact. He doesn't smile. His face remains impassive, detached. He then turns away. The door closes, and he and his sisters are gone.

Two officers invade her cultivated space. Charlotte is of the mind to bolt the door and call her attorney. But she doesn't act fast enough, and if she resists, they'll place her under arrest and cuff her.

One officer takes the empty glass from her hands. "Careful," she snaps. "That's an Artĕl. Do you know how much that costs? Of course you don't," she says, noticing the cheap watch on his wrist.

He sets the glass on her desk with a sharp thud. The other officer asks her to kindly come with them. They have questions about the murder of Benton St. John.

"Fine, fine," she says, gathering her coat and tote, already spinning a new story in her head. Dwight murdered Benton, not her. And he'd threatened her life if she ever spoke of the truth. Only now that he's dead does she feel safe to talk about that horrible night so long ago.

Dwight is already buried, she calculates, settling into the back seat of the cruiser, but she won't hesitate to dig him a deeper grave to save herself.

42

The limousine Lily sent for Lucas at the hotel she put him up at rolls to a stop in front of Grauman's Chinese Theatre in Hollywood and a teeming mass of prepubescent, screaming kids. "Fuck me." Lucas gapes at the crowd through the tinted window and swallows audibly. He's already sweating, and he hasn't even left the vehicle. His hand swipes across his forehead and returns damp. He rubs off the moisture on his thigh and considers telling the chauffeur to keep driving, but he's already left the limo. And Lucas would hate himself if he missed Lily's premiere showing.

His door opens, and the noise rises to on an earsplitting decibel. Lucas rears back when he notices everyone pointing at him and waving to get his attention. They're probably trying to guess who he is. Lily told him this morning the studio had sent invites to half of Hollywood, touting the premiere as a family event. People those screaming kids could paw at, beg a selfie with. Perhaps snag an autograph from when he struts down the red carpet.

But he's nobody. And he sure as hell doesn't strut.

The best he's done was buy a new pair of dark-washed jeans and steel-toed boots to go with his favorite Pearl Jam shirt. He got a haircut, too, rubbed in some product Olivia gave him, and styled his hair the way she showed him. A messy, textured look. Apparently, it makes him look hot. But what matters most, he's dry.

He checks his watch.

Thirty-six days, eleven hours, and seven minutes sober.

His mental health has a ways to go, but physically, he's never felt better.

Before him the red carpet stretches from the sidewalk to the gaping mouth of the theater. At the end actors dressed as Lily's characters entertain the crowd. Banners fluttering in the afternoon breeze flank the entrance. Photographers snap photos of guests posed before a backdrop, a blown-up version of the movie poster.

He has to walk past all that.

For a wild moment flashbacks to Lily's signing when the police tackled him rear to mind. His breath comes quickly. Fingers dig into the leather seat.

"Sir?" The chauffeur inches the door wider, impatient for him to get out. Cars have lined up behind them.

"Yeah." He can do this. With a grunt he heaves himself from the limo and faces the crowd. He swears they scream louder when he does.

They have no idea who he is.

Then he remembers his stint at the signing made the news.

Head down, Lucas strides up the carpet, dodging outstretched hands. A girl hollers for a selfie, and a reporter sticks a microphone in his face. He keeps on walking.

Near the end of the aisle, a giant Tabby's Squirrel grabs his arm and ushers him before the photographers. "What the—" It takes effort not to punch the ginormous plastic nose off the bobble head as he turns to face the cameras with a grimace. Flashing lights blind him. How does Lily stand this kind of attention?

He starts to walk off.

"One more, Lucas! One more," they shout.

How the hell do they remember his name? He's a nobody.

He holds up a hand to block his face and rushes into the theater. The front of the house is high ceilinged with a red-and-gold art deco aesthetic. It's crowded, but not nearly as crazy as outside. Lucas breathes deeply, waiting for his heart to slow down, and looks around. He spots

Lily right away. She's all smiles and surrounded by people, her hand weaved with that of the man beside her. He's tall with close-cropped hair and a button-down shirt with rolled-up sleeves. Boring, but Lucas likes the look of him. He especially likes how his entire focus is on Lily alone. He must be Kavan. And he adores her. For that he has Lucas's respect.

Off to the side are Olivia, Blaze, and Josh. His sister sees him and waves him over. But before he can make his way to her, someone shouts his name. A body slams into him.

He looks down and grins. "Sunshine Girl." Happiness lightens his chest. They've spoken on the phone about hers and Sophie's plans for their summer move to California City, but he hasn't seen her since his arrest.

"You made it." Shiloh looks up at him, dancing on her toes.

"Told you I would. Ready to work this summer?"

She rolls her eyes and groans. "Buzzkill."

He laughs. "Missed you, kiddo."

"Can I meet her for real this time?" Dressed in high-waisted jeans, new Chucks, and a *Tabby's Squirrel* shirt, she can hardly contain her excitement. She glances over at Lily, but the woman approaching behind Shiloh has his attention.

Sophie smiles, and something tightens inside him. "Hi."

The edge of his mouth draws up. "Hey."

"Is that a smile?" Her grin broadens, and so does his.

"Yeah. I think so." In the past, he would have denied it. But he's been smiling a lot more lately.

A wide headband holds back her mass of tight curls, making the freckles stand out on her nose. Studs and hoops march up her ear shell. From his count, not that he's counted before, she's added another piercing. She looks down at her sundress and combat boots.

"I don't usually wear dresses." Her hand smooths down the front. "Skirts get in the way of hunting."

They share a smile. So, she's still pursuing bounties. "You look nice."

"It's really yellow."

"Reminds me of the mustard fields in Napa Valley. Have you been?"

She shakes her head. He hasn't either, not for a long time. An unexpected desire to take her this summer rises. They'll bring Shiloh and make a weekend of it.

Her eyes meet his. "Ready for us to move in?"

"We're ready." He just finished updating the kitchen and bath in the apartment Sophie's renting. Ivy even furnished it.

"Shi just wrapped up school. I have to close up my place in Redondo Beach for the summer, but we should be there by Tuesday."

"I'm sure Ivy will make sure there's plenty of lasagna."

"And you? Would you want to share a sunset and soda with me?"

He feels a lightness in his chest. "I look forward to it."

Speakers crackle before a woman's voice announces the movie will begin shortly. She invites guests to take their seats. The people surrounding Lily disperse. She says something to Kavan. He kisses her and disappears into the darkness of the theater. She grabs Josh, and they make their way to Lucas.

Shiloh gasps. She grabs Lucas's arm. "She's coming." She stares, gobsmacked.

Lily smiles at them. Shiloh stares back, mute. Lucas snickers, and she tosses him a dirty look.

Lily's attention stops at Sophie. He almost forgot they're friends. Or were before Sophie betrayed his sister.

"I hope you don't mind I came," Sophie says.

"I'm glad you did."

"I'm sorry—"

"Stop." Lily grabs her hand. "You could have handled it better. We all could have. But it worked out in the end."

Sophie looks relieved. "Thank you." They hug, and Shiloh clears her throat, finding her voice.

"Hi," she squeaks.

"Lily, this is Shiloh. Shiloh, Lily," Lucas introduces.

"Hi, Shiloh. Nice to officially meet you." Lily shakes her hand. "I've heard so much about you."

"You have? That's . . . wow. Sick." She wipes her palms on her jeans.

"Lucas told me you draw."

"He did?" She looks at him, worried. "Cool. I mean, what did he say?"

"Only good things. I understand you want to be an animator."

She nods vigorously. "I've watched all your videos."

"You're staying with him this summer?"

She nods again. "In the apartment next door."

"Tell him to bring you to visit. I'll give you a tour of my studio. You can show me your work."

Shiloh's mouth falls open. "For real?"

"Definitely," Lily says, but she's looking at Lucas. "My brother and I have a lot of catching up to do."

He nods. He gets it. He feels the same.

Beside him, Josh fidgets, smoothing his hair. He pets his chest like he's trying to iron his shirt's wrinkles with the sweat on his palm.

"Nervous?" Lucas teases. Josh's eyes haven't left Shiloh.

"Shut up," he says out of the corner of his mouth.

Lucas chuckles. He grasps the back of Josh's neck. "Relax, dude. Shiloh." He feels Josh tense under his hand. "This is my nephew, Josh."

Shiloh waves, shyly. "Hi."

"Hey." Josh's voice cracks, and his cheeks flame red. Lucas holds in a smile. He's been there, and he won't dare laugh.

Someone runs through the entrance, and they all turn toward Tyler, Josh's father. "Hey," they say collectively.

"I didn't think you'd make it in time," Lily says.

"Almost didn't. Traffic was insane." He drops a kiss on her head and gives Josh a fist bump. Then his gaze swings to Lucas, and his eyes widen. "Dude, been a long time."

"Sure has." Lucas gives him a man hug, slapping his back just as Olivia and Blaze join them.

After another round of hugs and introductions comes another announcement that the movie is starting.

"Should we go in?" Blaze asks.

Tyler agrees and Sophie turns to Lucas. "We'll see you inside?" He appreciates that she senses he wants a moment with his sisters.

He nods.

"We'll save you a seat," Shiloh says.

"Thanks, Sunshine Girl."

She snorts at the nickname but doesn't complain. The endearment's apparently growing on her.

Everyone disperses to take their seats, leaving Lucas alone with Olivia and Lily.

"So." He shoves his hands into his pockets.

"So," Olivia echoes.

"Here we are." Lily swings her arms.

"Anyone hear from Mom?" Lucas asks. He's been thinking about her a lot lately, the lies she'd told him. How she'd manipulated him. She was far from an ideal parent, but she was his mother. He loved her, often worried about her well-being given how his father treated everyone in the family, his mom included. Their arguments had been explosive. He's had a difficult time choking down her betrayal. Confronting her the other week hadn't been easy.

"As if she'd call me." Lily removes her sweater and folds the garment over her arm.

Olivia shakes her head. "Unless St. John's case makes its way to court and they need us to testify, we won't hear from her."

Lucas isn't sure how he feels about that.

Olivia rests a gentle hand on his shoulder and meets his eyes. "I know you miss her. But she left us long before she actually did leave."

He nods. He realizes that. He's been trying to accept it.

"Our parents were toxic," Lily adds.

And like the alcohol he gave up over a month ago, he needs to cut his mom out of his life. Stop thinking about her. And stop feeling guilty about his mistakes.

His cheeks puff as he looses a long breath and looks around. *Tabby's Squirrel* banners fill the house front. The theater is packed. Lily's movie will be this summer's blockbuster animation. There's already Oscar buzz. Incredible given how his baby sis started out. The odds she'd faced.

He takes in his sisters. His family. The three of them aren't their parents. Never have been and never will be. They're good people. People who've been broken, struggled, and have put themselves back together. Lucas is trying to do that now. He'll get there, that he believes. They have the power to break the cycle of abuse and neglect and are doing so.

They've done so, he amends.

The best thing Lily did was run away. Distance herself from them. Because look at her now. Her smile takes up the entire room.

Lucas does something he hasn't done in a long time. He makes the first move. He reaches for Lily. His palm cups her face. Emotion tightens his throat.

"I've missed you," he whispers thickly.

Her eyes shimmer and smile quivers. "Missed you, too."

"Gawd, you guys, you're gonna make me cry." Olivia throws her arms around them. "You have to come to the lake for Christmas. Both of you. The house should be done by then. Bring everyone."

"Only if you come to the beach for Thanksgiving," Lily says.

They look at him.

He groans as if visiting them is the most tedious chore. Then he laughs and strong-arms their necks, dragging them against his chest. They both shriek.

"Yes, I'll be there. Ow." He grunts when Lily punches his chest. Olivia pinches the underside of his arm. "Stop it. Fuck." Sisters. He lets them go only to drape his arms over their shoulders.

Like Olivia's superheroes, Ruby, Titian, and Dahlia, they're stronger together.

And like Lily's characters on *Tabby's Squirrel*, they still know how to have fun.

Arm in arm, Lucas walks with his sisters into the theater.

The Carson siblings. Together again.

EPILOGUE

Two months later

"That's a wrap." Lucas adds the last suitcase to Ivy's car and closes the trunk.

"Thank you, Lucas. You don't realize what you've done for me."

He has an idea. He gave her the freedom to live out the rest of her days as she sees fit. And she gave him more than he could ever repay her for. A purpose, an expanded family, and a home.

After he learned about the money his mother left him, and after they sold the house in Seaside Cove, Lucas made an offer on the Dusty Pantry.

He hugs Ivy, smiling at Shiloh and Sophie over her head. They stand to the side, waiting for their turns to say goodbye.

"I'm going to miss you, Ivy."

She snorts a laugh. "You're going to miss my lasagna."

"That too." He winks.

"Come here, girl, and give me a hug." She turns to Shiloh. "You make sure Lucas eats his salad."

Shiloh grimaces. "No promises."

Ivy cups her cheeks and looks her in the eye. "You're one lucky girl. I thank my lucky stars every day Lucas found you."

After Lucas left his sisters in Seaside Cove, he returned to California City and filled Ivy in on everything: who he is, who Shiloh is, and how their paths had crossed. Ivy, bless her, was surprisingly understanding despite him deceiving her, and she still wanted to sell him her building. *You need it more than me*, she told him.

"Me too." Shiloh gives Ivy a hug, meeting Lucas's gaze. He still gets sick to his stomach whenever he thinks what could have happened if he hadn't pulled Shiloh out of the homeless encampment when he did.

Sophie steps forward with a chilled bottle of Italian soda. "For the road."

"It's not that long a drive." Ivy's moving in with her sister in San Diego, and in another month, the two ladies depart on a six-month voyage around the world.

"Then enjoy it tonight when you get there."

"We'll be celebrating with something a little stronger than this, but I'll take it," Ivy jokes, tucking the bottle under her arm.

She settles into her car and starts the engine when Lucas says, "Forgetting something?" He holds out his hand, and she stares at his palm. Then she rolls her eyes and drops her apartment key in his hand. Lucas slips his hand in his pocket. "Thank you."

"No, thank *you*." Ivy takes one last look at the Dusty Pantry. "Wish I could say I'm going to miss this place, but . . ." She shakes her head. "You all had better come visit me."

"We will. Now get out of here before we don't let you go." He knocks the roof of the car and stands back.

"Bye, Ivy." Shiloh waves.

Ivy waves back, reversing from the parking spot. Just before she turns away, Lucas catches her wiping off a tear. The woman's going to miss this place more than she cares to admit, and he's going to miss her. He's sure they'll see her again before she leaves on her trip.

When Ivy turns out of the parking lot, Shiloh turns to him and Sophie. "Can we go now?"

He exhales, still not 100 percent sold on this idea of theirs. "Hop into the truck."

They pile in, Shiloh in the middle and Sophie on the other side. Lucas doesn't take the road. He cuts across the dry land, brambles and weeds scraping his undercarriage. The city has been cleaning out the homeless encampment. Most of the residents have left, some checking into the local shelter. Bob, Barton, and Ricky disappeared a while ago. Lucas checked. He wouldn't allow Shiloh anywhere near the encampment if they were still around. But there was one resident left, and Shiloh didn't want him living alone on the streets. They've just been waiting for Ivy's apartment to become available.

They reach Irving's Caprice, and Lucas parks the truck. Sophie pulls a box of latex gloves from her bag. "Put them on."

"Why?" Shiloh asks, and Lucas slips on a pair.

"Hepatitis is rampant in encampments."

"Ew." Shiloh makes a face.

"You got lucky, kid." There is much she could have been—and probably was—exposed to during those two weeks she lived out of a car.

"What's the plan with this guy?" Sophie asks. She isn't too keen on the idea of bringing a homeless man to the apartment complex. But Shiloh insists he's harmless.

"We get him cleaned up." His body and system. Lucas has a strict no-drugs policy. If Irving brings any of that into his building, he's out. "Then we put him to work." He'll make the perfect janitor.

"And then we find his daughter," Shiloh adds, jumping out of the truck after Sophie.

Lucas grunts. He's heard about Irving's stories and isn't confident a daughter exists.

Irving is waiting for them by his car. He brushes a hand down the front of his button-up dress shirt that's several sizes too large for his bony frame. Lucas can only imagine where he dug that thing up.

"Itchy Irving, look at you." Shiloh whistles. "Did you get all fancy for us?" He's wearing a suit and wing tips. He's also carrying a briefcase.

Lucas will be checking that before Irving moves in. He catches a look from Sophie, and her eyes flare in agreement. She's thinking the same thing.

Irving grins at Shiloh. His teeth are stained, some are missing. But he pushes back his shoulders. "Daisy Ray. I knew you'd come back for me."

"Told you I wouldn't forget."

Sophie leans in close to Lucas as they walk over to Irving. "She's got a heart of gold."

"Yeah, she does." And he's been grateful she's had room in it for him since the day he met her. "Come on, kiddo," he says to Shiloh. "Let's get this man home."

ACKNOWLEDGMENTS

To Danielle Marshall, Chris Werner, Gabriella Dumpit, Jen Bentham, Ashley Vanicek, and everyone else at Lake Union and Amazon Publishing. As always, I am blessed to be working with such an incredible publishing team. Series are always a gamble. Thanks for rolling the dice with me so that I could share the Carson siblings with the world.

To Tiffany Yates Martin, Hannah Buehler, and Ashley Little, without whom I'd never know when to use *further* or *farther*. My editorial team pushes me to push my characters, and because of them, my stories shine.

To Rex Bonomelli, my cover designer throughout the series, who gave the No More trilogy its daring and mysterious vibe. The covers are emotional and powerful, and among my favorites.

To Gordon Warnock, who always has my best interests at heart in this crazy, ever-changing industry.

To all the bloggers, book reviewers, book boutiques, booktokkers, bookstagrammers, and my early reader team who shout, promote, and share their love of my books. I'm forever grateful.

To my family, who gets me.

And to you, dear reader, for being a forever fan. Thanks for hanging out with Olivia, Lily, and Lucas. I hope you enjoyed their stories. The No More trilogy has been a ride—the Carsons that family you love to hate. If you think they're dysfunctional, then you must meet the

Donatos in the Everything series. I recommend starting with *Everything We Keep*.

Love exclusive content? Join me in the Tiki Lounge (www.facebook.com/groups/kerrystikilounge). All readers are welcome. Also join my Beach Club (www.kerrylonsdale.com/for-readers/) for new release announcements and giveaways.

ABOUT THE AUTHOR

Photo © 2021 Dana Moran

Kerry Lonsdale is the *Wall Street Journal, Washington Post*, and Amazon Charts bestselling author of *Side Trip, Last Summer, All the Breaking Waves,* the Everything Series (*Everything We Keep, Everything We Left Behind,* and *Everything We Give*), and the No More series (*No More Words, No More Lies,* and *No More Secrets*). Cofounder of the Women's Fiction Writers Association, her work has been translated into more than twenty-seven languages. She resides in Northern California with her husband and two children. You can visit Kerry at www.kerrylonsdale.com.

ABOUT THE AUTHOR